JES DREW

BETRAYAL & BANDITRY

SUNSET AT DAWN

ONE

BETRAYAL & BANDITRY

SUNSET AT DAWN VOLUME ONE

JES DREW

BOO'S BOOKS

Printed in the United States of America

First Printing, 2023

ISBN: 9781088086308

Boo's Books Publishing https://agencyofbooksandspies.blogspot.com/

Cover by @saintjupit3rgr4phic

Under the jacket art by @chicken.doodle

Omnibus cover by Hannah Rogers

Logo and couple art by Maddy Moore

Single character art by @mageonduty

Map by Almond Abordo

Author Photograph by Amy S.

Edited by Katy Mauerman

Formatted by Atticus

Dedicated to everyone I used to know. Those I lost, those who left, and those I long to see again.

And to the Creator God Who made us all.

CONTENTS

SYNOPSIS

She's a noblewoman turned thief.
He's the Sacred Prince.
Neither recall being betrothed.

When Elspeth loses everything in one night for the crime of being born an elf, she wants vengeance. Forced to resort to banditry in order to survive, her forest becomes a safe haven for others dismissed by the Empire. But becoming the Bandit Queen isn't enough to compensate for the castle she lost; only the royal palace will do. To become the Empress, though, she first needs to save the Sacred Prince.

After a devastating decree, Prince Otello intends to put his empire to rights and make restitution. If that means taking on a false name to better investigate the crimes committed against the elves, so be it. Perhaps he can even locate the noblewoman who plagues his dreams like a lost memory. The last thing he anticipates, though, is the vexing maiden on the wrong side of the law— and his own growing desire to rescue her from the clutches of the Bandit King.

A prophecy of destruction tore them apart. Now a vision of doom will unite them.

PRAISE

For Embrace of Shadows:

"I loved this!!! These characters are *heart eyes*"

— Brittney Rogers, reviewer

For Red as Blood:

"Red as Blood is a fun jaunt through the Wild West coupled with all the trappings you want in a fairytale . . . The setting was fresh and interesting. A sweet, clean read."

—Skye, author of *Falling Snow*

For The Bachelor Missions:

"Normal life and romance are difficult enough for a secret agent, but time-traveling doppelganger girlfriend-wannabes who use futuristic weaponry were not covered in the training courses. Jes Drew's The Bachelor Missions follows our hero, Kristian Clark, through three separate but connected espionage adventures with plenty of romantic difficulties. Because these stories are e set in the real world, characters plainly discuss Christianity and some common arguments for and against the faith. Still, God-talk and two conversion scenes remain light in favor of the stories' light and humorous tone—like Men in Black but without the aliens."

—Lorehaven Magazine

EHYPTIO
GAELIA
UPPER IMPARIA
ACADEMY OF BLOOD
MIDDLE IMPARIA
CANTER
HEAVEN'S GRACE FALLS
KREUZSCHLAFEN PALACE
SITZVONNE
RODEN
HOFF
GREAT WALD FOREST
HAFEN VILLAGE
NEUES VERSPRECHEN
SOUTHERN IMPARIA
(FORMERLY HAYA
VENICAN ISLE
CONSTANTINIUM

PREFACE

"*What has been stolen must be returned four-fold.*"
—from the Second Scroll of the Elder

PROLOGUE

Lady Elspeth

Kreuzschlafen Palace Sitzvononne during the thirty-first year of Emperor Augustu's reign . . .

"*My lady.*"

At the sudden slaughter of the silence, I nearly tumble into the garden fountain I had been sitting at, watching the water in tranquility. Water has its own sort of music that can flow into one's soul with quiet burbles as surely as any minstrel's note.

"I did not mean to startle you."

Since whoever has intruded on my solitude seems determined to remain, I turn to see who else would walk the palace gardens in the wee hours before dawn.

The sight of the figure veiled in white almost sends me tumbling into the fountain again.

But my mind summons enough sense to remember gysts are found only in legends. Then I recall the person who wore the same white tunic inlaid with gold threading when we were introduced but yesterday.

Jumping to my slippered feet, I drop as gracefully of a curtsy as I can manage in my haste. I have to draw upon all the blessings my elvish heritage affords me, but I manage not to fall on my face before the Sacred Prince of the Sun. "My liege."

"Please, rise."

Obediently, I stand up and quickly smooth out the dress that could not be more different from the one I wore when I was presented before the court and the crown prince. That dress was the finest piece I ever wore, created from the finest silks my father's merchants could trade for, pearl white and pure.

But now I stand before the Sacred Prince dressed in a simple gray woolen morning gown. I pulled it on over my shift when I found myself unable to sleep in a room filled with so many strangers and not one of my kin.

Unless one counted Meredith, though I suppose I cannot since we share neither the same blood nor the same heritage, merely the same manner of heart and a close proximity of our families' baronages.

"I am so sorry; I did not realize you would desire to visit these gardens." I move to dip another curtsy before moving past him, my focus on the palace wing reserved for the noblewomen who were presented to the court yesterday.

"Actually, it is *you* that I desire."

I stop fast and turn to face the Sacred Prince.

With his face veiled, I cannot make out any clues except that, by the sudden rigidity of his body, I'm not sure he meant to say that.

"My prince?" I whisper.

He clears his throat. "That is, I was hoping we could speak again. And what a pleasant surprise to find you in my mother's garden."

"I'm sorry; I should have known that the Empress's gardens were sacred. Creator rest her soul." I touch my forehead and then each shoulder in respect.

The prince grasps my hand in a sign of . . . well, I'm not sure even he knows, as he freezes at the same time that I do.

"Please do not upset yourself, Lady Elspeth," he whispers.

"Y-you remember my name?" Granted, I was just introduced to him yesterday. But so were dozens of other young women, all at least as fair as I.

"How could I not? You were so different from everything I've ever known."

Reaching up with the hand that isn't held captive by his, I touch the point of my lengthened ears. The most noticeable trait of my elf blood that sets me apart from all the other noblewomen presented today.

"I would be honored to take a stroll around the gardens with you."

"So, you can make sport of my heritage?" I snatch my hand from his. How could I have thought that the Sacred Prince would somehow be different from the majority of his people?

"What? No!" He pulls away as though I'd slapped him. "I have not come here to mock your heritage, but to discuss our future."

I stare at him. "*Our* future?"

"I mean only that when I saw you, something shifted. I don't know what, only that I believe it's worth exploring." The Sacred Prince sighs. "I'm going about this all wrong, aren't I?"

"I am more befuddled now than when you first approached me, so I would say that there is certainly room for improvement in your communication style." I slap my hand over my mouth, but too late to stop those bold words.

To my utter surprise, he snickers, and I am quite perplexed at the thought that the Sacred Prince is capable of such an ignoble sound. It seems so . . . human.

But he is a mortal, after all. And I am elvish. And no one would allow our bloodlines to mix at such a great height as the royal line.

"I am quite flattered, my prince, but there are several more beautiful girls far more eligible than I." I turn.

"Wait!"

I pause and glance over my shoulder at the veiled man. "Is that a command?"

"It is if that's what will make you stay."

Sighing, I turn back to him. "For only a moment more. It is hardly appropriate for us to both be out here alone, after dark, without even one of the other girls to chaperone."

"It would be hardly appropriate for one of them to be present when I remove my veil. Even the purest maiden must not be allowed to gaze upon the face of the Sacred Prince before the Sun claims him at his first coronation."

"Of course, that would be inappropriate. Wait—" My gaze snaps to him. "Are you saying you intend to remove your veil?"

"I alluded to something along those lines, yes." He gently tugs off one of his white gloves.

"But how could you? I am also a maiden!" I glance around, wondering where the guards are hidden, about to come down on me for such scandalous conversation. Or worse, a matron ready to write home to my parents about my shameful behavior.

"I believe you are more than a mere maiden." He slides off his other glove and places both on the ledge of the fountain I had been sitting on just moments before, when life was normal. "You are a true hero. After all, you saved my life this day."

My gaze snaps from tracing the grace of his long fingers to his veil. "I—what?"

"Surely you remember? It was only this afternoon."

I think back, racking my mind, but find that I only remember walking up to his throne and dropping into a curtsy.

And then preparing for bed. No, that can't be right. What happened in between?

The Sacred Prince takes my hands in his now bare ones, and I gasp at the contact, my skin suddenly warm and my mind desperately searching for memories.

Because this is not the only time we've touched; I know it.

Then he kneels before me, and I almost drop to the ground so that I'll be lower than he is.

But while I may curtsy to royalty, I will grovel before no one, so I remain on my feet. "My prince?"

"Otello. My name is Otello."

"Otello?" I squeak, and I'm surprised lightning doesn't come from the sky and strike me down for my impertinence.

"Do you trust me?"

I stare at him, this man I only met yesterday but have heard of my entire life. The mortal who is to rule over my people after his ancestors conquered them. The man who most certainly cannot mix bloodlines with an elf.

Who remembers things that my mind does not.

Still, my mouth utters words I do not quite understand, yet still feel to be true. "Yes."

"Then remove my veil, Lady Elspeth."

With determination I do not feel, I shake my head once. "I cannot."

"You could, as my betrothed."

I stagger backward, and if it weren't for his hands holding mine, I'm sure I would have fallen into the fountain already. "My prince!"

"Otello."

"My Otello—" My face heats when I realize what I've said.

Releasing my hands, he stands up, and I wonder if I've gone too far.

"Then will you allow me?" His voice is lower than it was before, and my insides skitter strangely to hear his voice like this.

"I— " I clear my throat. "You may do whatever you wish, Sacred Prince. How can I stop you?"

"With but a word."

I shiver, but I'm not cold.

He reaches up and grasps the top of his veil, and I hold my breath.

"Lady Elspeth?"

"Yes?" I whisper.

"Do you wish me to stop?"

"No."

My answer startles me, but I don't take it back.

Prince Otello lifts his veil away from his face, revealing a firm jaw and large lips before he twists his torso to toss it next to his gloves. Then he turns back to me.

I'm immediately caught in the spell of his violet eyes. They give an otherworldly quality to his face that is otherwise the expected standard of handsome, with a strong nose and a stronger jaw. His brown hair is mussed from the veil and ruins the illusion of perfection, though in the most adorable, boyish way.

"Lady Elspeth?" His tone has also become boyish in its nervousness, though he is as much a man as I am a woman.

"Elspeth," I whisper. "Just Elspeth . . . Otello."

His face breaks into a beautiful grin, and he steps forward again. Takes my hands in his. "I didn't have a chance to thank you for saving my Empire."

"No need. I would do it again." Whatever it was I did, and whatever it might take to do it again.

Otello's smile softens as he steps closer, and I'm glad to see that he has several inches on me, which is not always the case between young men and myself thanks to my elf blood. "What an excellent answer from a future Empress."

If he weren't the Sacred Prince, I'd laugh in his face. "A lovely thought, but—"

"Marry me."

I blink. "Very well."

He blinks back. "Really?"

At this point, I'm not sure if it's possible for either of us to be more stunned. Someone could knock us both over with a finger. "I suppose so."

His face brightens as if the sun itself shines out of it. I feel his hands grasp my waist, lift me up, and spin me around.

When he sets me back down, I grab hold of his forearms to steady myself.

Otello smiles down at me. "May I kiss you?"

"You may." Once again, my tongue moves without my mind, but I cannot bring myself to recant.

He leans forward, and it strikes me that my very first kiss will be with the Sacred Prince. My . . . betrothed?

Just wait until I tell Meredith.

Otello lowers his face to mine so close that I can feel his exhale on my skin. My lips swear they sense his even though my eyes have slid shut as I anticipate the moment that I never allowed myself to even daydream about.

Then something grabs my hair and yanks me backward.

I cry out in shock and pain, and my eyes fly open to see a stunned Otello staring after me. His gaze moves to something beyond me, and anger flashes across his face.

He charges forward, but then someone else grabs him and holds him back, a figure in swirling green robes.

"It seems your prophecy was correct." rasps a voice behind me.

Goosebumps prickle on my skin, and I crane my head to see who has a hold on me.

I see brown robes. The official garb of a mortal magic user.

"Let her go!" Otello yells. "You have no right to touch her!"

"Neither do you, boy," answers the brown-robed man, finally dropping his grip from my hair to my upper arms. Still painful, but not as debilitating.

"She is my betrothed!"

Despite the terror at this sudden change in circumstances, a strange sort of happiness fills me to be so claimed by the Sacred Prince before witnesses. Even witnesses such as these.

"I am sorry, my prince," says the man in the green robes, and there is something about him that seems . . . familiar. "But I've seen your future. This betrothal must not be so. At least not yet."

"You don't get to say that. *He certainly* doesn't get to say that!" Otello glares at the man holding me.

The man lifts me from the ground and carries me backward.

New terror fills me, and I fight to loosen his grip, to escape from this dream turned nightmare someway, somehow.

Otello strains against his captor, but not as hard as he could. He seems to be holding back against overpowering the man, who is clearly older and weaker than he.

Is it out of respect for that man he holds back, or lack of desire to rescue me?

Then I see him slide a hand into his pocket. To fetch a hidden weapon, perhaps?

The man holding him grabs his arm and tugs it out. "You cannot, my prince. You must not expose the true nature of your Heritage Magic before Adalbert; he is not to be trusted."

"He can't be trusted with Elspeth!" Otello cries.

"He will not hurt her," assures the man in green, whom I realize suddenly is an elf like me. Why is he against me, though? "He has bound his magic with a vow against it."

I'm sure that should give me relief, but I don't know why they were even speaking of me.

Otello seems to wilt before my eyes, and I realize he's giving up.

"*How could you?*" I demand.

His eyes are brimming with desperation when they meet mine before quickly sliding away. "It doesn't matter where you take her, Adalbert!" His words become more and more muted as I'm dragged farther and farther away. "I will find her!"

"No, he won't," Adalbert whispers hotly. "He won't even remember this night."

I turn to him. "What?"

"Not to worry, she-elf. Neither will you."

"You can't make me do anything," I hiss. "Mortal Magic has no jurisdiction over kin blood."

"But Kin Magic does."

Turning, I see the elf in green robes stepping through the night, this time without Otello.

"Where is the prince?" I demand.

"Safe," he assures, his voice too kind for the situation as he steps up to me. "This is the only way to keep him safe."

I glare up at him. The green robes. They set him apart as the Keeper of Knowledge. The highest rank an elf can have in Constantinium. Well, besides Empress, apparently. Why did it take me so long to place him, though? "What do you mean?"

"You must not remember what I mean. I am sorry, kinswoman, but you must forget one more time."

"One *more* time?!"

Instead of answering, he places his fingers on my forehead, and I feel his magic moving from them, overpowering mine.

And then I feel nothing at all.

CHAPTER 1

Lady Elspeth

Roden Keep, Middle Imparia during the thirty-seventh year of Emperor Augustu's reign . . .

"I don't know why I always see danger lurking around every corner."

When the stars I'm staring at don't answer, I shake my head at myself. "I also don't know why I talk to myself and think that the universe will respond. To think, my people believe I'm fit to rule a baronage."

I turn from the night sky and abandon my balcony for the shelter of my sleeping chambers. And startle to see a shadow towering over my bed.

My hand goes to my side, where I am accustomed to keeping my dagger sheathed. But as I am undressed down to my shift for bed, with only my cloak pulled over it for the chill, it isn't there. In fact, it is under the pillow that the shadow is lifting.

For the first time since coming of age, I wish I were something I'm not. If only I were a child of man, I could protect myself with the sheer force of magic alone.

But the Kin Magic of the elves is tied up entirely in our own bloodline. If someone or something is not connected to my blood, I have no power over it.

As if the thought of my abilities summons it, a sharp pain suddenly sears through me, just below my ribcage.

Biting my lip to keep from crying out, I see nothing that could have hurt me, and the shadow is still at my bed.

Which means it was not I who was injured, but one of my kin.

Forgetting everything else, I rush past my still oblivious intruder, out the door of my sleeping chambers, and toward the sleeping chambers of my closest kin now that both my parents have made the final ascension to the Creator.

My feet slide silently over the cold stones of the floor as I expertly tread the terrain I grew up in, as though I were highly trained in the all-but-forgotten elvish skill of Silent Footfall.

Unfortunately, the Silent Footfall is useless when an enemy looks directly at you, as the man standing out in my hallway is doing. Even more chilling than the cold, hard hate in his eyes is the power emanating from the bejeweled blade in his hands that give evidence that he has already ransacked my late father's sleeping chambers and looted his greatest weapon.

The weapon that was laced with my ancestors' blood to seal the enchantment to make it beholden to all their kin and descendants.

Father's voice echoes in my head.

"My child, if you forget all other ancient Davars, remember this one alone."

The cloaked being before me charges, the blade pulled back so he can make a clear swing with it once he reaches me.

Obeying my father from beyond the grave, I assume the appropriate position drilled into me for such prayer Davars. My right arm reaches out while my left arm pulls back, my spine in a gentle lean. "In my day of need, my weapon shall take heed!"

I speak too loudly, and the man ransacking my room charges to meet us in the doorway even as his companion makes the swing.

Making the slightest move with my right hand, I watch as the blade arcs over me and then embeds itself into my doorpost, slicing the hand of the first intruder.

While the first man roars in pain and the second tries to pull the sword out of the doorway, I step back, careful to keep position except for gently pulling back my right hand.

The blade in the doorway dislodges itself at my command, and then I throw my hand backward, causing the sword to rip out of the thief's hand and come sailing through the air to me.

Reaching up, I clasp the hilt and straighten. "I am Elspeth, daughter of Ephraim, and Baroness of Roden. You shall leave my home with all haste!"

The cloaked form of the sword thief snarls at me even as his companion presses his hand to his chest. Even though the garments mask any discernible features, I can still sense the hatred emanating from beneath its hood. "And I am Vontrapp, a veteran from the Crusades, and future Baron of Roden. Your filthy elf blood doesn't belong in this land at all."

His words do not match his accent, which is foreign to this valley, but that name— that name I know.

My father served alongside a Vontrapp.

I clutch the hilt more tightly to hide my shaking; whether it's from fear or from the powerful Davar flowing through my blood, I know not. "*Your* filthy trespasser blood is about to be spilled all over my nice floor." The sword is not my weapon of choice, but after my father went to the Crusade, I made sure I could use the blade should the need arise.

Vontrapp throws off his hood, revealing matted brown hair and a grimy skin, but most hideous of all is his snarl. "I am ready for death. Can your kin say the same?"

The blade almost falls from my hands at his words that don't even carry the power of a Davar. *"Irwin."*

My foe takes the opportunity to charge at me, and I just barely lift my sword fast enough to block his blow, which nearly tosses me into the wall. With our lightweight bones, elves were meant for speed, not strength. I need to use my speed against his strength, or I shall surely die. And then no one will rescue my cousin.

With a shout, I dive to the side and drop to the ground.

"Kneeling already? I may let you live after all."

I swipe my sword at his ankles. He moves one foot in time, but not the other, and it's his turn to fall against the wall.

"Impetuous little thing," Vontrapp mutters, whirling around to face me and halt my blade from piercing his back as he leans on the wall while his ankle bleeds. "Such a shame. I could have had such fun with a pretty little pet like you."

Rage overpowers me, and I swing at him again when I should block his blow. I duck instead, which spares my life, but throws my swing, and I hit the wall more than I hit his waist.

Then arms are wrapping around me and dragging me backward, away from VonTrapp. Hands, one of them oozing warm, sticky blood, grasp my wrists and twist them until I drop the blade of my ancestors.

Vontrapp straightens as much as he can with his injured foot and waist. He limps forward, raising his sword. "Hold her steady. I want to lop her head off just so."

I grit my teeth. "The Emperor will avenge me." Actually, I will not even let it come to pass, but he doesn't know that I am training my gaze on him so he won't notice the way my ancestral sword is rising behind him. "My father served him faithfully."

"Oh, but it was the Emperor who decreed this violence against your home and every elf keep."

I stare at him in disbelief, and then my sword wavers, giving away its position.

"Behind you!" cries the bleeding man holding me.

Vontrapp turns just as the sword arcs toward his neck.

Then, before my very eyes, Vontrapp vanishes into nothing, and the sword moves through air.

My jaw drops and the sword falls. What nightmare reality have I been awakened into? Mayhap I'm being influenced from fumes of one of Irwin's potions gone wrong.

Irwin!

I throw my arms back, crashing the hands of the man who holds me against the wall. He bellows in my ear, and I wrench my hand free of his bleeding hold. With all but one arm free, I whirl partially away from him. Then I kick his arm that still clutches my wrist.

He releases that wrist too and goes down, clutching his hand to his chest.

Then I turn and run down the hallway, my focus on my last living kin, Irwin and his mother, my mother's sister.

My sword flies into my waiting hand as I turn the corridor and make my way to their chambers.

The door is already ajar, and my heart freezes as though one of the ancient, forgotten *Davars* has been used against me.

Sliding inside, I stare into the darkness. First, I turn to where I know Irwin's bed is and find him sleeping still. Then I turn to the canopy bed of my mother's sister— and find another form standing over her.

A figure who plunges a blade into her.

"No!" I scream.

The figure turns to me.

"May the blood you have spilled return upon you!" I scream, hurtling my sword forward. I hear it make contact and watch the form crumple to the ground.

I hurry to my aunt's side, ignoring the man who doesn't make any move to stand; who doesn't even writhe.

"What's going on?" Irwin mutters behind me, stumbling in his sleep.

Reaching forward in the darkness, I touch my aunt's neck and feel the sticky ooze of blood.

"No," I whisper. This cannot be happening. There has been enough death in my clan these last few years to last a century.

I press my shaking hands down on Aunt Orpah's sticky neck. "By the strength of our blood bond, I strengthen the blood flowing in your veins."

I wait desperately for some sign that the *Davar* is working. But there is no glow from my hands to signify the Kin Magic is at work.

And Aunt Orpah's chest refuses to rise.

Desperation seizes me. "By the strength of our blood bond, I strengthen the blood flowing in your veins!"

A hand grasps my arm and I turn, my entire body shaking now.

Irwin is looking up at me with wide eyes. "She was just alive. How can she . . . How can she?!" His voice breaks as he dives forward, trying to heal her likewise.

And something else sounds like it's breaking outside the room.

I turn to my last living kin. "We have to escape."

"What is happening?" he asks, his eyes wide as he tries to process in vain the corpses before us even as he seems to be trying to put his mother's blood back into her body. The sight reminds me so painfully of the way my mother tried to bring back my father, and died trying.

"Death," I whisper. Then, my hands still wet with his mother's blood, I grab his arm, wrench him off our fallen kin, and drag him into the antechamber that served as a sitting room before he had it converted into an alchemy lab. I pause only to reach out my other hand to summon my sword back to me.

Irwin suddenly pulls free, and I turn in terror at the thought that he would be stolen from me as well.

But his slight form is reaching to grab several potions from the higher shelves before he hurries back to my side. "These will help us make our escape."

Since I have very little training in the ancient art, unlike my cousin, who could do little else but study during his bouts of sickliness as a child, I just nod. Then I pull him toward the doorway that leads to the hallway.

Three dark forms look up in unison with my movement.

I freeze.

Then a deep, guttural sound erupts beside me.

Turning, I watch as Irwin launches one of his recently collected vials at the guards.

They hit the stone ground in front of them and explodes.

Then Irwin and I turn and run in the opposite direction. We don't stop until we reach the kitchens.

"Elflings, is that you?"

Irwin flings the curtains separating the kitchens from the outer rooms shut behind us, and I turn to Cook, armed with a rather large cutlery knife.

She drops it at the sight of me and throws her arms around me.

I hug her rotund form back, breathing in the smell of flour, herbs, and a distant childhood when she served as my nursemaid and fed me with food and tales alike.

"I was just coming to fetch you young'uns," Cook says, pulling away and then moving to the farthest kitchen. "Now hurry, this way."

Irwin and I follow her to the passageway she showed us when we were too young to understand why our ancestors once needed hiding places and escape routes from our human neighbors.

Cook hastily digs out the brick that causes the door in the wall to slide open. Then she turns to us. "Hurry. If Abel is worth his salt at all, he's waiting on the other side with two saddled horses."

Irwin steps into the dark passageway that once was merely a forbidden plaything. But I stay by Cook's side. "You aren't coming with us?"

She shakes her head. "These monsters are only after your kind. They seem to be under the impression that they are 'liberating' us mortal servants."

I reach to grasp her hand, scared at the thought of losing another piece of my life. I'm more terrified in this moment than I would be if estries had me bound to a pagan altar for their Dark Ritual.

When I see my reaching hand, though, I see the blood still staining my fingers and pull back from tainting Cook's apron. "But they might hurt you if they learn of your kindness to us."

"They'll learn nothing about you from me. Nothing but pain and suffering, that is." Her eyes flash, and despite her small stature, I know her to be a mighty force to be reckoned with. "I know just which of young Lord Irwin's potions to mix in with their supper."

"But Cook—" I forget about the blood and grasp her hands desperately. When this night is over, what will I still have left that I call mine?

She stubbornly shakes her head. "I must look after the others, especially the maids. But you must go. Your father's line must not end with you."

Cook always knew just what to say to convince me to do what she thought was best for me.

"And don't forget your winged rodent." Cook scoops the family *Shamir* out of her apron pocket where it prefers to nap with a tenderness that belies her harsh words.

I gasp as I take hold of the creature that fits well curled up in the palm of my hand. Its long tail wraps around my thumb, and I feel the power in my blood swell. How could I have forgotten even to think of the precious gift of our Creator to my kin, the creature that somehow shares no blood with my kind but strengthens our bonds with each other?

It blinks up at me with eyes that make it appear to be an infant, even though I know it has been in my family for at least three centuries. Its tiny form resembles something like a cross between a monkey and a mouse with its butterfly-like wings folded together.

"I have you now," I whisper before placing it on my shoulder. Its tail releases my thumb to wrap around my ear instead, as is our habit. Thankfully, it retains its minuscule form. Not that I should expect it to grow now after all these of smallness, grieving my parents.

Then I look up at Cook. "I'll never forget you."

"Well, I would hope not, child. I changed your nappies. Now go!" She pushes me into the passageway after Irwin and closes the door behind me, bathing us in darkness.

Until a glowing vial appears in my line of view as Irwin shakes it, apparently to activate it.

He holds it up and outward. "This way, Cousin."

Listening for the sound of the enemy on the other side of the wall, I follow him until the vial illuminates a dead end.

The smell of horse manure would normally drive me away, but after all I've been through, such mundane inconveniences mean nothing anymore.

Irwin activates the entrance on the other side of the tunnel before I get there, but he stands frozen in the dim light from the stables.

I hurry to his side. "Is something wrong?"

"I just didn't want to leave without you," he whispers back.

"Oh." Leaning out, I glance to the left and to the right, but I don't see anyone. Then I jump out.

Irwin stumbles after me, and we make our way over the crunching hay toward the darkness that we know our horses to be stationed in.

"Who goes there?" A voice whispers.

"Elspeth," I answer.

Suddenly, a light flares out in the darkness, illuminating the cloth falling from it to the ground, and the young man behind it whose hair is the same texture and color as the hay that is always sticking out of it.

I press a hand to my chest, suddenly aware of how hard it's beating. "Abel."

"What's happening?" he whispers, glancing around erratically, as if the shadows might pounce on us at any moment.

"We're under an attack," I gasp.

His eyes widen. "The keep?"

Irwin almost chokes. "Our family . . ."

Abel nods. Elves may have equal rights with mortals here, but socially, not so much. And deep down, we all knew, and our servants with us, how tenuous our safety truly is.

"I prepared three horses." He moves toward them.

"Mother won't—" Irwin's voice breaks.

"It'll just be us two," I answer.

Abel reaches my mare, Omen's, gate. "Well, I'm coming with you."

I glance back toward where I left Cook. "They're not attacking your kind."

"You've been a good Master." He hands me the reins for my mare. "Well, Mistress. Somehow, I doubt that those who come to plunder and kill by night will be better than you."

He helps me up and I clutch Omen's reins in one hand and her mane in my other. "I appreciate your loyalty. But I can promise you nothing."

"My freedom is all I ask." He hoists Irwin up.

I sit up straight. "They would have to take my life before they took our freedom."

Abel mounts the third steed. "Then lead the way, my lady."

Omen follows my silent orders to charge out of the stable. Irwin and Abel ride at our heels as we make our way to the forest that borders my estate for cover.

The moment we are all three in the shelter of the trees, I allow the others to pass me as I turn back.

My family keep looks the same as it has always looked from the outside looking in . . . except that I have never had to see it from this angle at night.

Now, though, it no longer houses my family.

I glance back at Irwin, who has stalled his stallion, to wait for me. My last living kin.

Turning Omen toward him, I make one last promise, this one to myself.

I will reclaim what was stolen from me. From us. And for both our sakes, I will never let myself be weak again.

CHAPTER 11

PRINCE OTELLO

Sitzvononne during the thirty-seventh year of Emperor Augustu's reign . . .

"This show of 'strength' was absolutely unacceptable."

Emperor Augustu Constantine III barely looks up from his papers. "Leave me, Otello." His voice sounds almost hollow as he repeats the only phrase I ever get from him anymore.

I close the study door behind me so we can have a measure of privacy. There is never actually privacy from the Guardians of the Holy Emperor of the Sanctified Empire of Constantinium, who never leaves the Emperor's side. I've grown used to ignoring all of them— except for their leader, the Emperor's Shadow, the only estrie permitted in court. Or allowed to live at all without being hunted to extinction like his brethren for their blood-drinking, soul-sucking ways.

Taking advantage of my privilege as the one person who could march up to the Emperor with no consequences from the Guardians or the Shadow, I do exactly that and slam a royal decree down on his desk in front of him. The one that flies in the face of our duties to our citizens, our divine right, and the Emperor-God, who gave us both.

My father stops reading his papers simply because they are obscured by my addition.

I clench my teeth together. "Since when do we make decrees allowing our people to turn against each other?" Leaving him to read the decree he signed into order not three morns ago, I turn away. I can barely bear the thought of sharing blood with someone who would callously let so much of it be spilled, let alone be in the same room as him.

He used to be such a just Emperor, a kind man. Or so it seemed when I was a child.

I run my hand through the thick dark hair I inherited from my father, though the resemblance is less clear now that his has turned all too white and is starting to fall out in clumps that his servants work hard to disguise.

Then I turn back to face my father.

And find that he has moved back to staring at his previous work, leaving the decree I brought hanging half off the desk.

"Father!" I cry. How can he be so unmoved by this when it has stolen into every moment of my life and banished all sleep from my eyes? When every time I'm alone, I can swear I hear screams of my people as others come to slaughter. And when every time I close my eyes, I see the form of a beautiful woman standing before me in purest white. I can never quite make out her face as her long, brown tresses flow around it. But there is no mistaking the betrayal in her voice when she whispers, "*How could you?*"

A woman I've never seen before, yet somehow feel as though I've known forever, living only in my mind and apparently determined to drive me insane.

Suddenly, my father's shadow shifts, bringing me back to reality, and I almost startle to see that the Emperor's Shadow is still in his place in the far corner of the room, barely visible in the black cloak of his title.

But my father has one other shadow, though the man carries a different title. From the dark corner, a man adorned in the brown robe of his title steps forward.

I narrow my eyes. "Adalbert."

The High Sorcerer studies me with amber eyes I'm told he was not born with. "Your father is weary and should be left alone."

"My father is my responsibility, not yours."

The Guardians of the Holy Emperor of the Sanctified Empire stir.

I nod toward them, almost causing the thick golden circlet awarded to me at my Unveiling to slide off my head. "And theirs, of course. But he allowed our people to slaughter each other! I need to understand why." I try to look past Adalbert to my father.

But I almost wish I hadn't, since none of my impassioned words seem to have had any effect on my father, who continues to stare blandly at his other decrees.

"Father? We need to right this great wrong somehow. They are *my* people as well." The words come from a deeper place inside me than I meant to display to this room full of hostiles and those more loyal to the sitting leader than to the future Emperor.

I close my eyes as the weight of the evil that has been done against my citizens alongside the burden of the evil worked by my people comes crushing down on me.

"As the greatest Empire in the world, the eyes of all are upon us. And we have shown ourselves to be simultaneously merciless and weak. Ehyptio is always looking for vulnerabilities, and now there are rumors of gysts escaped from Purgatory with Heavens only know what intentions. And we have exposed ourselves before them all."

Father finally turns to me, and I'm struck by the expression in his eyes. Or, more accurately, by the complete lack of one. It is as if my father has somehow departed from his own mind.

I stumble backward, my gut telling me to flee. But my heart tells me to go to him, hold him, and somehow protect him from whatever has sent him into this state.

"My liege."

Startling, I turn to find the only titled Elf-folk of my father's court standing in the doorway, studying me.

"Uriel," I say, going to the Keeper of Knowledge, the man who trained me to harness the magic of my royal bloodline. Indeed, the only person other than my father and myself to know the manifestation of the Heritage Magic our bloodline carries. "My father— I believe something is wrong."

Uriel holds out his arm, causing his green cloak that he wears to separate his station from that of the High Sorcerer to drape out. "Come with me, my prince."

I allow my tutor to lead me away from my father, holding my tongue until we're out of earshot of the man I trust far less than the elf before me.

Heinrich, my valet and closest companion, falls into step behind us. He follows me everywhere but into the Emperor's presence.

Once we reach the library, though, I close the door with Uriel and me on one side and Heinrich on the other to make sure that we are not disturbed.

Then I turn to the man who sometimes seems more of a father to me than the man who sired me. "I think something is wrong with my father. The man who raised me would never sign such a law into being. Your kinfolk . . ."

A flash of sadness moves across Uriel's face, and he bows his head. His long fingers touch his forehead and each shoulder in the tradition of his people when speaking of either the dead or of evil.

Both apply to this situation.

"I fear the court may not be the safest place for you, my prince."

Startling, I study my tutor, but he's no longer looking at me. "Uriel?"

He clears his throat, his expression a mask. "I mean only, you should go and find those who survived the Night of the Broken Walls. Make restitution where restitution can be made."

I rub my face. "You're right. We can't undo what's been done, but we can try to restore it. *I* can try to restore it."

"As a Prince ought."

Dropping my hand, I frown. "But my father . . ."

"I'll watch over him, or as much as he needs to be watched over with the Guardians of the Holy Emperor of the Sanctified Empire already bearing that duty."

"You're right. I'm being foolish, worrying for nothing." Moving past Uriel, I swing open the library doors, startling Heinrich, who appears to have been trying to eavesdrop through.

"Heinrich," I say, "oversee the packing of my belongings. We will leave at dawn."

Obviously, the doors were too thick to eavesdrop effectively through, because the face that eerily resembles mine frowns. "Where to, my prince?"

I stride past him as the weight of my necessary mission settles on my shoulders. Then I glance back at him. "The entire Empire."

CHAPTER III

Lady Elspeth

The first Heaven opens, and pouring rain helps in covering our tracks.

It also serves to make me as miserable physically as I am emotionally. The sky seems to grieve what I have no time to mourn yet.

"Where should we go?" Abel asks.

Irwin whimpers behind me, and I know he's in even less of a condition to think about the future than I am.

But I have to be strong. For both of us. Well, all three of us. Four if I count the *Shamir*.

It squeaks and nuzzles closer against my neck. I feel its frightened heartbeat pulsating opposite my pulse.

"The woods," I say. Say again? I feel like we're in some sort of tortuous cycle. Every time I close my eyes, I see my aunt murdered again and again. See myself shed my first blood on repeat. Watch my agonizing escape from all that I know and love.

So, I keep my eyes open and facing forward. "They will give us shelter from both the enemies and the weather."

They follow me unquestioningly to the woods because I suppose they want direction. I do too, but there is no one ranked higher than I here. The command is mine whether or not I like it.

I lift my chin and shove my weakness back for another day. Then I push on.

And on, and on, and on.

"Please don't be mad at me, Miss, but I learned how to build a shelter from my days going pheasant hunting with my brothers."

I shudder as I hold the large stick Abel gave me steady as he places a blanket over it. "Why would I be mad at you?"

Even as Abel's hands continue to be deft in their work, his face slightly flushes. "It was your woods. Only because we had heard your family was kind and never hanged poachers."

"Well, I'm glad you didn't starve."

Irwin finishes tying our horses to a nearby tree and comes to stand by us. Elvish men are generally not as tall as their women, with him being a good head shorter than me. But seeing him now, his dark brown curls plastered to his pale face and his white shirt loose and long over trousers, he looks even smaller and more vulnerable.

He lifts his colorless face from studying the ground-turned-marsh. "We're all going to have to be poachers now."

I look away as the truth of Irwin's words hits me. Never in my lifetime have I committed any crime against the Emperor or his people.

But now that's all going to change. All because the Emperor and his people committed a grievous crime against us.

Something burns inside me, driving me to my feet. "No, we will not poach."

Abel and Irwin both turn to me. "What?"

"We will not poach, and we will not steal." The rain has plastered my hair to my face and seems to have soaked through my skin, but I feel no chill compared to my rage. "We will merely take back what was ours. Our restitution."

"Abba, Abba!"

Father looked up from poring over the Roden records he was always reading. "What is it, my little Starlight?"

I stumbled toward him, almost anchored in place by the history tome that weighed almost as much as I did. "Today, I learned our people didn't begin in Constantinium. We came from Southern Imparia. The Empire conquered us!"

For a long moment, Father just stared at me, and I waited for him to tell me that Constantinium was the villain all along.

Then Father set his ledger down. "The Empire did not conquer us."

"But Tutor said—"

"The Creator gave us over. There is a difference."

I frowned. "But why would the Creator do that? I thought He loved us. We're His people, aren't we?"

"We are His people and He does love us, but that means sometimes He has to take things away from us to lead us back to Him. Because without Him, we can never know joy."

"Elspeth. Elspeth, wake up."

I peel one eye open to find Irwin shaking me. I blearily look at him before the sunlight drives my gaze downward, to where my long brown hair is tangled with the grass staining my shift. "What is it?"

"Abel is gone."

That wakes me up. I sit straight up, memories of last night mixing with vertigo as I scan the woods.

I conclude that Abel is, in fact, gone, just as I remember why Abel and all of us are in the woods.

And realize why it's a very bad thing that Abel is not here. "We have to go."

All the blood drains from Irwin's face. "You think they snatched him?"

"Or he betrayed us." I move to grab the few possessions I still have left. Which is only the filthy shift that falls to my knees, my hooded cloak, my father's sword, my mother's ring, a couple hairpins that I apparently missed removing before going to bed last night, and the keys to my castle I wear on twine around my neck, though it's useless to me now.

All three horses are grazing where we left them tied to tree branches. Abel didn't go far.

A twig snaps.

We both jump, and I turn to find Abel along with three more straw-haired lads behind him, each one taller and broader-shouldered than the last.

“I brought my brothers,” Abel says, looking way too innocently proud to be a traitor. "To be thieves, too."

His words are not at all what I expected. "What?"

The tallest and broadest brother steps forward. “And we know who our first mark should be.”

I turn to him, still somewhat dazed by the sudden turn of events. “What?”

“A traveling freak show,” he adds.

Pursing my lips, I shake my head. I need to reclaim control of this situation, if I ever had any semblance of control to begin with. “We will only steal from those who stole from us."

“These bandits have already taken more than their share of the town crops as payment no one offered, and we even heard that he’s stolen people.”

I nod. “Then we take the crops back and claim the four percent retribution for ourselves.”

Irwin and I crouch behind a set of barrels, fugitives in the town we used to govern. I’m still wearing only a filthy shift that leaves far too much of my legs exposed to be decent for a noblewoman.

“They say they’re the circus,” whispers Geoff, the eldest brother. “But all they’ve done since they arrived two days ago is steal from the people in every way possible.”

“Then we steal it back,” I say for the umpteenth time, hoping that I can make myself believe that it is right. But somehow, mixed with all my rage, is still a trace of guilt.

I study the tents thrown up haphazardly in the town square. One tent appears to have cages tucked in the darkness. “We should strike that tent first. If there are people in those cages, they can help us if we liberate them."

Irwin turns to me, his blue-green eyes wide. "We're just going to run in?"

Biting my lip, I turn to him. "Do you have any other ideas?" I genuinely want to know. I know I don't have any other ideas.

Irwin looks somewhat offended at my answer. "I just don't think we should be reckless."

I bite my lip harder and taste the copper and buzzing power of my blood. "You're right. You should stay here, Irwin. Just in case something goes wrong."

He looks even more offended by that.

"We should all just walk in," Geoff says. "With us brothers forming a wall around Elspeth, since elves are a bit more noticeable. We'll just stride in all normal like and then ambush."

I nod. Then I reach under my hair and feel the *Shamir* entwine around my finger. Then I hold it out to Irwin to take. It looks at me with its wide, yellow eyes, looking somewhat betrayed. Then it reaches its little arms toward Irwin obediently.

He stares at it. "You need it, though."

"No, I need to use stealth. And you know our little friend likes to expand at the most inopportune moments." Before Irwin can point out that he has not changed his size since my parents were taken too early by the Creator, I face forward, studying our mark.

And then wait. Wait for some normalcy to return to my life. For the elders in my family to warn me to caution. For my servants to remind me that my actions affect more than just me. For fear of losing all I have to the wrong side of the law to control me.

But my elders are all dead. My servants are subject to another. And the law has already betrayed me.

So, I stand, feeling strangely weightless, like when I fell from the top of the tallest tree in our courtyard.

Then I rush forward before I can hit the ground.

I keep running, all the way into the tent, until I collide with large body.

The body topples backward, and I stumble forward, stepping on it before I hit the cage. I grasp the bars to steady myself before glancing back.

The body I collided with appears to be a man twice my size. But he's now prostrated on the ground, his eyes closed and blood pouring from his nose where I stepped by mistake.

"Have you come to rescue WolfBear?"

I turn back to the cage to find the most pathetic figure I've ever seen in my life, even for one thrice my girth and at least an elle taller than I am. From one perspective, the person appears to be a human. A woman. But she is also not quite so.

Her ears are neither small and curved like a human's nor long and pointed like one of my kinfolk. Rather, the closest resemblance seems to be a wolf. The rest of her face does not appear entirely human, elvish, or wolfish, but like a mixture of all three and something else.

For a moment, I just stare at her in wonder. I had heard the legend of such creatures, the product of another legend: the werwölves. Humans and elves alike who drink the blood of animals as part of a dark ritual to gain their properties at will. And should two werwölves bear a child together, the result is what some call the elioud, with no choice over their animalistic resemblance.

As I stare at this strange being, she turns to me with mournful eyes not unlike my old hound used to give me. "Please."

I feel both my heart swell with pity and my face flush with shame to be gawking at her when she obviously needs help. "I will release you."

Taking the pins that once held my hair in place, I put two into the lock and begin to work it.

The sad creature studies my work, making my hands clumsier with the knowledge of being watched.

I swallow hard and keep at it. "And what is your name?"

"They call WolfBear . . ." Her voice is deeper than any female's voice I have ever heard, making me doubt my earlier analysis. Even so, there is something somewhere that seems feminine. "They call WolfBear Wolf-Bear."

At her words, I realize the qualities are not merely wolf-like, but perhaps bear-like as well? One ear is long and gray, but another ear is short and brown now that I see her face from another angle. Long, white hair falls between those two ears filled with braids, adding evidence to my theory that she is, in fact, a female.

"Do you like to be called WolfBear?" The lock finally clicks, and I pull out the pins.

"That is good." WolfBear nudges at the door, and I step back as it swings open. Then she steps out and pulls herself to her full height, which is closer to nine feet than my own once impressive height.

She looks down at me, wiggles her unorthodox nose, and smooths out the dress of rags covering her frame. "WolfBear thanks you, mistress."

I accept her gratitude with a nod. "You are free now, WolfBear."

"WolfBear is free to serve you." The tall creature bends her great height and breadth down in a crude variation of a curtsy.

"I appreciate your gratitude—" Something explodes outside the tent. "But I will not keep you from your family."

I move toward the tent entrance, a shadow far taller than mine following close behind.

"Family sold WolfBear. Mistress is WolfBear's family now."

Pausing with one foot just outside of the tent, I turn to WolfBear, wondering what to say to that.

Before I can speak, though, WolfBear grabs hold of me, picks me right off the ground, and sets me down to the side just as what appears to be a firework whizzes past.

Then WolfBear pounces on a stranger dressed in a colorful circus uniform who had been coming up behind Abel. WolfBear jumps up, leaving the circus man curled up and cowering on the grass, and gestures to Abel. "Is this Mistress's?"

I wordlessly nod.

WolfBear picks him up and sets him down beside me before bounding toward where Abel's brothers and the other circus people are fighting over fireworks.

"Who's that?" Abel asks, his eyes still wide as he takes in the fray.

"WolfBear."

"Is she coming with us?"

"Do you think you can stop her?"

As I speak, she picks up two men and smashes their heads against each other before dropping them.

Abel grunts. "Guess we have a new member of the band."

Suddenly, a massive explosion throws us both backward, into the tree line.

Irwin hurries to my side. I see his mouth moving, but I can't hear anything but a ringing in my ear. I shake my head in confusion, and Irwin keeps mouthing words.

"What happened?"

Not sure how to answer, I let Irwin pull me into an upright position. I see the circus tents on fire, with the remaining conscience circus folk and villagers hurrying to put the fires out.

"Do you think it was the newest member of our party?" Abel asks.

Abel's middle brothers come stumbling forward, the edges of their hair and garments singed. Geoff is just behind, beating back an even more singed circus man with a half a tent pole.

With a heavy sigh, Abel sags against a tree. "Never mind. I should have known."

Once the circus man goes down, Geoff spins around to smack it at his singed brothers. "Don't do that again!"

Amid the chaos, WolfBear trots over happily, a basket that appears to be filled with food under her arm. "This is WolfBear's new clan?"

Abel sighs as the two arsonists both try to wrestle the pole away from Geoff and fail. "If you'll have us."

CHAPTER IV

LADY ELSPETH

Our three horses graze within the crude log pen WolfBear fashioned for them. The rest of us sit around the green-hued bonfire Irwin built with sheer alchemy for the sole reason of wanting to feel like he was contributing. Something about how Abel and the two middle brothers do all the hunting and Geoff and Wolf-Bear chop our firewood.

I guess I contributed best by daring to go into town with my cloak hood over my head and my ears sharp to hear what news there was. When I can't bear to hear the constant bird whistles between the brothers while they hunt that I can somehow hear no matter where I wander in these woods.

"The bards haven't stopped singing about our escapade with the circus," I say, choosing to put some pheasant on my crude wooden plate. WolfBear also contributed to the meat today, but I'm frankly not sure what it is, and I don't have the stomach to find out. "Both the local bards and the traveling troubadours have picked up on our other petty thefts and spun them into glorious tales."

Geoff grunts, with a full mouth, his appreciation of being appreciated.

Personally, I rather like that they see our escapades as heroic and not desperate means of survival, like getting the tools we need to survive long enough to become avenging heroes. And I can't fault their creativity. "You should hear the yarn they've woven about how we stole executioner's silver ax the night before he was to kill one of our own."

Irwin glances at the rusty ax propped against the fallen log we plan on hewing for more firewood. "You mean when we slipped that off the back of one of VonTrapp's goons when he kept threatening the merchants in a drunken rage?"

Abel's eyes widen in wonder. "And what do they make of how we snatched your bow and quivers?"

I glance down at the lovely wooden weapons I keep close to me now that my preferred weapons have come back into my possession. I've had too many failed attempts to clumsily hunt with my enchanted sword. "You mean when I stole back my own pieces from the crooked fletcher VonTrapp sold them to?" I hate to confess it, but even if the fletcher were not crooked, knowingly purchasing stolen goods, I would have taken my bow back from him. Even if it isn't blood-bonded to me like my ancestors' sword, it is bound to me by memories.

My mother engraved it with my name. My father first taught me how to shoot from it, straight and true. So many moments of my childhood were spent at our archery range, pretending to be Ælfric, Ruler of the Elves, risen again to lead his people back to our promised land in safety and peace.

Or mayhap just a type of elf like Ælfric. The ancient elvish is a little tricky to translate at that point. But we all anticipate the day when he or one like him will prophesy that the Creator has finally decreed that we can return to *Haya,* the land of our ancestors long since dubbed Southern Imparia, without fear of the Plague because our ancestors' infidelity has been forgiven.

Geoff seems bored. "Heard that one. I think we stole it in order to free the soul of the dearly deceased Lady Elspeth that was bound to the weapon that couldn't defend you." He yawns. "The tales paint glamor where is none. Only us surviving by willpower and our own wits alone."

One of his middle brothers, identical twins I haven't learned to tell apart yet, belches in his brother's face.

I frown. Mayhap it has far more to do than our willpower than our wits. "It has been a long fortnight, but at least they actually are sharing something else than the rumored gyst sightings."

Abel shudders. "What are those things, anyway? Old Man Ben says they look like us and act like us, but they come from another world. And you only know it when they pass through walls or even disappear entirely."

Irwin frowns as he picks at his clothes, where a piece of meat fell. "Shades aren't real. They don't walk among us and steal our sheep and our womenfolk at will."

One twin scoffs at that. "Not to worry, Irwin. You have no womenfolk to steal from you."

The other, either Helmut or Hubert, swats his brother. "What are you talking about? He's the only one who's got womenfolk here." He gestures at me while staring at his twin like he's the biggest *dummkopf* in the forest.

His twin glares back at him. "Not like *that*. You know what I mean."

The blank expression he gets in return makes me think he does not, in fact, know what his brother meant.

Irwin snorts. "Gysts are the real *dummkopf*. People just tired of saying the same stories about estries and werwölves. Even the Dark Ritual gets trite after too many whispered rumors."

Abel shudders again.

"*Anyway*," I say, not wanting to talk about those who suck out one's life force by night or take on the forms of vicious animals at will when there are no castle walls around me. "They have taken to calling us the band of the Bandit King."

Geoff chokes on his bite. "I suppose the circus did not want to admit to being thwarted by a band led by a Bandit *Queen*."

"Bandit Queen." I try the words out again in my head, liking the feel of them. I suppose it is a suitable title to replace Lady Elspeth, Baroness of Roden.

"Our fame is spreading," I add, moving my plate to my other side in order to shield it with my body as WolfBear tears into her catch of the day like a wolf might. "But not enough to have reached the ears of those we require vengeance from."

"You mean the robber baron sitting in our home right now?" Irwin asks, an uncharacteristic rage hardening his words. "Because I think he's heard. I saw a fresh wave of troops being brought in there."

"VonTrapp." I wince at the pain of uttering the name I've heard too many say in the marketplace. They say his limp is an injury from the crusades.

I will never not find joy knowing that it came from me.

That monster is no wartime hero. Not when he makes no distinction between killing enemy soldiers in battle and slaughtering innocent women in their beds.

I raise my face to look Irwin in his eyes. "No, not just him. He is only the hand of the monster who came for us. We need to go after the very head."

Though VonTrapp's blood will be mine. I am my aunt's kinsman avenger.

Abel chokes on his pheasant. "You mean the Emperor?"

Irwin studies me. There was once a time when he would have said to leave such matters in the Creator's hands. After all, the Creator is all of our Kinsman Avenger. But that time ended when his mother was slain while he slept.

"They all owe us retribution. And since no retribution can pay for the life they took, I also require revenge." The Creator may have decreed that we surrender *Haya* to Constantinium for our sins, and then exiled us Himself, but I committed no sin against the Creator worthy of my exile from Roden.

So I will not submit to it. And if the Creator will not help me reclaim what is mine, I will do it myself. Even if it means going straight to those that the formerly pagan Empire claims have the divine right to rule over all.

Geoff actually puts his food down in order to rub his hands together. "And what's the plan for that?"

I chew on my lip, all my tough words falling away with no aim behind them. "I-I don't know yet. I just know that we are far from reclaiming what belongs to us."

A scrap of WolfBear's meat lands on my skirt, and I reach to swipe it off quickly, noting the discoloration of my nightgown that has been reduced to near rags these past few days. Any more wear and tear, and I'll have to hide myself from all the menfolk. "And I know what we need next."

Irwin glances down at his own garb with even more disgust than I feel for my own. "And who are we going to steal from? Our own castle?"

We are far from ready to re-infiltrate that— physically or emotionally. "No, the next township over. He turned a blind eye to our plight. It's only right he should be reminded of it when he goes to dress and finds no more clothes to change into."

Irwin considers this. "They also had an excellent lab, if I remember correctly. If you go, don't leave me behind this time. Especially if there's a chance that we might see Meredith."

I lick my suddenly dry lips at the name of the girl who was once my dearest friend. "We'll see how Baron Hoff likes it when he is infiltrated." I look off into the sunset, hoping to draw strength from my words and the surrounding nature.

However, my focus is disrupted by WolfBear pointing at the scrap of meat next to me. "Mistress eat that? Or can WolfBear?"

Irwin and I stare up at the castle that we may not know as well as our own, but whose walls we were once welcomed in as children.

"Do you think Meredith retained her sweetness?" I ask, thinking of the daughter of the baron whose playmates we used to be.

Before Baron Hoff's wife passed to the highest Heaven and proved to be the only reason elves were allowed inside his walls.

"She had a special sweetness." Irwin's voice holds a hint of wistfulness. "One not even her father could touch."

I glance at him. "Her beauty was also apparent, even from childhood."

Irwin's face flushes, confirming my long-time suspicion of his tender feelings for her. "Perhaps we should steal her away as well?"

He looks away from me, not that it does anything to hide where the pink has become red on the back of his neck. "I'm only here for the lab equipment."

"Of course you are, Cousin. Of course, you are."

Under the cover of darkness, Irwin and I lead the others through the forest around the wall to the broken gate that he, Meredith, and I used to play next to, hoping we might catch sight of a beast in the forest beyond.

Irwin takes the lead as I wring my hands together. I have half a mind to tell Irwin to stay back, like last time, to keep him from being in danger. But he is the only one other than me with the information we need to properly infiltrate the castle. He's the only one who knows which tools he needs from the lab. I'd have to take it all. Maybe I should instruct him to do that anyway as a stab against Baron Hoff.

And I know he would not listen to me. The rage I sensed before is still there, and I fear that if I had him remain behind, he would go in alone to seek Meredith for nostalgia— or worse, her father, for revenge. Because we both know that it was he who put a stop to our visits and never permitted her to come to us.

I reach out and grab WolfBear's wrist.

She stops moving and turns completely to me. "Yes, Mistress?"

"WolfBear, instead of you coming with me, I need you to stay with Irwin."

Irwin glances back at me.

I give him a small smile and turn back to WolfBear. "To . . . help him carry his equipment."

WolfBear plants her large hand on my shoulder, somehow not scratching me with her claw-like nails. "WolfBear protect Mistress's kin."

Smiling, I nod my gratitude. "Thank you."

"The gate is still busted!" Irwin calls.

I gesture toward him, and WolfBear walks over to him, grabs two of the busted metal bars of what was supposed to be a hunting entrance, and pulls them apart.

Abel's jaw drops, but the rest of us rush past him and in between the bars.

Irwin and I lead the way to the castle, using the overgrown garden as cover. They used to be a legend in our part of the Empire for how well-trimmed, colorful, and exotic the flowers that grew here were. When the Baroness yet lived.

The kitchen door is ajar, just like it used to be. I suppose the cook still has her moments of great warmth. It is comforting that this, at least, hasn't changed.

The kitchen is dark, with the hearth boy snoring drunkenly by the dying embers.

I turn to Irwin. "This is where we part ways. I'll steal the clothes and you go to the lab in the tower. Take the brothers with you."

Irwin frowns. "You can't send everyone with me and leave yourself unprotected."

"The lab was barely used during our time here. I doubt that has changed. And you'll need many hands to steal every piece of lab equipment. I need more stealth to steal the clothes, which are considerably lighter, from the bedrooms, which are also more occupied."

Irwin's jaw drops slightly. "The whole lab?"

I smirk. "He doesn't use it, you need it, and it will make quite the point. Our reputation will spread and where better to start with revenge than with the person who banished us from our home for merely being elves."

Irwin's eyes flash. "It won't be fun transporting all that equipment, but it will be done."

He moves in the direction toward the tower, and WolfBear follows, along with Abel's brothers. But I grab Abel himself before he follows.

"Stay by this door and make sure everything stays secure."

Able nods and salutes me as though I were the general of the Emperor's own army.

Then I clutch my cloak more tightly closed. The thought of being seen by those who knew me before, in my present state, is strangely unnerving. It is the last vestiges of my noble birth, I suppose.

But I am also a thief, and I hurry out of the kitchen to the staircase I that will lead to the bedrooms.

I pause outside the room that used to belong to the Baroness. Meredith told me on the last day we were here that after her mother was laid to rest, her father shut the door to the Baroness' room, and no one was allowed in. Doubtless, all her dresses are still behind the door, and I only need one. Well, two, so I can wash the one.

My hand goes to the door, but then freezes. There is no love lost between the Baron and me. But it seems cruel to take such a treasure from a grieving widower, even if he is otherwise a monster.

And these dresses are Meredith's inheritance.

Turning from the door, I go to the room that belonged, at least at one time, to Meredith's older brother, Leopold. His clothes are undoubtedly too large for Irwin, but I'm sure I can tailor it. I used to do embroidery while my maids stitched; I'm sure I can figure out their part of the job. And for the brothers, too.

But I still need something.

My eyes slide toward Meredith's door. I used to borrow her dresses all the time. And I know she'd prefer if I took hers than her mother's.

I go to what I hope is still her room and try the door.

It opens easily. I suppose she wouldn't need to lock it, since there are no legal decrees to murder *mortal* women in their beds.

Carefully easing into her room, I note the moonlight shining in through the window, illuminating the room enough to reveal it has changed little. The wardrobe stands in the same place, as does the bed. But there is a larger form on it this time.

Avoiding the bed, I move toward the wardrobe and open it.

It creaks loudly, and I clench my fist. Of course, I forgot about that squeak.

The lump on the bed moves.

I plaster myself to the wardrobe, hoping the moonlight doesn't find me.

But then a candle flickers into existence suddenly, illuminating the face of a grown-up Meredith, her red hair escaping the fat braid on her shoulder. "Who are you?!"

Throwing off my hood, I gesture at my face. "I'm Elspeth. I'm not here to hurt you!"

"Elspeth?" Meredith pushes aside her sheets and comes closer to me, holding the candle to my face. "It *is* you." She smiles, but it suddenly wilts. "Why are you here?"

"I-I needed a dress." I push aside my cloak to reveal what used to be as fine a sleeping shift as hers.

Meredith blinks in confusion. "What about your dresses?"

"They were stolen from me, along with my keep and lands."

"What? What happened?"

Even though I am currently trespassing in the home of a known elf-hater and facing someone I haven't seen in years, it all comes rushing out.

Next thing I know, we're sitting on her bed, and Meredith is shaking her head and holding both my hands while the candle flickers on the table beside us.

"I had no idea," Meredith whispers. "My father had been bragging that soon we would not have to see your kind around here anymore, but I didn't realize it could be anything but a drunken rage. He has kept me isolated in this castle. Oh, but your aunt." She lowers her head.

"I'm sorry I came to steal from you. At the time, I was only thinking about getting revenge on your father for separating us."

"I also want revenge for that. Here." Meredith releases me and goes to the wardrobe, squealing it open the rest of the way. "Let's get you some dresses."

"Really?"

"Yes, and then I'll grab some of my brother's tunics for us as well. Dresses won't be the most practical in the forest, after all."

I stand up. "'*Us*'?"

Meredith spins around, holding out a dress to me. "I am coming with you."

"Wait, I don't think you understand the state of our lives."

"You live in the woods with no one to tell you what to do. It is you who misunderstands the state of *my* life."

I chew my lip nervously as two dresses get thrust into my arms. "But your father . . ."

"Is so drunk he won't even realize I'm gone. He'll think I'm finally being obedient and staying silent and in my room."

"And your brother?"

"Is not my guardian, no matter what he thinks." Meredith grabs a satchel and starts sliding items into it.

I chew my lip a little harder. Leopold may have teased me mercilessly after learning our mothers intended us to wed someday, but he's not heartless. I know he cares for Meredith. Even as I care for Irwin and would do anything to protect him.

But Irwin would also appreciate it if I reunited him with our childhood friend.

Then, because I have little of a choice in the matter, I allow Meredith to drag me out of her room.

A moment later, I find myself standing outside Leopold's room with four dresses now, only to have more outfits placed in my arms when she emerges.

And then we're in the kitchen with Abel and the kitchen boy still snoring in the corner.

Abel gawks at us. "Who's that?"

"The newest member of your merry band," Meredith gushes, wielding her somewhat ornate dagger that she'd taken from the display on her mantle.

Footsteps draw my attention, and I turn to find Irwin walking into the room.

"Be careful not to drop anything." His face turns away to properly address those behind him as he carries some glass twisty thing in his arms.

Then he turns back around, takes one look at Meredith, and promptly drops the glass thingy, causing it to shatter.

The kitchen boy gives a startled snort.

"Go back to sleep, Carl," Meredith orders.

Carl's breathing evens out, and he apparently does just that. Then she turns back to Irwin. "Look at you, all grown up. You're almost tall enough to fit in one of my dresses."

With that, she turns and trounces at the door, leaving Irwin wide-eyed and red-faced.

I will have to speak to her about not addressing the fact that male elves are normally a head shorter than their female counterparts, though he is at least the same height of most mortal women, including Meredith herself.

Right now, though, all I can muster is, "Be careful not to step on the glass, Irwin. Or else I'll have to have WolfBear carry you out."

Irwin mutters something under his breath, but I ignore him as I step out. We'd had another successful heist, our merry band is growing, and I finally have a proper dress to wear.

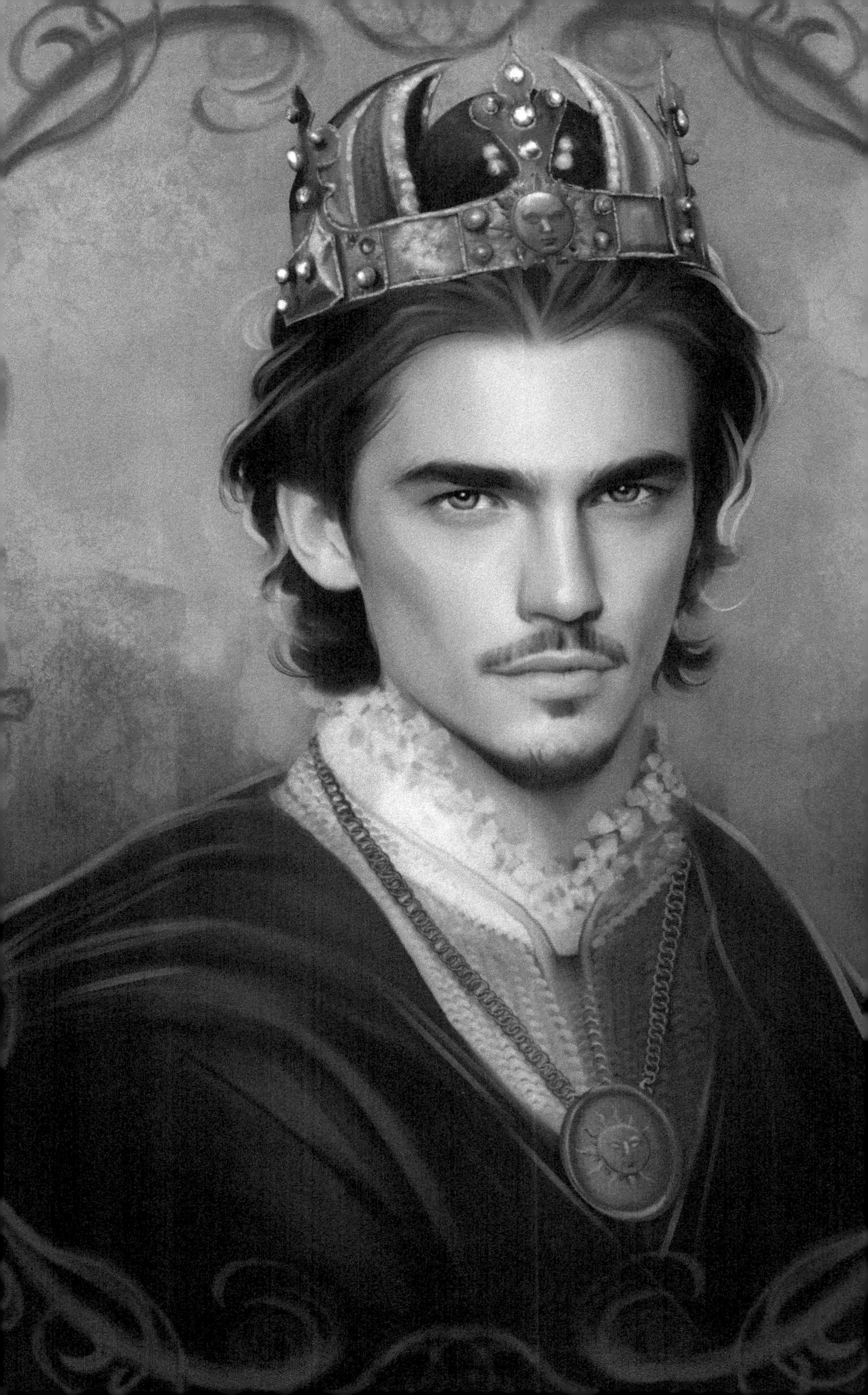

CHAPTER V

Prince Otello

I rub my face wearily as I slump back into the chair provided me by my ever-thankful host.

"So, we were quite protected in this castle because of its placement on the cliff because of my wise ancestors," Baron Abijah is saying, his pointed elf ears somehow bending with his words. "But I much appreciate the very son of the Emperor himself coming to check on us and give a personal apology."

I am beginning to regret that apology as the Baron waxes poetic on it for the fourth time. I'm also regretting stopping by at this castle first. And at this point, being born, to be honest.

Heinrich, my most faithful companion, first as my official playmate and then as my valet, clears his throat. "And speaking for the entire royal court, I am very pleased that you are doing so well, Baron Abijah. But it has been a hard day's travels and I would be deficit in my duties if I did not start preparing the Appointed Son for slumber."

Baron Abijah seems to realize the late time and how far back I am slumped in my chair. "Oh, yes, yes. Allow me to show you your chambers for the night. The very best in the entire castle, with the most beauteous view of the precipice below us and the shoreline that my people have sailed for centuries."

His words continue to wash over me, but I can barely listen as I stand to follow. Heinrich falls into step beside me.

"You are a hero," I whisper.

Heinrich grins and lowers his own voice. "Nonsense, my prince. The act drew purely motivated by self-preservation."

"I present the Lady Elspeth."

I lifted my head from where I had let it hang, heavy under the ceremonial veils I had to wear to establish my purity before the noble daughters of age being presented in court. The first official responsibility that my father has appointed me.

A tall, slender maiden moved forward in a pristine white dress adorned by her golden-brown tresses. She dropped into a curtsy before me and lifted her chin to face to me.

And even though I cannot quite make out her features, I felt myself straighten in respect of the awe-inspiring beauty before me.

She slowly rose. Her eyes seemed to look everywhere but at me. Her gaze moved far above me and then widened.

Suddenly, she launched herself at me, and slender frame or not, she sent me flying off my pedestal. I went sliding across the polished floor, her on top of me.

Then a terrible tearing sound filled the room, and for one horrifying moment, I thought my leggings tore.

But then the gold chandelier laden with amber stones to best imitate the sunlight came crashing down onto my throne, where I had just been standing.

I looked up at the young woman lying on top of me, apparently completely unaware of the way we were touching, as she craned her head back to look at what she saved me from.

My smile bloomed behind my veil, and I hoped she could sense it even if she could not see it when she turned back to me. "You have rendered a great ser—"

The look in her eyes stops me cold. They are simultaneously furious and heartbroken, wretched and defiant. "How could you?"

I wake up in a cold sweat and stare straight ahead in the darkness as my mind feels like it's swirling around in my head.

"Did you have a bad dream, my prince?"

"I think so." I rub my hand down my face. "And you know it's 'Otello' in private."

Heinrich stirs from his cot on the floor. "That sounds like it would be very forward of me, my prince."

After the dream I had, I don't feel like humoring him, so I just roll over on my side. "It feels like it was more than a dream."

"Oh?" His voice sounds groggy, and I wonder how long I have before he falls back asleep. "And what was it about?"

"A beautiful woman."

"Sounds like you'd better get back to that dream, my prince."

"*More* than a dream." I roll back onto my back. "Fuzzy like a memory. But anticipatory, like . . . like my destiny?"

Heinrich makes a borderline affirmative noise, and I know he's past the point of caring, and probably even listening.

"Fine, I'll let you go back to dreaming about Lady Adela."

That wakes him up a bit, and I hear him choke on nothing. "With all due respect, my prince, shut up."

I snort. Then I lie on my back and wonder where I've heard the name "Lady Elspeth" before.

Once the royal carriage has delivered us safely down the steep hill of Baron Abijah's impenetrable castle is situated upon, and more importantly, away from his chatter, I exhale dramatically.

Heinrich, my only companion in the carriage since the twelve guards accompanying us are mounted, smirks. "Do you think all elves are like that?"

"Uriel isn't. I believe it may have something to do with the isolation."

He nods in mock solemnity, causing his hair to shift. It was once a shade off of gold but has since been dyed to match my own dark hair so he can pass as my double if necessary. "Indeed, my prince. You are quite wise."

Groaning, I throw my head against the cushions. "How many times do I have to inform you that you are allowed to call me by name?" We were raised together. My nursemaid was his nursemaid and neither of us had our mother. I at least had my father. He had only me.

"Only as long as it annoys you to be called 'my prince.'"

I shake my head at him and then glance out the window. "I would suffer many a fruitless conversation in the future if it meant that all the other elvish barons survived the Night of Broken Walls."

"On that, I agree wholeheartedly, Otello."

Turning back to him, I give him a weak smile. "Do you think my father is . . . well?"

At my words, Heinrich's expression becomes solemn for real. "It doesn't seem like my place to speak upon the Emperor's wellbeing."

"You've known him as long as I have, Heinrich. That decree wasn't like him. Nothing he's done these last couple of months has been like him, actually. It is like he is a mere shadow of what he used to be. I haven't even had a proper conversation with him in months."

"His skin is so fallow. And his smell." Heinrich wrinkles his nose before glancing at me. "I'm sorry. I misspoke." His tone is insincere, a mere pleasantry tossed over the loathing for my father that he hides so well from everyone but me.

I sigh. "No, you haven't. I've noticed as well. Surely the court physician has him well taken care of, though."

Heinrich nods, though he doesn't seem very convinced. "Surely."

Sitting at the pub booth on a stool, I do my best to ignore the stares of the other clientele. Heinrich is the one wearing the princely robes and crown for this stop, sitting just to my left, but we are both surrounded by the guards. Except for my Captain, Gerrard, who is in the kitchen, now monitoring the preparation for our dinner.

Heinrich and I swap places like this so often that I'm as used to seeing Heinrich wear my crown as I am to seeing my reflection doing so. Something I'll never get used to, though, is seeing him wear my Heritage Medallion.

It always makes me a little sick to my stomach at the thought of someone attempting to assassinate Heinrich while he's disguised as me. But Heinrich has two specially made wrist bands that serve as sheaths for a dozen throwing knives. He can protect himself. Of course, so can I, but with my Heritage blood, I must submit to every protection.

My valet leans forward, and I see the gold pendant about the size of my palm dangle from its chain. Even though I can't see its engraving at this angle, I know it bears the family seal of the sun. And it calls to my blood and the magic flowing through my veins.

The first Keeper of Knowledge used his knowledge of Kin Magic and strange alchemy to bind that Medallion to my ancestor's Heritage Magic. Uriel taught me how to utilize the Medallion to augment my magic passed down from that ancestor.

I take another swig of ale and wish it would take away my headache. Between the exhaustion of the journey and the pressure of all that is ahead of me in my mission, as well as what I left behind, I'm surprised I have any capacity to think.

"Long journey?"

Turning, I find a stranger has taken the only stool near me that isn't being used by someone in my entourage.

He lifts his mug at me, giving me a world-weary grin. His dark blonde hair is probably not its actual color, only because of travel filth rather than for a disguise like Heinrich. His clothing is equally dirty, a thin tunic over leggings that have mud up to the knees.

The man notices my perusal of his appearance. "I'm Callistus. I'm not normally so filthy, but as my town's bard, it seemed only right to come to these parts to investigate the emerging tales of the Bandit King."

"The Bandit King?" I ask, hoping he doesn't notice my deflection from giving my own name. Perhaps I'm superstitious, but I feel as though lying during the first conversation is bad luck. Especially since I'm to be the head of the Church as well as the nation one day.

Callistus nods eagerly, a light sparking in his green eyes. "After the province was shaken by the Night of Broken Walls, a new legend arose. The avenging Bandit King. No one quite knows who he is, whether man or elf. But they say he steals from the rich and delivers the poor."

I rub my jaw. "Fascinating. It is certainly something to investigate while in the area."

Jumping off his stool, Callistus bows to both Heinrich and me. "I would be honored to assist you, my liege and my lord." He stands and frowns. "That is, unless such a noble entourage already has their own bard."

"You know what?" I look over Callistus' head to make eye-contact with Heinrich. "We forgot the bard and brought only a fool."

Heinrich sticks his tongue out at me.

Grinning, I turn back to my new acquaintance who will hopefully be able to introduce more useful rumors as I seek the scattered elf-folk. "Consider yourself hired, Callistus, for both entertainment and investigation."

"Thank you, good sir." Callistus slides off the booth to give me a bow at the waist before turning to Heinrich and doing the same. Then he turns back to me. "And since I shall now be traveling with far more esteemed company than just my donkey, I believe I shall go bathe."

He ducks out and I turn back to my mug, musing over who this Bandit King may be and what kind of complicated matter lies ahead of me. Somehow, though, I think it will be an excellent way to keep my mind off the darkness in my Empire and in my own family until I can discover how to resolve both.

"I must say, I am absolutely honored to be in the presence of not just a courtier from the Emperor's court, but his own son, and now two nobles beside!"

Callistus's chipper tone is quite a contrast in the tension almost smothering us in the dining room.

At least I do not have to be in the focal point of the tension as I am not sitting in the place of honor. Since the Captain of my division of Guardians of the Holy Emperor of the Sanctified Empire of Constantinium, Gerrard (or Gerrard the Guard, as I prefer to call him) is uneasy with the presence of Callistus, we are maintaining our disguises. Hopefully, Baron Hoff's time away from court will make it so he doesn't recognize that we are duping him while eating from his table.

But as the highest-ranking Baron in the province, we must stop at his castle first. And hopefully he can offer more information about the elvish barons in the area as well as the rumored Bandit King during our stay.

Personally, though, I'm rather thrilled to be sitting here in Baron Hoff's castle, attending a royal function without being the royal in question. It is freeing. The long-winded conversations won't be addressed to me, after all.

I don't envy Heinrich at all as he sits across the red-eyed, sallow-faced Baron Hoff. Not that I have much of a better conversation partner as the surly faced firstborn son glares across at me and doesn't say a word.

Casually as I can, I bring a spoonful of soup to my mouth.

Callistus proves to be as indifferent to the tension, because he suddenly leans forward and says, "Baron Hoff, have you had any trouble with the Bandit King in your serfdom?"

The son's fist hits the table hard, splashing my soup. Baron Hoff stands up so quickly his chair falls over.

Gerrard the Guard tenses, and I fear that any moment he'll send the Guardians in to extract Heinrich and me.

"Don't speak to me of this 'Bandit King'!" Baron Hoff picks up his plate of pork and throws it at the wall. Lean hunting dogs pounce on the food ravenously. "He stole away with my daughter in the dark of the night!"

I choke on my pheasant. "What?"

The son— Leopold, I believe— crushes his bread to crumbs. "He came into my room and stole my garments while I was sleeping, and I never knew it. Till I awoke and my Meredith was gone with only a note behind."

"How long ago was this?"

Leopold grinds his teeth together. "This past night."

Callistus wrinkles his forehead. "And you are not out searching for her?"

Baron Hoff collapses in his chair. "My health is too terrible for such a journey."

"And I *was* out searching." Leopold is hard at work making it so his teeth will become useless. "But I was called back to entertain the Prince." He glares at Heinrich.

That would explain his mood during this meal.

Why must injustice and treachery run so rampant in my Empire? My Constantinium?

I stand up. "This is a terrible travesty. I shall go out this very moment to search for her."

Gerrard whips his gaze from Leopold to me, the new greatest threat to my wellbeing.

I silence him with a Look to prevent him from blowing my disguise and causing further turmoil in this house. "You can come with me, Gerrard. The rest of you stay with the Prince."

Heinrich frowns to miss out on out the action.

Callistus stands up. "And I will accompany you, good sir. What a tale this could be, rescuing a fair maid from the clutches of the Bandit King." He turns to Baron Hoff. "What was her name again?"

Baron Hoff seems to consider this for a moment, as though he's not sure if he remembers, but Leopold says, "Meredith."

Callistus frowns. "That will be hard to find something to rhyme with, but I will endeavor to do my best."

I grab my cloak from my chair. "Let us make haste."

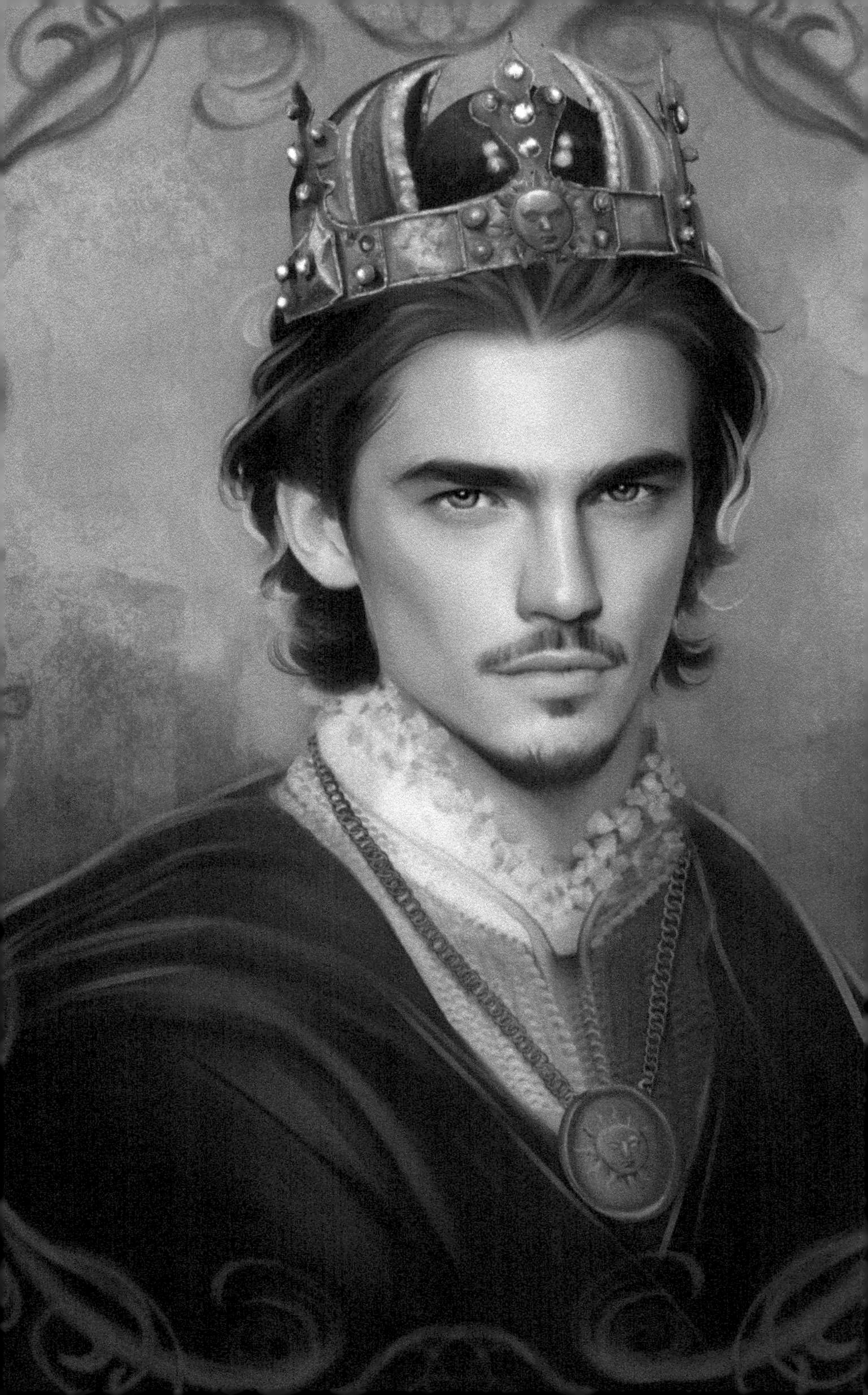

CHAPTER VI

PRINCE OTELLO

Mounted on one of the guard's steeds, I lead my party toward the woods lining the grounds, which grow thicker the farther away from the castle they are. It seems more than likely that Bandit King would hide in the forest, and it's at least worth a perusal. If that fails, though, we can always go to the village and ask the citizens for rumors.

"Stay where I can see you!" Gerrard calls from his mount, not looking at all pleased to have broken up our company.

Callistus grins at the Captain. "Not to worry, good sir. I'll stay quite close to you in case we find our Bandit King. Your sword is a lot bigger than my knife."

Ignoring Gerrard's order, I keep riding because I'm sure my sword is much larger than whatever the Lady Meredith has to defend herself with.

Riding parallel to the forest, I scan the area for any sign of people, and abduction, or even a path wide enough for me to ride through.

I see a flash of red and force my horse to a halt as the red material vanishes behind a large tree.

Sliding off the horse, I charge into the forest. "Who goes there?"

There is only silence other than the sound of my riding boots chomping through the foliage.

But I see the red garment disappear behind another tree further down.

Whoever this is, they are certainly nimble. Or perhaps terrified. Fear can give one abilities that one has never previously learned.

"I mean you no harm!" I call, hoping I'm talking to a peasant or Meredith, and not the Bandit King or one of his men, because I am fairly certain that I mean *them* harm.

There is no more movement, and I continue to the tree I last saw the red beside.

Despite my earlier assurance, my hand goes to the hilt of my sword as I round the tree.

And find nothing.

I unhand my sword and lean against the tree wearily. Glancing around, I find no more trace of red.

Of course. I actually have a lead, and I let it get away from me. How am I supposed to rule an empire if I can't even find a single abducted maiden?

The tree seems to want to comfort me, because it sends a flower drifting slowly down to me.

I reach out and grab it, wondering what kind of tree this is. Despite Uriel's extensive work in leading my studies, I am far from identifying every plant. Though, this red flower looks suspiciously like a poppy. Which, lack of botany expertise aside, I'm fairly certain is a ground-growing flower.

Glancing up, I see not six feet above me, perched on a thick branch, is a maid wearing a long red dress. The kind of dress a baron's daughter would wear, but a peasant could never be able to afford.

My eyes travel up the fine dress— and fine figure, if I'm being honest with myself— to the wide blue eyes of the young woman staring down at me. Her brown hair is pleated around her head several times, with flowers tucked into the braids.

I stumble backward, not at all prepared to see a verifiable nymph perched above me.

The nymph parts her plump, pink lips. "Would you kindly not look up my skirt?"

Of all the words that could have come out of her mouth, I would have been less surprised if she had spoken in the Tongue of the Dead.

I blink and stare dumbly like the dolt I am. "I'm sorry?"

She narrows her eyebrows, and those light blue eyes of hers somehow darken. "You're not forgiven."

"What?" I jump backward as her words finally register in my mind that appears to have fallen under some sort of dulling enchantment. "Oh, I wasn't looking up your skirt! I was seeking a maid." I furrow my brows. "Meredith?"

"I have not been abducted," she answers with a lift of her chin. "And I certainly don't need rescue."

"Your father and brother are worried sick with the thought that the Bandit King may have already debauched you."

"Bandit King?" The nymph— Meredith?— raises one finely shaped eyebrow.

"Yes, the man who abducted you." I glance around, scanning the area to make sure he isn't here right now, preparing to attack.

I turn back to her and find her smirking at me. As if the thought of abduction is somehow hilarious. Maybe it has not been that horrible for her. Her skin is yet flawless despite the surrounding dirt, and her hair has barely an errant wisp from its plated bread. It won't remain so for long, though, if she remains in these woods.

"The forest is no place for a noble lady as yourself," I say, grabbing one of the lower branches to pull myself up somewhat.

"Oh, is that so? At least you have the taste to recognize my breeding."

I take another step up and wrap my arm around her waist.

She glances down at me. "What are you doing? Unhand me at once!"

Praying to the Emperor-God of the Three Heavens that I don't drop her and break her neck, I half-throw her over my shoulder and then jump back down.

Her legs, which are hanging over my shoulder on the side where I can see them, start flailing wildly. Her arms hit my back.

"Let go of me!" she screams.

Her skirt flares up to reveal her ankles. I avert my gaze as I walk toward the edge of the forest. Her time in the wilds must already be influencing her. No mortal noblewoman would ever display such flesh. That is something a wild she-elf would do since their culture holds fewer restrictions on modesty.

"I am rescuing you, milady," I say, trying to discern how I can get her to my horse without dropping her or accidentally flashing her ankles to one of my hunting party should they catch up to me before then.

"You are *abducting* me!"

"Your father and brother are anticipating your return."

"My father and brother are dolts, and I ran away from them to save myself!"

I stop, suddenly frozen by her words. "You chose this?"

Her limbs still, much to my relief. "Please put me down and let me explain it to you, since you are determined to not leave me in peace."

Sighing, I bend over and plant her on the ground before placing my hands on her waist to keep her from running before I can be sure that she is safe.

She glances down at my hands, and I feel my face redden at my boldness. I'm not sure if I have ever touched a woman before. I suppose not since my nursemaid, but she certainly doesn't count.

Clearing my throat, I find some courage deep inside to retain my hold. "Please explain."

Meredith blows a newly escaped strand of hair from where it has fallen in the middle of her face. I have to fight the urge to reach up and tuck it away for her.

"I have been kept locked away in my room almost continuously since my mother passed. I have to wait until my brother can escort me if I want to even step foot on the grounds, and he rarely has time for me." Meredith's eyes flash dark again. I've never seen a mortal woman's eyes change shades so rapidly. Not that I have been this close to any woman's face before.

"So, you ran away with the Bandit King?"

She shrugs one shoulder. "I saw an opportunity, and I took it. He has been nothing but kind to me, far gentler than my father ever was."

"And he is not taking advantage of you?"

"He has not touched me." She glances down to where I am, in fact, touching her. Then she lifts her chin with pride. "We have a friar in our company who is preparing to wed us."

I feel a strange twinge of sadness that this beautiful nymph will soon belong to another. But I smile and nod. "So, you are happier in this life? Safer?"

"Indeed I am." She looks up at me, her eyes lighter now with what appears to be hope, a greenish tint in her gaze.

"Then I will assure your family of your safety and happiness." I release her waist and then hide my hands behind my back before they reach out and take hold of her again.

"Oh, thank you!" she cries, throwing her arms around my neck.

I stumble backward, startled. She seems undeterred, though, and presses her full lips against one side of my face and then the other.

Then, just as quickly as she grabbed hold of me, she releases me and runs deeper into the woods.

And I remain frozen where I stand, not completely sure that she wasn't, in fact, a nymph who'd just spun a spell over me.

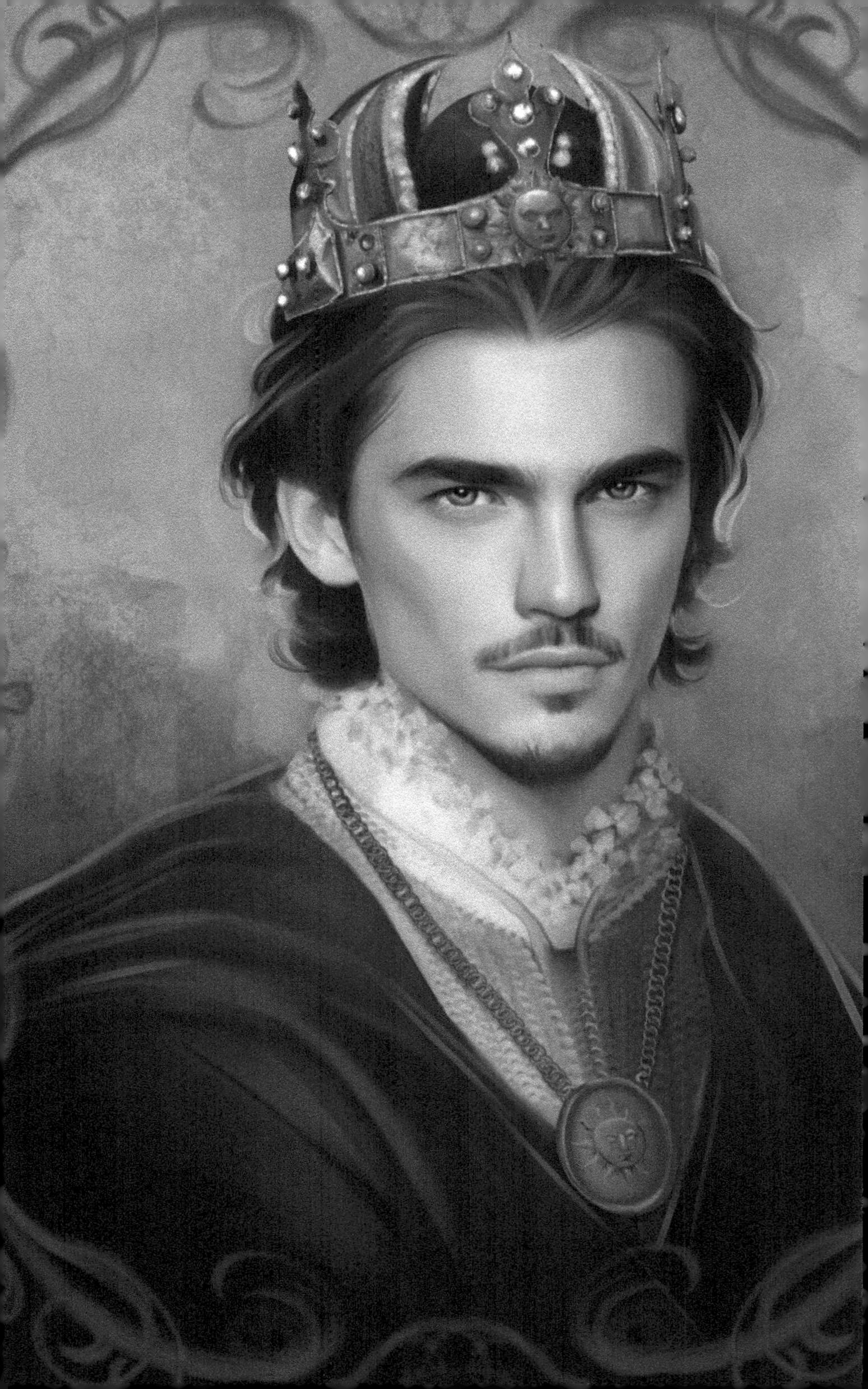

CHAPTER VII

Lady Elspeth

One hour previous . . .

I stare at my reflection in the river, absolutely dazzled by how beautiful I look wearing Meredith's red dress.

I feel like a lady again. With this soft cloth against my skin, I can almost imagine that my keep was never invaded; that my life continues as it was.

"Are dresses really practical for life as an outlaw?"

I open my eyes again to see Meredith's reflection in the water beside mine, combing her hands through her damp hair she just finished washing. She has chosen to wear one of her brother's tunics and leggings.

"I will change eventually. But I need to wear a proper dress for a little while lest I forget myself." Turning to her, I shake my head. "You look like a she-elf."

"And you look like a noblewoman."

"Well, I am." I turn back to the water and reach for my nearly dry hair.

"Here, let me." Meredith comes behind and takes my hair.

We carefully go to a nearby rock for me to sit since I am significantly taller than she is. Not that it matters if her skirt is a bit too short on me. The elves have long understood the need for speed and stealth, and have harnessed it as part of our Kin Magic, so it is understandable that a she-elf's skirt cannot drag on the ground.

It is only the standards of our rulers, the mortals, that decree that no inch of female leg may be exposed. Not that there is anything in the Scrolls of the Elder that they usurped from us and took to be their own commandments that say anything about what constitutes as complete female modesty.

"Thank you for allowing me to come with you," Meredith says, wrapping the braid around my head, collecting more tendrils of my hair as she does so.

"Your company is most welcome. I'm just sorry we were parted for so long."

"I meant come with you to your bathing river. I knew Irwin won't dare come by for a peek if you were also over here."

I choke on absolutely nothing.

"There." Meredith knots my hair together and then bends over to collect the wildflowers growing by the bank.

Standing, I go to the river and take in my reflection. With my hair wrapped around my ears, I not only resemble a noblewoman but also a mortal noblewoman, one who would be accepted anywhere.

"Here." Meredith comes up beside me and holds out some flowers.

I take a couple of red poppies and start weaving them into my hair.

"A flower crown," Meredith says. "Fitting for the Bandit Queen."

Smiling, I grace her with a curtsy.

Meredith grins before frowning. "So, what are we going to do? Do you have a heist planned out?"

I snort. "We just did one. Today we will live off the land until the next need or vulnerability presents itself."

She pretends to pout. "Well, that sounds absolutely boring."

"More boring than staying locked in your room to satisfy your father's whim?"

She wrinkles her nose. "I sometimes get to go out. When my overprotective brother finally deigns that he had some time to escort the sister he claims to cherish so much around the yard. Otherwise, I certainly couldn't leave the castle. It was outside the castle that mother perished, after all."

I reach out and grasp her hand. "I'm sorry about your mother. And the rest of your family."

She squeezes my hand. "And I'm sorry about your parents. And your aunt."

"At least I still have Irwin. And now we have you."

Meredith smiles. "Let's go torment your cousin now."

When we get back to the camp, all four brothers are surrounding Irwin and his now completely set up lab system. At least, I believe it is set up, sans the beaker that he dropped last night. I focused more on archery than alchemy, so I am not completely sure. Irwin seems perfectly happy tinkering with it as it is, though.

Not too far away, WolfBear is putting together large logs, probably for the shelter Irwin asked to be built around his precious new equipment.

"What are you going to concoct first?" asks either Helmut or Hubert.

"An invisibility potion?" the other adds.

"No," Irwin says, not looking up from his equipment. "Something much more powerful. But I'll need special ingredients."

Meredith skips. "Ooh, that sounds exciting. What can I get?"

Irwin jerks up at her voice and just stares at her for a long moment.

Coming to his rescue, I say, "Will there be any need for elderberries?"

Shaking himself out of his trance, he turns to me. "Yes, elderberries are part of it."

"I saw a patch of them growing near the forest's edge. I'll go pick some now."

Meredith turns toward me. "I can come with."

"No, I need you for something else." Irwin's face goes bright red when he realizes how that might have sounded. "That is, I also need clovers."

Laughing and shaking her head, Meredith walks over to a clover patch not too far from the tree where we hung our new clothes.

"Don't forget to hunt some dinner," I tell the brothers. I don't bother saying anything to Irwin, because he's already back to fiddling with his equipment.

Then I make my way to enjoy being in nature while wearing a new dress in peace.

Without a sundial to help me track the time and only the knowledge that darkness will tell me when it's time to return to camp, I feel as though there are no fetters on me as I go along, picking berries in my makeshift bark basket Geoff fashioned.

How odd, here in the forest, it is still my responsibility to care for those under me and make sure we all do our jobs to move forward, same as when I was in a castle. Yet it's different now. Because there is no fine chair at the table or private room or anything else but this new dress to show my differentiation from my servants. The only difference between us now is that they look to me for guidance and thus far have chosen to obey me.

I still would not mind having my own bed and kitchen chair again, though.

Beyond me, I hear a horse's whine and snort, startling me out of my reverie.

Turning, I see a strange man sitting tall on a pure white stallion just outside the woods.

Instinct takes over, and I summon all my stealth, heritage, and training to make my way behind a large tree.

I focus on my breathing to keep it silent enough to hear the rider dismount from the horse and start stomping through the leaves.

Definitely a mortal man.

Glancing up, I see that the tree I've sought shelter under is also a good climbing tree.

I hike my skirt way higher than even a she-elf should dare, plant my foot on a knot, grab hold of a branch, and pull myself up.

"I mean you no harm!" the rider calls. He has the voice of a young man, likely not much older than I.

I pull my skirt up around me and hold it tight around my legs as I press myself closer against the bark.

Then he comes into view. From my vantage point, I see he has thick, dark hair and a hand on the hilt of his sword.

Means me no harm, does he?

He scans the area where I had just been and seems very confused to not find me there. Unhanding his sword, he leans against the tree wearily and then scans the area again.

Just don't look up. I'm not even seven feet above him, so if he looks up, he can't help but see me.

As I'm staring down at him, I notice something drift past me.

A poppy.

From my hair.

I reach out to grasp it, but it's too late. I watch as it slowly drifts out of reach, a silent taunt.

The stubborn little thing flutters right in front of the man rooted at the bottom of my tree.

To my horror, he reaches out and grabs it. He spins it around, inspecting it.

Then he glances up.

His strangely deep violet eyes find me right away, and for a long moment, he just stares at me.

I stare right back down, assessing him. His ears are curved, confirming his mortal status. His face is hairless, but his jaw is firm and strong, evidencing his status as both youthful and full-grown.

My gaze drops to his garments, a fine green coat that matches the surrounding forest, a white shirt, dark breeches, and tall, brown boots that have been recently shined. HIs garments are simple, but of a good quality.

I have never seen him in these parts before, but he is surely too wealthy to be a lone traveler. Which means there may be more members to his party nearby.

His face goes from the pallor of shock to a pinkish color, not unlike what comes over Irwin when he looks at Meredith. He appreciates what he sees.

My hand comes up to touch my ears, but I find the tips of them covered by my hair wrapped around my head. Ah, that's why. He thinks I'm a mortal woman.

The man stumbles backward, still not looking away from me.

And I decide to play into his apparent attraction and surprise until I can figure out how to get away. "Would you kindly not look up my skirt?"

He blinks in confusion. "I'm sorry?"

I'd not expected an actual confession. I narrow my eyebrows, somewhat offended. No man would have done such a thing to me while I was a Baroness. "You're not forgiven."

"What?" He looks as taken aback as if I'd slapped him, which I really ought to do. "Oh, I wasn't looking up your skirt! I was seeking a maid." He creases eyebrows. "Meredith?"

Meredith? That's who he thinks I am? Did her family send him for her? "I am not abducted. And I certainly don't need rescue."

"Your father and brother are worried sick with the thought that the Bandit King may have already debauched you."

So, they did send him. And still cannot accept my new title. "Bandit King?" I raise one of my eyebrows back at him.

"Yes, the man who abducted you." He looks around, as if searching for the Bandit King— while ironically speaking to me.

I smirk to myself.

He turns back to me. "The forest is no place for a noble lady like yourself." Then, to my horror, he grabs hold of one of the lower branches to pull himself up.

"Oh, is that so? At least you have the taste to recognize my breeding." I glance around, wondering how a noblewoman like myself can get down without breaking my leg since he's taking up what was going to be my exit.

Suddenly, his arm is around my waist.

I go rigid and stare down at him. "What are you doing? Unhand me at once!"

Instead of heeding me, the barbarian tosses me over his shoulder and then jumps back down, shaking my upside-down body and making my death seem to come plummeting up toward me.

The moment I stop descending and am merely upside down, I flail my arms and legs, hitting his back as hard as I can. "Let go of me!"

"I am rescuing you, milady," the barbarian says, walking, I assume, back toward his horse and his party and away from my horse and my party.

Panic grips me more than vertigo. "You are abducting me!"

"Your father and brother are anticipating your return."

"My father and brother are dolts, and I ran away from them to save myself!"

He stops, suddenly my words finally getting through his stubborn skull. "You chose this?"

I still my limbs, wondering if perhaps I can get through this yet. "Please put me down and let me explain it to you, since you are determined to not leave me alone."

Sighing, he bends over and my world spins around again as my feet hit the ground. I reach up to hold my temple as I steady myself and then feel two other hands grasping my waist.

I go rigid again and look down at his hands. What is with this man's boldness? Glancing up, I find his neck has gone red, and he seems to be wondering that himself.

He clears his throat but doesn't release me. "Please explain."

I blow the newly escaped strand of hair from where it has fallen in the middle of my face. This bold knight or whatever he is— or thinks he is— has ruined the real Meredith's hard work.

With my friend in mind, I summon her story to myself. "I have been kept locked away in my room almost continuously since my mother passed. I have to wait until my brother can escort me if I want to even step foot on the grounds, and he rarely has time for me." I clench my fists at the thought of what she went through.

It is a difficult world even for noblewomen.

"So, you ran away with the Bandit King?"

I shrug one shoulder. "I saw an opportunity, and I took it. He has been nothing but kind to me, far gentler than my father ever was."

His eyes search mine, as if looking for lies. "And he is not taking advantage of you?"

"He has not touched me." I look away before he can find out my omissions. I stare instead where I am actually being manhandled at the moment. "We have a friar in our company who is preparing to wed us."

He smiles sadly and nods. "So, you are happier in this life? Safer?"

"Indeed I am." I look up at him and find myself somewhat struck by the authentic nobility and innocent trust in his violet gaze.

"Then I will assure your family of your safety and happiness." He releases my waist and then hides his hands behind his back.

"Oh, thank you!" I cry before deciding to thank him like a mortal damsel would and throwing my arms around his neck.

He stumbles backward, apparently startled. He probably doesn't get a lot of gratitude.

Even though he doesn't deserve it, I give him the customary kiss on each cheek before remembering that it is customary to my *people,* and not my rank.

Before he can realize what I've done, I release him and rush into the woods for refuge.

Hopefully, for my sake, he believes me and won't try to pursue me. And hopefully, for his sake, we never cross paths again.

CHAPTER VIII

LADY ELSPETH

I reach the camp despite my circuitous route intended to shake the man in case he followed me. Not that I ever saw any sign that he was.

Irwin is now actively brewing something, even without the berries that I left behind in my flight.

"What are you making?" I ask breathlessly as I approach him.

"Some basic sleep powder. Thought it might make our robberies a little easier." He looks up from his work and frowns at me. "What happened to you?"

"A passing gallant mistook me for Meredith."

The real Meredith glances up from where she's cutting one of her brother's breeches into little sacks, probably for the sleeping powder. "For me?" The *Shamir* looks up from where it was napping on her shoulder, apparently tired of Irwin's ignoring it in favor of his alchemy.

"Your family sent someone after you. He was quite certain the Bandit *King* captured me to make me his *Queen*." As if I needed any man to make me a queen in my own forest. Both my parents bore me into the world as a noblewoman. Only for the title Empress would I have to depend on a man, namely the Sacred Prince, to grant me.

Not that such a thing was anywhere in the realm of possibility, since no one would allow an elf to taint the Heritage Magic of the royal family. But I remember being introduced to the Sacred Prince while I was being presented in court. I wore all white to represent my purity, as did all the other girls being presented.

I remember when we were all lined up, them giggling about how handsome he had to be behind his ceremonial veils to establish that he was not only pure but also sacred. They weighed how likely it was that one of them might catch his eye, and when they counted us, they excluded me as part of the variable.

At that moment, I wanted to wed him just to spite them.

And there was a moment that I thought perhaps it was more in the realm of possibility than I originally gave credence to . . .

"They did?" Meredith asks, looking confused and snapping me out of my thoughts. "I guess I should have expected that from my brother, but not my father. Who was it? Obviously not Leopold. Was it Old Brom? He does have terrible vision."

"No, it was a young man. Not one I've ever seen before."

Meredith creases her eyebrows. "Did Father hire a mercenary?"

Geoff raises one eyebrow from where he's reclining against a tree.

"I don't know. I hope not." I press a hand to my temple and sit down on the tree stump WolfBear left for us. "That could really complicate this."

"We can't move the camp," Irwin mutters. "My lab is set up and functioning."

"We can set it up somewhere else," I say.

"But what if something else gets broken?"

"Just don't look at Meredith," Geoff offers helpfully.

Irwin glares at him.

And Meredith gets up to pace. "Maybe he's one of Leopold's friends. I don't really know any of them because he keeps us far away."

"We should just be very vigilant," I say. "And if there is any change in the wind, we need to be ready to leave at a moment's notice."

They nod, and I try to take the burden of my encounter off my shoulders.

But not only does the burden of care for my cousin and myself remain, but also the need to protect all these who have chosen to follow me.

I can only imagine how heavy the burden would be for whoever marries the Prince and becomes Empress over all these souls.

I lie on my makeshift bed— two of Leo's tunics laid over some hay that the brothers found for us. Meredith is lying behind me, and I can see Irwin from my vantage point by the moonlight. He already got up twice to fidget with his lab, and I wonder if I should just throw one of his sleeping powders at him to calm him.

Closing my eyes, I try to find some peace for myself.

Until I hear a twig snap.

I sit straight up and scan the area, looking for the source of the sound that is probably a squirrel or a rabbit.

But it could also be the gallant knight again. Mayhap a mercenary. Worse still, a bear or a bigger animal.

Sliding my feet to the cold grass beneath my bed, my bow is instantly in my hands, an arrow pulled taut and ready, my childhood mantra echoing strangely in my head. *I am* Ælfric, *Ruler of Elves.*

Another twig snaps, and I turn to face the source of the sound.

I find myself aiming at the face of a strange man, with several other people standing behind me.

My heart begins to pound, and I keep my arrow in place, the sinew straining under the pressure of my arrow pulled against it. "Who are you?"

The strange man doesn't so much as flinch. He stands with perfect posture despite his almost ghoulish frame. "My name is Kennen. My people and I are searching for the Bandit King. Have you encountered him?"

"Why are you looking for him?" I glance back at the camp, wondering if anyone else has awakened. Should I scream, or would that just cause a panic and possibly bloodshed?

Everyone appears to still be sleeping, except for WolfBear, who is curled up on the ground by the fire. Even though her eyes are closed, she has one ear perked up and is listening.

I have one ally in this.

Kennen and his people don't move forward or backward. "We have come to join him."

"Join . . . him?"

"My village and I have known only poverty and tyranny. We are ready to take what is rightfully ours. A good life."

Licking my dry lips, I glance around, not sure what the best move is. WolfBear can certainly take some of them out, but their number is so great I cannot even see the end of them.

So, I decide to go with honesty and hope that if that fails, mayhap the Creator will have mercy on me for telling the truth and deliver me. And not hold my thieving against me.

I lift my chin and hope that despite my sleeping in my new dress and more of my hair having escaped from its braid, I still look every inch the noble. "*I* am the Bandit King."

Kennen steps forward, and I can make him out better now. He is exactly my height, but at least a generation older than I with his dark hair is laced with silver. The clothing draping off his narrow frame is brown and tattered, yet there is something in the way that he carries himself that demands a sort of respect. Like he has the heart of a noble in the station of a serf.

His gaze scrutinizes me, and his expression betrays neither disbelief nor acceptance. "Is this true? Are you the Bandit King, she-elf?"

"I'm sure you've heard of the tales. That elioud by the fire is whom we rescued from the circus. And the lady on the straw is the woman I supposedly abducted from Baron Hoff's castle."

"So, the legends are true."

I'm taken aback that he believes me just like that and puts so much stock on the "legends."

"We were the serfs who ran the land belonging to Baron Tragott and the surrounding baronages."

I glance past him to the crowd and then back to Kennen. "Why are you here?"

"Because we heard of you, and it gave us hope."

"What kind of hope?" I'm feeling a little less like my entire camp is going to be slaughtered this night, but still a little hesitant to hope.

"Hope for a better life. Serving you."

With that, Kennen goes down on one knee, the position reserved only for swearing fealty.

Behind him, the mass of people do the same, looking as if a wave is moving over the sea.

And I stare in shock as my kingdom grows.

"Are we sure about this?"

I turn to Geoff, surprised that he's voicing concerns. He never showed much concern with anything beyond what he was going to eat next in the past.

"Sure about what?"

"Going from a small team to . . ." He gestures to the people working on making a place for themselves in our little clearing and around it. "There have to be at least a dozen people here!"

Actually, it's closer to a hundred, but Geoff was never good at counting. "What are we supposed to do, Geoff? Drive away a mob of people?"

"Well, no. But we could make them want to leave . . ."

"Or we could embrace our new numbers. Our new power."

Geoff turns to me. "You think we can keep the power, though, and not be swallowed by it?"

I never knew that Geoff thought so philosophically. Or thought at all, really. "We can if I don't fail, at least not in front of them."

As Geoff ponders that, I go to stand by Irwin where he's now suspiciously glaring at anyone who comes too close to his lab set. "How is the potion making coming? Will we need to test any soon?"

He gestures to where the twins are napping beside him. "They already volunteered."

"Oh. Well, that seems effective. How long have they been out?"

Irwin thoughtfully holds up a vial to inspect its contents. "They are going to be quite surprised when they wake up to find a hundred and twelve new faces."

"A hundred and twelve?" I glance around again, somehow overwhelmed by the additional twelve to my original count.

"Yeah . . ." Irwin doesn't seem enthused as he turns from his vial to glare at a child who wanders too close. Then he turns back to me. "Did you bring me elderberries?"

"Um, no . . . But I can go get them now."

He shakes his head. "I'll have one of those kids get it. You're too important now. You are what stands between our small band and these new people. Only important things for you from now on."

I purse my lips, not sure about going from being charged over many friends, to few friends, to few friends and many strangers in such a short time. "Have a couple of the kids go together. I don't want them to get lost."

Irwin nods, and his focus shifts back to his work before I can remember to ask him what potion the elderberry will be for, since I know enough about alchemy that they aren't for the sleeping powders. But by the look on his face, I know I've lost him and he won't be resurfacing any time soon.

Turning again, I take in the impromptu village again. And then I lift my eyes to the skies above us. There is a darkening in the horizon as gray clouds draw in. We will soon need shelter for all these people. More shelter than our circus tents will be able to provide for all of them.

"What are you thinking?"

I don't turn to face Meredith as I continue to think. "I'm thinking that my holdings included a stockpile of tarps from our recent trades with the gypsies. And they are no good where they are now."

"Your people would surely not hold it against you if you took what was yours."

"And if we do not find my people there, then I don't much care what they think."

Meredith nods in agreement with my words, and I try to find my own assurances as I prepare to face the place where I lived and loved and shared with my family.

And saw my aunt be slaughtered.

"You need to remain here," I say.

Meredith stops nodding. "What?"

"I need you to make sure Irwin doesn't follow. I can't risk him doing something reckless."

"And you *won't* do something reckless?"

"Everything I do is carefully plotted out. Even revenge." I gesture to the ornate dagger tied to her waist. "Which is why I need that."

Meredith looks down, her lips twisting with uncertainty.

I gesture to the enchanted sword lying on our cot. "Use that if necessary before I can return the dagger. But I need a weapon of stealth."

She chews her lips now, but nods and removes her dagger from her side and hands it to me.

Squeezing her shoulder, I nod my thanks before touching my forehead to hers. Then I leave Meredith to distract Irwin so I can find Kennan.

Creator, give me the fidelity to keep these people's faith, the strength to provide for their needs, and the honor to avenge should the opportunity present itself.

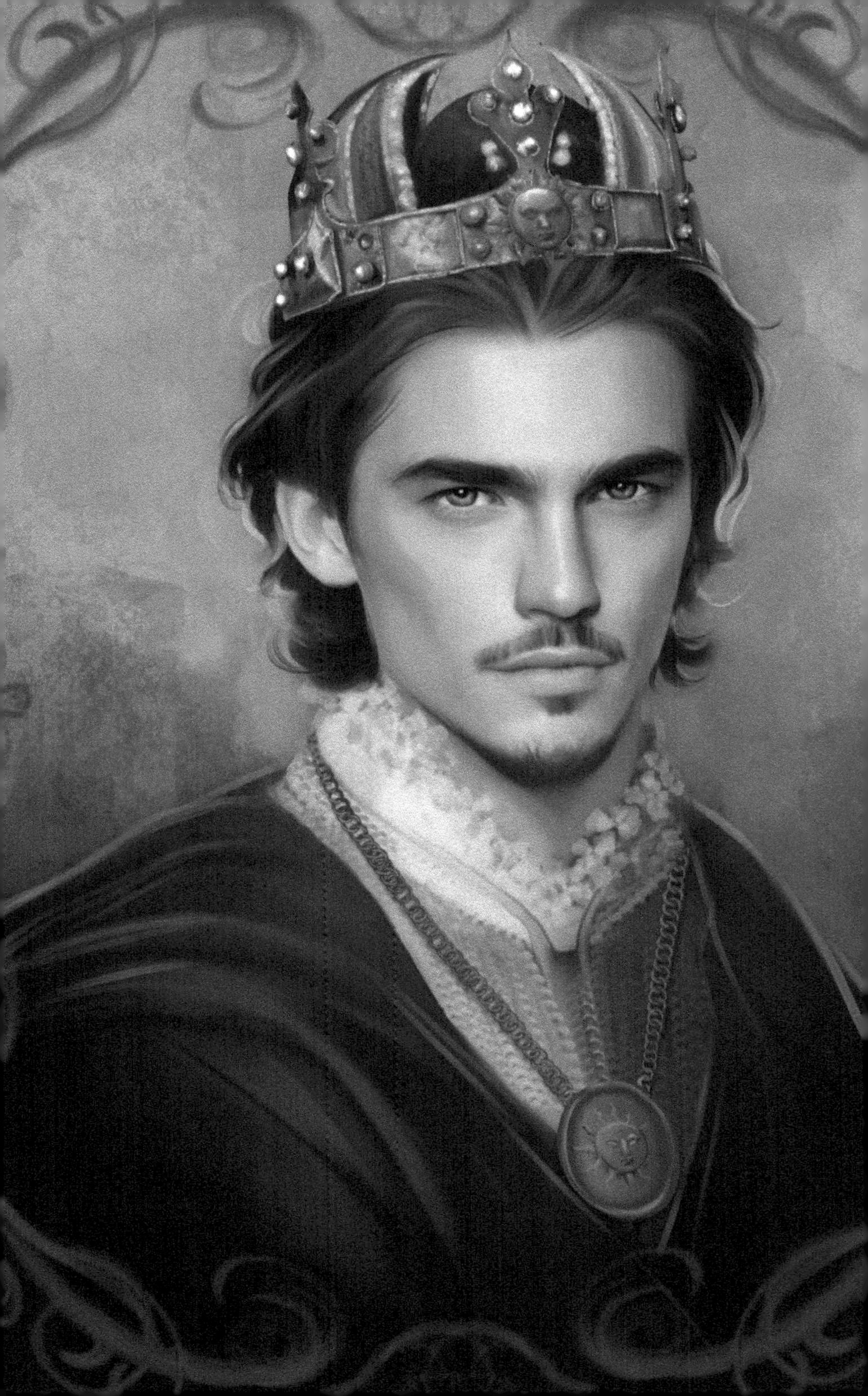

CHAPTER IX

PRINCE OTELLO

"My prince, it is my greatest honor to host you here."

I almost answer before remembering my disguise. Pressing my lips together instead, I wait for Heinrich to address the large, sinewy Baron before us. The man's tanned skin says he is no stranger to hard labor under the sun.

"The honor is mine," Heinrich answers, eying the shortness of the Baron's traditional fur coat that is the ceremonial apparel for a Baron in this region, "Baron . . ."

"Baron VonTrapp," he answers, not bothering to leave his throne long enough to give a proper bow.

"I'm sorry," Heinrich says without a hint of apology in his tone. "I have just come from Baron Hoff. He had been under the assumption that it was an elf Baron who resided here."

The obviously mortal Baron VonTrapp ducks his head, and I notice that *all* of his livery appears too short on him, as though designed for a male elf and not a mortal man. "Indeed, this castle was once commanded by an elf by the name of Ephraim. His she-elf daughter inherited when the crusades took him." Baron VonTrapp touches each shoulder, his forehead, and his chest in the mortal manner. Yet it is somehow devoid of all religion despite the symbology of the gesture. "I took the maid for a bride, but the poor thing was heartbroken after what happened to her people during the Night of the Broken Walls."

I step back, startled by this baron's great boldness in questioning the Emperor's command in the presence of his own son. A sentiment that I agree with, but surely he cannot be aware of that within moments of our meeting.

"Of course, I have received word that you have come to make amends with the elf-folk on behalf of your father." Baron VonTrapp smiles slyly.

Or perhaps he is aware, after all. Mayhap Baron Abijah's excitement over the plans for restitution spread beyond his province already? As a port baron, his words may have spread to the entire Empire by now.

"Not that there is any form of restitution that can restore my beloved Elspeth to me." Baron VonTrapp makes great ceremony of dabbing at his eyes.

The utterance of the name strikes me as suddenly and searingly as though the Emperor-God Himself threw down a lightning bolt to pierce me. That name . . .

Baron VonTrapp continues, oblivious to my turmoil. "But as your humble servant, I appreciate any and all gestures."

I glance at Heinrich to see if he is as taken aback by the man's boldness as I. He nods just once before turning back to the Baron. "Indeed, we will have much to discuss. But first, I require a place to lay my head."

"Anything for my great guest of honor." Baron VonTrapp claps his hands together, and an older maid with a hunched back appears, pale wisps of hair covering her face.

"Show the Prince and his companions to the sleeping chambers," Baron VonTrapp instructs her. "Be sure to supply them all that they request. Sustenance, ale, or one of the younger maids. Whatever they request."

The *frau* nods quickly without looking at him once. "Yes, my liege."

She moves to our side, and two men, large and sinewy like their Baron step forward as well, apparently to assist her in assisting us.

"This way, my prince," the woman whispers to Heinrich before moving toward the opening to a new corridor without another word, the men attempting to take the parcels containing my possessions from my guardsmen.

I gesture for them to give it over as a sign of trust. Even though trust is the last thing I feel toward the Baron. But too much of my hand has already been revealed in this court before I ever stepped foot here, and it is imperative that we all play along in order to find out the truth of the elf-folk who once lived here.

Callistus, who has been silent for the longest period since joining the company, sidles up beside me. Somehow, despite having to remain silent for so long, Callistus has the wherewithal to keep the words that come to his lips now a whisper that only I can hear.

"His tongue tells of a tragedy, but his eyes reflect a cruel hunger."

I nod once. "Indeed."

Heinrich raises an eyebrow at me from his bed, the finer of the two in the room offered to us. Because apparently, the perks of being a Prince must continue behind closed doors if he is to "be expected to maintain this masquerade."

I raise an eyebrow back at him.

He leans back on the fine mattress, arms folded behind his head. "You have asked me to pass as yourself, my prince. To be obedient, I must be authentic, even when there are no obvious witnesses."

Shaking my head, I slide back on my second boot.

"But back to the question at hand." Heinrich raises his second eyebrow, now in response to my new attire being a black leather jerkin and breeches instead of my nightshirt.

"I came to find the elves who were displaced and restore them where restoration can be made." I stand up and grab my blackest cloak. "And here we finally have an example of a baronage that once belonged to an elf . . . but is possessed by a mortal."

"And what evidence do you think you can find of our host's lies dressed like that?" Heinrich's eyes drift closed, and I feel as though he would pay better attention if he hadn't chosen the more comfortable duvet for himself.

"If he truly was widowed, then there is undoubtedly a monument to his lost bride in the family catacombs. Or at least the beginnings of one."

At this, Heinrich's eyes widen. "You intend to break into catacombs at this hour of night?"

"It seems more likely the attempt would be successful now than at broad noon."

Heinrich nods slowly. "From a practical sense, yes, but you forget the supernatural aspect."

I roll my eyes. "There is no such thing as phantoms."

"What about estries?"

"There have been no estries sightings in this province for three decades. My father's Shadow is the only connoisseur of blood we have to concern ourselves over."

"What if that is because all the estries of the province decided to lurk around in this elvish crypt . . ." Heinrich gives an exaggerated shudder. "This is exactly how you become the next victim of the Dark Ritual."

"That is ridiculous. There would be no blood for them there." I move toward the window. "Besides, the Dark Ritual can only be completed by a willing victim."

"I'm sure there's always an exception." Heinrich frowns. "Please tell me you're not going out the window."

I take the grappling hook crossbow out and hook it to the tower ledge. "Both our guards and the Baron's men are stationed outside our room. You know, this is the only way I can get out undetected."

"Apparently you're not concerned with the living dead, since you're so eager to join them."

I secure my hook to the windowsill that has been updated from an arrow slit to something that barely allows the sun in— and hopefully me out— in our more civilized age. "I've scaled higher."

Heinrich slides out of bed to come help me with stabilizing the hook. "What is so important about this Lady Elspeth that you must investigate her fate so thoroughly?"

The blurred face from my dream comes to mind. "I-I don't know. But I *need* to."

"Then at the very least, be careful, my prince."

"Aren't I always?"

He snorts at that and hands me my leather gauntlets.

I tie the cord of my grappling hook around my waist before pulling the gauntlets on. Then I wiggle my legs out the window.

"What will you do if you get stuck out there?" Heinrich asks, still steadying my grappling hook.

"Probably cry." I feel my shoulders pop out, and then there's not enough of me keeping me in place, so I plummet.

Darkness conceals the ground and the tower, and even the cord I have to take by faith to be there. *Saints save me.*

My hand grasps the cord coming from around my waist, and I use it to steady myself. Then I send my legs out, searching until I feel the stones of the tower rushing past me. Or rather, I'm rushing past them.

I plant both legs onto the stone and do my best to use it to slow my descent. Until the rope goes tight around my waist, feeling almost as though it is cutting me in half.

I'd gasp if it didn't knock the breath out of me. Then I gingerly take one foot off the now still tower and search below me. It just barely brushes over what feels like grass.

Lifting my other foot, I take my knife out of my boot, unsheathe it, and then cut myself free of the rope.

The ground proves to be a foot lower than I expected, and I land with a jarring thud.

"Ow," I moan before checking to make sure nothing is broken. Then, not bothering to stand up, I reach to tug on the now sliced rope three times to indicate to Heinrich that I'm on the ground safe and sound and he can pull it up.

As the rope rises out of sight, I roll over onto my stomach and brace myself. Then I push my sore body upward and wait a moment for my eyes to get accustomed to the darkness and ascertain that there is no one else around.

The stars finally decide to lend their light, illuminating the fact that I have chosen the right time between guard patrols to make my landing. I decide not to waste that time and make a mad dash toward where I can see trees grown in an orderly fashion. A garden of some sort. Which is where nobility traditionally keep their dead, hidden between growths of new life.

Stumbling toward it, my eyes make out what appears to be a mausoleum in size, though there are no torches lit around it to illuminate the details.

How odd that there is no evidence of a guard keeping watch or ceremonial fires lit for a beloved bride lost too soon.

When I reach the building, I feel along what can only be cold marble until I find a door. I realize too late that most people lock their mausoleums at night to protect against grave robbers.

But fortune appears to be smiling on me this night— or else the Baron is even more negligent than I had previously supposed— and the door opens for me.

I check the handle on the other side to make sure the door won't lock if I shut it behind me. Then I ease my way inside and close the door as gently as possible behind me.

Then I turn to face a greater darkness than what I faced outside. This darkness is the type to feel like a substance itself, the kind where I have to take even the existence of my hands by faith and not by sight.

I sense a drop before me and carefully feel out stairs. I descend them practically on my hands and knees to keep from plummeting until I feel the ground even out before me.

Standing up, I notice the dampness in the air. The mustiness. The smell of not quite death, but lifelessness at least. And I realize I am sealed underground in darkness with no one else but the dead.

Panic rises in my chest, and I focus on who I am and what I have the power to do.

Reaching into my satchel, I take out a torch stick in one hand and a pouch of lava rock in the other. At least, I hope they are my lava rocks.

I kneel to steady my torch stick between my knees and place my hand on the top, where it has been treated with sulfur. Then I place two fingers of my other hand into the pouch and grasp the stone that was forged by the drying of lava after an eruption from one of the islands under my father's jurisdiction.

"*Umwandeln*," I breathe, drawing on the focus word, or *Davar*, Uriel gave me to help me reach deep into my bloodline and channel the heritage of my forefathers through my fingertips.

My hand touching the lava rocks burns with new power I feel passing through my body, causing a glow to fight the darkness from beneath my skin.

Then the power I pulled from the lava rocks reaches my other hand, and the torch simmers. I focus more until its head completely bursts into flame.

Dropping the lava rocks and pulling my hand back away from my torch, I close my eyes and try to focus on who I was before the fire flowed through me. Before the fire *was* me. *"Rückgabe."*

I feel my skin cool. My blood flow slows. And then I feel . . . mortal once again.

Opening my eyes, I scoop up my pouch of lava rocks and pocket it next to my other pouches of minerals before picking my torch up in my other hand and standing.

I hold it out to take in my surroundings.

The crypt is much larger than it had appeared outside, giving credence to the fact that it is indeed an elvish crypt, since they believe they must make the dead comfortable for their first three days underground, while they believe their soul still lingers. The sarcophagi are enmeshed into the walls, which are hollowed out. Unlike mortal coffins, the engravings in these display only the title and name of the deceased, no sculptured image of the person now interned in the stone. The elf-folk view such carvings as blasphemous, as though their likeness is too similar to the Creator to dare attempt to replicate.

I approach one of the small tombs and read an inscription. The name does not match Elspeth, so I move to go on but catch sight of one piece of decoration on the coffin. A deeper chasm within the indentation in the cave is fit around a book with a cover painted in vibrant colors. Its title simply says *The Life of Baron Ephraim.*

Stepping back, I look as far as I can see across the wall before the shadows take over and see an identical shelf above each tomb with a differently colored book secured within.

Then I turn and notice for the first time the benches set around the central support pillar of the mausoleum. So, it is true; elvish tombs are built for the living to come visit their dead instead of to honor them with final rest like we do.

As I shine my torch across the room, I notice something that seems off in the otherwise perfect symmetry of the mausoleum. One corner is not as open as the other three are and is shrouded in darkness.

I step forward, expecting perhaps a pile of building supplies.

What I do not expect to find is a woman.

My torch almost falls from my hands in my surprise as I take in the view of hair perfectly plated around a sculpted face crowned with eyes a shade of blue I've seen only in one woman, and only for moments before the color shifted to another shade of blue.

"Meredith?" I whisper.

"You?" she says back, her eyes wide as she stares at me.

How long has she been here? I would have noticed if someone came in after me— which means she was here before me.

Did she see my display of Heritage Magic? The sacred secret kept safe in every royal family, known only to the sitting Emperor, the direct heir, and the Keeper of Knowledge, who teaches the royal line to use their abilities through the generations?

Meredith doesn't know I'm the Prince. Perhaps she'll mistake my ability as an expression of lesser magic, the more common noble bloodline magic or a watered-down peasant bloodline magic.

She opens her mouth, and I prepare to lie in order to protect matters of national security.

"What are you doing here?"

That question catches me off guard, though it is a good question to ask. "Wait a moment . . . What are *you* doing here?"

"I'm a friend of the family." She straightens up and crosses her arms over a dark tunic that falls over dark leggings that showcase the shapeliness of her legs.

I quickly lift my gaze to her face. "Why are you dressed as a man?"

"I was in disguise." She plucks at a piece of black cloth around her neck that was probably up over her nose and mouth before she came down here and expected to remain alone. "Now you have yet to answer any of my questions."

"I, uh, heard that the lady of the house was recently interned here and came to pay my respects." In the dark of night. Alone. With a magical torch I lit only after I thought I had no witnesses.

Meredith creases her eyebrows. "Baroness Eden was laid to rest two years ago."

"No, her daughter. Lady Elspeth."

She gasps. "Who told you she would be here?"

"Baron VonTrapp—"

A sliver of light interrupts us, a shaft of brightness from above joining my torch in its fight against the darkness.

Until I smother it to conceal our location.

The sound of voices descends with the invading light.

I place my hand over Meredith's mouth as she does the same to me. Then we usher each other into the corner where she had been standing, with her against the wall and me pressing into her. My body responds as if I were still holding the lava rock, heat flowing through my blood at the contact, as if she were fire itself, yet unable to consume me.

"He wants us to convert one of 'ere reserved tombs into one for Lady Elspeth, right?" rasps a man of obviously low bloodline.

"Nah, that'll take too much time," answers another gruff voice. "Just convert one of 'ere existing tombs into one for Elspeth. A lot of them have similar names, ya know."

I feel her heart beating against my chest. We are entirely too close. I need distance before I become as dull as one of my rocks in my pocket under her enchantment.

Dropping my thankfully gloved hand from Meredith's lips, I then remove hers from my mouth. Then I lean toward her ear. "We need to be ready to run."

She shakes her head, causing her lips to brush against my jawline for the barest second. "You can run, but I must fight."

"What?" I whisper a bit too loudly as the two men carrying torches descend into the tomb with us.

"They must not be allowed to deface this sacred place," she answers, dropping her hand and reaching for something.

And I reach a deeper level of knowledge of how very close we are and how much of her is in contact with me as her hand brushes over my legs, searching for something.

She produces a knife and then leans toward my ear so close I feel her lips on my neck. "You can run while I distract them."

I resist a shudder at our proximity and pull myself together. "I cannot leave a lady to fight two men alone."

"Then I hope you brought a weapon."

CHAPTER X

Lady Elspeth

One hour previous . . .

Dressed in the darkest tunic and leggings that we stole from Leopold, I crouch on the border of the forest that skims the environs of my inheritance.

Due to the reduced capability to protect this territory despite my stone wall that goes through part of the forest, no one lives out here. The huts here serve pragmatic purposes, like smoking the meat caught in the forest or storing supplies we have no immediate need for.

"There don't appear to be any guards in this area," I say. "Unless they are hidden inside one of the huts, which is unlikely. I doubt this part of my land was a foremost priority for Vontrapp's taking over my baronage."

"Won't the doors be locked?" Kennan asks from his crouch beside me.

I take the chain holding my keys from underneath my tunic and hold it up to him.

He nods. "So, this should be simple, then."

"If the Creator smiles upon us." Trying not to think about how the Creator seems to frown often lately, I gesture for him to follow me, but for the other dozen men who came with us to wait in the shadows.

Kennan and I approach the hut that I know is for storage, and I unlock it.

I gesture for Kennan to stand back while I cautiously open it, in case there is a guard with a bow and arrow on the other side.

But there is no one, just as I suspected. Just barrels of building supplies for when we were ever going to have enough manpower to better cultivate this land.

Waving the other men to come over, I gesture to the barrels and rolled up tarps. "Take as many of these as you can carry back to the camp. Kennan, you keep watch in case a patrol comes by on their rounds."

Kennan frowns. "Are you not staying?"

"I—" I glance away from the silhouette of my old home, where it stands stoically before the setting sun. I so desperately want to go to it and be home. But I also want to flee from the knowledge of the blood that was shed there. The life that I lost on my last night there. And the life that I took.

"I must go to my family crypt one last time and honor my aunt."

Kennan doesn't seem very certain about that decision, but he seems to remember that he has no ranking over me. "Should we wait for you?"

"No. Get back to the camp as quickly as possible and prepare it for the oncoming storm. I know my way back and will return by sunrise."

He gives me the barest nod. "As you say, my lady."

"Good man." With that, I tug my hood over my hair and my makeshift mask over my face to buy myself some time before I am recognized if I were to be spotted. Then I move toward the shadows of the trees to disguise my approach as I begin the trek up to the final resting place of my ancestors.

Using another of my keys to gain entrance through the hunter's door, I press myself to the inside of the inner wall, thankful that the sun has now completely set, and the darkness shall aid me in my journey.

My ears pick up the sound of stomping men, and I am careful to avoid their approach. These men are too comfortable in their strength to bother concealing their presence, as I was trained to do from childhood.

Finally, I reach the mausoleum my ancestors have been buried in since the Creator banished us from *Haya* and drove them to pledge their fealty to a mortal dynasty.

Until the latest Emperor proved himself faithless to those who served him and betrayed my people.

Using a third key, I let myself into the crypt and then quickly close the door behind me.

I reach up and grab one of the *Kochav* Orbs set in the fixtures of the crypt. At my touch, it immediately lights up, responding to my shared kinship to those buried here. These orbs, created by an ancestor to guard our deceased and guide our living, are the only type of magic allowed in the presence of the dead. After all, for my people, it is our unity with each other that strengthens our magic. In the face of loss, we set aside our strengths and choose weakness even as we set aside joy for mourning.

As I do today, in respect for my lost aunt.

Holding the *Kochav* Orb that is the size of my palm, I descend the staircase, breathing in the underground must I've known since childhood, when my parents began teaching me how to respect our dead.

Before they joined our dead.

My feet take me to their coffins, the most recently added in the tomb. I trace their names and look up at their Life Books. For a moment, I consider taking those with me. After all, I can no longer come every day to read them and remember. But how disrespectful would that be?

Tears prick my eyes at the thought of losing them all over again, but I have other responsibilities to tend to before I can think about losing myself to grief.

I move to the section of the grave that was reserved for my aunt, who may never have the honor of lying here, for I know not where they placed her body.

Reaching up, I take the reversed Book of Life from its stand where it had shown only the dark back cover. Then I take it down and open it.

There isn't time to write everything that needs to be recorded from the last time Aunt Orpah wrote in this journal in the custom of remembering life while surrounded by death, to the night she died.

So, taking a quill and ink pot that can be found at the end of each bench surrounding the central pillar of the mausoleum, I turn to the last page.

Death took her as a coward in the shadows of night while she slept. I, Lady Elspeth, daughter of Baron Ephraim, of the tribe of Benji, take upon myself the duty of Kinsman Avenger.

I set the book down open to allow it to dry, thinking of everything that I owe my aunt, both in life and in death. She became a second mother to me when my own perished of a broken heart. Her own heart had always been strong, even while she was physically weak from the same wasting disease Irwin was born with.

But even though she was too weak to make frequent pilgrimages to the family crypt to update her Life Book, Irwin's potions always strengthened her in between bouts of Kin Magic. We thought we had many more decades with her ahead of us. After all, there are only two things Kin Magic cannot heal. The Plague sent by our Creator to haunt our promised land, and death itself.

My eyes grow moist as I close the book and turn it cover-side out to place it in its resting place. The cover of the book had been painted by Aunt Orpah when she was yet a child on the first day she was introduced to the family crypt and our ancestors.

I glance deeper into the crypt where our own plots are reserved, and books are facing inward. There should be centuries ahead of us still to honor our dead as we live in the home they passed onto us, but life is cruel, and men are crueler. All I know is that I cannot bear to lose the last of my kin before myself.

Please, Creator, grant me this grace at least. Let the elder perish before the younger.

Closing my eyes, I continue silently plead with my Creator even as I ask my aunt for forgiveness for failing her and say farewell to the rest of my kin.

Until I hear the crypt door open above me.

Panic tears the strange peace I found in these shadows away from me, and I throw myself toward the nearest corner, in between the coffins bearing my great-grandfather and my fourth cousin.

Then I remember the *Kochav* Orb.

Snatching my hood off my head, I wrap it around the *Kochav* Orb, which fades when it loses my touch. Then I stuff the covered orb down my bodice.

Just as my eyes re-accustom themselves to the darkness, a shadowy form crawls down from the stairs.

I hold my breath at the chilling sight.

I watch as the mysterious shadow stands up, and then bends down again, fiddling with objects I can't quite see.

"*Umwandeln*," the shadow whispers, and then he's not a shadow anymore, as his body begins to glow, starting from his left hand and spreading across his body.

My eyes widen as the shadow becomes the man who tried to abduct/rescue me as Meredith earlier. Only with golden, glowing skin.

He is indeed a noble, then, to have such a powerful ability. Though, I do not recall any noble I ever met or learned about having that magic in their bloodline. But mortals can be so complicated. We elf-folk have the same Kin Magic, all of us. Those of us with the purer blood are better at manifesting it than others, but we all possess the basics of it for the protecting and healing of our kin. Mortals' magic is different with each line.

The glow passing through the boy causes the wood he's holding to suddenly combust. I jump slightly before seeing that it is a controlled flame on a torch.

Even as my heartbeat goes back to normal, I feel my blood simmer. Who does he think he is to come into my family crypt and display his magic so openly? Has he no respect?

The boy seems to sense my anger because he whispers, "*Rückgabe.*"

At his word, the glow fades, and he appears to revert to his normal form, illuminated only by the torch.

He pockets something and stands up before using his newly lit torch to illuminate the surroundings.

I hold my breath as the light draws dangerously near to my corner, but then he is distracted by my father's tomb.

My hands clench, and I wonder what he'll do, but he appears to just be reading the inscription. Then he steps back and continues to study the neighboring tombs and the central pillar of the crypt.

Why would this mortal come to my family crypt? Did he serve alongside my father in the crusades?

He turns his torch once again to the rest of the room. This time, the light reaches me, exposing my location.

He steps forward, and I brace myself.

The man's violet eyes widen in surprise as he takes me in.

I study him as well. His chin-length dark brown hair is unkempt, as though he just fell out of bed, and his dark tunic and leggings match mine very well.

"Meredith?" he whispers.

"You?" I whisper back, since I still don't have a name for him, not even a wrong one.

His expression twists in concern, though I'm not sure for what. Perhaps it's merely confusion at finding the "abducted" maid in an elvish crypt?

Unlike him, though, I have good reason to be here. "What are you doing here?"

He stumbles back a step, but then gestures his free hand at me. "What are *you* doing here?"

"I'm a friend of the family." I straighten up to my full height and cross my arms, daring him to challenge me, to question my right to be here.

He doesn't seem to be listening to me as his gaze drops to my legs.

Of course. No wonder mortal woman have to wear such long skirts; their menfolk are quite savage.

The man finally catches himself and quickly lifts his gaze to my face. "Why are you dressed as a man?"

Because I didn't want to tarnish one of my new skirts or risk tripping while potentially fleeing for my life. "I was in disguise." I wish I did not have to discard my hood. I may even yet have to flee since apparently, I cannot hide from this man. "Now you have yet to answer any of my questions."

"I, uh, heard that the lady of the house was recently interned here and came to pay my respects." He ducks his head, probably because he realizes how outlandish that sounds when he comes here under the shadow of night.

But my heart still pangs with grief at all the former ladies buried here, and I crease my eyebrows. “Baroness Eden was laid to rest two years ago.” Unless . . . does he mean to say they are planning on honoring my aunt by interning her amongst her own?

“No, her daughter. Lady Elspeth.”

I gasp. Is this his way of telling me he knows who I really am? “Who told you she would be here?”

“Baron VonTrapp—“

Pure rage floods my blood at the name of the robber “baron” who stole everything from me, including my aunt’s last breaths.

Before I can say exactly what I think of that monster, a light comes down from above. But it’s not my *Kochav* Orb or his torch.

The boy drops the torch and smothers it until it darkens , leaving us with only this new light that is coming closer, along with new voices.

My instincts take over, and I plant one of my hands over this very talkative mortal’s mouth even as his own instincts seem to mirror my own, and he plants his leather gauntlet over my lips. It tastes like rope, somehow, and I have to fight the urge to push it away or gag.

Then in one swift move, the man presses me back into the corner so that the cold of the underground, the stone, and death itself soaks through my clothes and skin and into my bones from behind.

But before me, I find the mortal’s body pressed into me, his body heat coming through me to combat the chill.

Beyond us, a voice speaks.

“He wants us to convert one of ‘ere reserved tombs into one for Lady Elspeth, right?”

The speaker is obviously male. I’d wager mortal, too. A peasant by birth, but not born around here, his speech pattern is similar to those of the northern provinces. Likely one of VonTrapp’s hired mercenaries.

Another voice, not unlike the first with the same accent, answers, “Nah, that’ll take too much time. Just convert one of ‘ere existing tombs into one for Elspeth. A lot of them have similar names, ya know.”

How dare they even *speak* of such a deed?

Suddenly, the leather glove falls from my mouth, and I feel the man moving my fingers away from his own soft lips.

For a moment, my anxious mind throws itself into the realization that I've never touched a man's mouth before. It was not wholly unpleasant.

Seeming to sense my thoughts, the mortal somehow finds a way to come still closer to me. "We need to be ready to run." His words are barely more than a breath.

I shake my clearing head. "You can run, but I must fight." How could I ever face my kin in the next life if I didn't defend them in this one?

"What?" he whispers a bit too loudly.

I wince and brace myself in case the two mercenaries turn toward us. Somehow, they missed the word, though, and I dare to speak— though far more quietly than he did. "They must not be allowed to deface this sacred place." I drop my hands, searching for Meredith's dagger and coming into contact with a great deal that isn't me or mine.

We are truly far too close.

Somehow, though, I reach my dagger. To his credit, the man doesn't jump back.

Since we seem to be allies in this predicament, I lean toward his ear so close I think my lips brush up against his skin. "You can run while I distract them."

He shudders, though I think it is from my breath rather than my words, because then he tenses. "I cannot leave a lady to fight two men alone."

Under my rage, I feel fear. Fear of taking another life. What if I'm weak?

Perhaps we will be allies for a little longer. "Then I hope you brought a weapon."

CHAPTER XI

Prince Otello

I reach for my sword before remembering too late that I couldn't exactly fit out my window with the Sun Sword.

"I think I have a knife," I whisper, searching my person.

Meredith squeaks, and I wonder in horror if I've accidentally searched *her* person in the process.

"Here, take this." She places my own knife in my hand.

Did she disarm me while arming herself? "I will defend you."

Meredith holds up her jeweled dagger. "We shall defend the dead." Then, without further ado, she reaches a hand down the front of her bodice.

I blink, not quite sure what I was expecting. Or continue to expect. Does she have more weapons stored there?

She pulls out a round object and wraps her hands around it.

Since I still have no idea what she's doing, I glance between her and the immoral men.

Then a glowing orb is suddenly flying across the room towards the two men, landing at their feet.

They both glance down. "What—?"

Suddenly, Meredith is no longer beside me and is coming up behind one of the men. I watch as she grabs hold of his wrist and twists it, making him drop his torch.

The other man unsheathes a sword.

I rush forward and put my dagger out to thwart the blow coming for Meredith.

"I order you to stand down!" I cry.

The man grunts. "You don't pay my stipend." He takes back his sword and then brings it back toward me.

I block it again, and the force of it throws me backward into the other man.

He stumbles out from behind me, gasping for air and clawing at Meredith, who is now on his shoulders, her legs wrapped around his waist and her hands wrapped around his neck.

I suppose wearing a proper dress would make that particular move significantly more difficult and even less appropriate.

The sword swishes next to me, and I just barely jump back, caught off guard by the distraction. Then I spin into the man and strike him in the face with the butt of the dagger before jumping away.

I flip it around and point it at him. "The next time, I will draw blood. Now, by my decree, leave this crypt and never return."

The man snarls. "And by what authority do you issue your 'decree'?"

Before I can answer, a pouch comes flying past me and hits the man square in the face. It explodes, with some kind of dust going all over his face.

Suddenly, small hands grasp my face and turn me away from the scene.

"I'm sorry," Meredith says beside me, her face also turned away. "I forgot I had sleeping powders on me."

"You have sleeping powders on you?"

She nods and then glances over to where the man I had just been talking to is lying flat on his back, snoring. His companion is doing the same off to the side.

My jaw slackens a little.

"I couldn't bear to shed their guilty blood in the face of the innocent dead." She releases her hold on my face, which is certainly not something I would ask of her, and goes to crouch next to the men. Then she glances up at me. "Would you mind helping me drag them out?"

"You think the first thing they are going to do when they awaken is go back to trying to deface the crypt?"

"No. Because I'm going to seal it off."

Her tone is so solemn all I can say is, "Oh." Then, because I can suddenly think of nothing better to do with my night but spend it in the presence of this mysterious maiden, I go to one of the men and grasp his shoulders.

After all, I need to find out how much of my display of magic she saw and what she deduced from it. For national security, of course.

Which also means she must not be allowed to learn my true identity.

"I'm Heinrich, by the way," I blurt as I lift the dead weight.

Meredith groans as she lifts the booted feet of the same man. "Charmed."

Together, we carry him up the stairs, grunting and groaning the whole time. I believe a silent agreement is made in those long moments that we will never share how much noise we made. After all, for all my years of training with the broadsword, this weight should be nothing to me. And a lady does not grunt.

Nor does she wear leggings and visit elvish crypts at night, but I suppose Meredith is not the typical lady.

We deposit the man unceremoniously just outside the crypt.

Meredith leans forward and grasps her knees that I shouldn't be able to make out as she pants. "Only one more."

"Indeed," I mutter, as I look everywhere but at those knees. I mean, I'm used to my own knees, but I've never seen a lady's knees. Is there any difference between male and female knees? I'm not sure, but I'm not looking long enough to find out.

"And now." With that, Meredith turns and descends back into the crypt.

Not to be outdone by a lady who doubtless never touched a broadsword a day in her life, I hurry after.

Meredith is waiting for me by the head of the other unconscious man. When she sees me, she bends down to grasp his shoulders. And then cries out.

I hurry to her side even as she stumbles onto the stone floor where the man had been, but is no longer.

Kneeling down beside her, I help her into an upright position. "What happened?"

She stares in wonder. "He was right there. You saw that, right?"

"I believe so." Still holding her shoulders, I scan the shadows to where the man has taken himself. Then I sadly release her to check in every corner of the crypt.

But there is no sign of anyone here but Meredith and me.

"*Gyst*," she whispers. "It must be. How else could he vanish into nothing?"

A disquieting thought, but not one that I have any power to do anything about right now. "Come on."

Meredith doesn't resist me as I pull her to her feet. Together, we climb the stairs sans one mercenary. I can't say I'm not relieved to not have to lug another one up, though.

Exhaustion from the night's events hits me, and I stagger. Without a word to each other, Meredith and I simultaneously lay down on the grass and stare up at the night sky as weariness racks our bones.

Meredith's breathing evens out, and she turns to face me. "Much obliged."

"A gentleman's honor." A gentleman lying very close to a lady. Her lips that kissed my cheeks are but inches away from my face now.

She seems to sense my thoughts, because she props herself up on her elbow, turning on her side to better face me. "So, you are called Heinrich?"

Of course, I have to deceive the first beautiful woman I cross paths with. "Yes, First Valet to the Sacred Prince."

Her eyes widen. "What an honored position."

"It is an honor. The Prince is the best of people, a real pleasure to serve." And apparently incapable of controlling his tongue in the presence of a lovely maid.

"Is he here? The Prince?" She sits up, as though she might be able to see him— me— if she gets a better vantage point.

I sit up, too, actually giving her a better vantage point. "Why do you ask?"

"I must meet with him."

The thought of Heinrich being introduced as me to her— and taking the opportunity to become better acquainted with an eligible noble lady in my stead— causes my stomach to squirm. "Well, he remained behind in Kreuzschlafen."

Her eyes flash, and the sweetness she'd exhibited between the fight and now seems to melt away. "I have a complaint to bring against him."

Oh. "Well, I'm his acting proxy. You can lobby your complaint with me, and I will bring it to his ears. Is it concerning the Bandit King?"

"No." Meredith pushes herself to her feet, and I inwardly berate myself for not jumping up and helping her up sooner. Then she brushes the tendrils of wet grass off her leggings, and I realize I have too good of a vantage point from here.

I jump to my feet, nearly falling back onto my face with the suddenness of my movements. "Then what is the complaint concerning?"

"This." Meredith walks over to the crypt and closes the door to it.

"The elvish crypt?"

"What has been done to those who were once its guardian. To all the elf-folk of any power."

My stomach twists at the memory of the offense from a bystander's perspective. What must she feel to have been friends with an elvish family? "Oh. Yes, that was a travesty. The Prince did not agree with that course of action—"

"Then why do I have to do this?"

I hadn't realized I had dropped my gaze to my own boots until she said that. Lifting my face, I see her looking back at me, and though the darkness masks their color, I can still see how violently they are flashing from rage and . . . tears?

Still staring at me, she reaches her hand into a part of the engraving of the crypt wall. I hadn't even realized such a move was possible, but it causes a small chamber to open in the stone, revealing a small lever her other hand finds.

Suddenly, a crashing sound echoes from the other side.

I jump and glance around for falling rocks but find none. "What was that?"

"I sealed the crypt." She pulls her hand out and then tries the door. It doesn't open.

Her hand drops as if she'd touched something hot, and she turns away from both the door and me.

"So, it can't be defaced?" I whisper, approaching her cautiously.

"It's what they would have wanted." Her voice that had been so strong with fury is fragile now, and her hands are covering her face. Her back quivers as though silent sobs are racking her body.

I place my hand on her shoulder, not sure what else to do. "Because of VonTrapp? Because of the Night of Broken Walls?"

"Because I couldn't protect what I was called upon to protect."

She spins around to better face me, I think, but runs into me instead. Instead of backing away, though, she seems to wilt.

Before Meredith can collapse, I wrap my arms around her waist and hold her tight as she now loudly sobs into me.

I have no idea what to say, so I say nothing. I just hold her, one hand even daring to move in circles across her back in an attempt to comfort.

"I failed them," she mutters into my tunic. "I failed them all. Even Irwin. I might have gotten him out alive, but he's not the same. *I'm* not the same. All because of evil, hateful *mortals*."

She keeps talking, but her words become even more mumbled and hard to understand. So, I just keep holding her and trying to remember that she is a stranger and that we are both in danger the longer we stand out here. But those thoughts are rapidly slipping away the longer I hold her, feel her, feel *for* her.

Finally, she pulls away and wipes at her eyes. "I'm sorry."

"No, I'm sorry I didn't think to bring a handkerchief with me."

She gives me a sad smile I can just make out by the starlight. "Isn't that what ladies give their heroes as a token of their affection?"

"Mayhap. I suppose the duty of the handkerchief depends on the one who is handing it out." I reach up to wipe away a last tear before I can think twice about it.

Meredith clears her throat and steps back. "We should leave before we're caught." She glances toward the very, very heavy man we carried. "Or he wakes up."

"Where are you going?"

"Back to the forest."

I frown, still not happy with the thought of a lady alone out there. Or even worse than alone— with the *Bandit King*.

"Let me escort you to the edge of the woods, then," I say. "I'm a guest here, so you're less likely to be in trouble if you're with me."

"You'll just let them come up with their own conclusions of why you were outside your sleeping chambers at night with a woman in leggings?"

I pray the darkness hides my flush. "Let us go now before we are caught, then."

Meredith nods and dashes off, somehow not making a sound, and I hurry to keep up with her the best I can without calling the attention of every guard and mercenary in the keep.

I want to ask her about her life now. If she still feels safe. If she would consider leaving the Bandit King for the Emperor's son. But of course, the last one is impossible because she can't know I'm him. And I certainly have enough to deal with between restoring my Empire and navigating these unknown waters with my father who has become a stranger to me without bringing this mysterious woman into my life. Especially if she realizes it was Heritage Magic that I used before her.

Suddenly, Meredith halts, and I nearly barrel into her. Then I see what she sees. A shadow bent over but moving.

My hand moves toward my borrowed dagger, and I prepare to fight.

CHAPTER XII

LADY ELSPETH

I freeze when I see the form bent over in the dark. A form I know all too well and have seen bent over in the same place dozens of time in this very garden.

But that was when my home was safe and secure and mine.

"Irwin!" I cry, rushing toward my cousin and away from Heinrich, First Valet to the Anointed Prince of the Sun.

Irwin doesn't even look up at my approach. If anything, he starts working all the faster in the garden that he used to toil over every moment he wasn't in the lab, tending to his mother, or with me.

I grab his arm and force him away from whatever plant he's fidgeting with. "What are you doing here?"

"I needed lemongrass," he answers, completely unrepentant and even trying to pull away. "It's hard to grow in the wild and impossible without seeds." He crosses his arms. "They don't deserve my garden or my lemongrass."

"No, they don't, but they also don't deserve you." I can't bury anyone else today.

Can't bury anyone ever again in my family crypt.

I feel a fresh wave of sorrow threaten to overtake me, but I throw the feeling far from me. I have to think of Irwin now.

"We have to go. Now." I grab his arm and try to drag him out of his garden.

He wrenches his arm away, causing it to fly free and high.

Heinrich steps forward, a menacing hunch to his shoulders. "Don't raise your hand to the lady."

Irwin seems to notice my companion for the first time. "I wasn't raising my hand at her."

I turn to Heinrich as well. "He wasn't. And I can take care of myself from now on."

My cousin bends down and harvests more lemongrass to place gently into his satchel. He doesn't tear it out quickly as a last act before leaving. Rather, his movements suggest he's tending to the plant, as though he might come back to it someday and find that it has grown anew for him.

But there's nothing to come back to here. Our crypt is gone. We can only move onward and upward. Take fourfold what was stolen from us because what once was will never be again.

Beyond us, I swear I hear the turmoil as my handiwork is discovered by VonTrapp's men.

I grab Irwin's wrist and yank him up to his feet. "We have to go. Now."

"I can take care of myself, El—"

I kick him gently in his shin to keep him from saying my name. It just doesn't seem like the best time to tell Heinrich that he's been calling me by the wrong name all this time. I still don't know this man enough to know how he'll react, and we're still in hostile territory.

"Hey!" Irwin cries, flailing backward.

Heinrich takes it the wrong way and rushes toward Irwin.

I spin around to grab Heinrich's shoulders to block him. His momentum is too great, though, and throws us both to the moist ground. I gasp as his body mostly covers mine, though not as hard as it would have if he had not been trying to avoid hurting me. Heinrich stares down to where my blade is dangerously close to his neck.

When did I get that out? Did I really lose myself to my reflexes that quickly?

My eyes go from his startled expression to his outstretched arm, holding his own dagger away from me. The dagger that he intended to use against *my* cousin.

Fury fills me, and I bring both my legs around his hips.

He makes a sound of surprise and is too stunned to fight as I roll us over so that I'm on top of him. My blade still hovers over his neck as I eye the dagger in his hand.

"I think you need to go now."

He frowns at me. "I will go. Once you get off of me."

Eyeing him and the dagger, I push myself up with one hand, not releasing my own blade.

In all my focus, I make the most ridiculous of elf-folk mistakes— the kind that can get you disowned— and lose my balance as one foot slips on the wet grass.

I come crashing down, My rump lands on his abdomen. He gasps as I knock the breath out of him, and eyes my dagger that I almost bring into his chest to stop my fall.

"Sorry," I mutter.

Heinrich just winces.

Finally, Irwin grabs my shoulders and pulls me up and away from the man who had been my ally just moments ago.

Clearing my throat, I smooth down my tunic with my free hand. Then I nod toward Heinrich. "Thank you again for your assistance." I won't let my manners be a casualty of my new lifestyle.

Still wincing, Heinrich sits up. "Again, it was . . . my pleasure." He doesn't look so sure about this now.

I nod again, grab Irwin, and then drag him away from Heinrich and our old home as swiftly as I can.

"Irwin, how could you?" I demand, resisting the urge to stomp through the forest from frustration and give away our position. I have already broken one sacred, unspoken elvish law by losing my balance, and don't need to add another to my ledger.

"I needed my lemongrass, among other things."

"Then you could have told me!"

Irwin grunts. "I'm not a child. I don't need a nursemaid."

I stop walking and whirl around to face him. "Where's Meredith?"

At the mention of her name, his expression turns from defiant to flustered. "I— uh— she's sleeping."

"Sleeping?" I narrow my eyes. "Why is she sleeping when she knew I wanted her to watch over you?"

"Some of my sleep powder . . ."

My jaw drops. "You actually used that on *Meredith*?"

He shrugs. "I needed the lemongrass. I told WolfBear to watch over her."

"Meredith will never forgive you."

He bows his head sadly. "You're not the only one who wants vengeance, Elspeth. It was my home, too. *My* mother. I am the closest Kinsman Avenger, not you."

Mayhap, but I'm the one better equipped to kill for Aunt Orpah. The one who's killed for her already.

Irwin doesn't need that burden on his soul.

I glance at his bag. "How is lemongrass going to help with vengeance? I may not be as good at alchemy as you, but I recall no poison that required lemongrass as an ingredient."

"No, but it's an ingredient in the *Chazah* Tonic."

At his words, I almost trip. Again. Another insult would be added to my heritage. "The *Chazah* Tonic? But only the most experienced Alchemists dare try that recipe."

"And since there are only us left of our kin, is it not time that I step up to take that title for myself?" There's no anger left in Irwin's tone, only resignation. "Isn't that why you took the title of 'Bandit Queen'? We must both assume new titles now."

I purse my lips together. "Let's get back to the camp and make sure everyone got back all right— and Meredith is fine. Then we'll see what else you need for your potion."

He catches up to me and keeps stride as we walk forward in silence until the sun peeks through.

"So, who were you with?"

I startle at his sudden question but keep my stride. "Heinrich, First Valet to the *Prince*. Apparently, he's here on the Prince's behalf to see how things are going in our backward province since the cursed Night of Broken Walls."

"Does he know who we are?"

"No, he thinks I'm Meredith."

It's Irwin's turn to almost trip. "Why does he think that?"

"Because it seemed better to allow a stranger to think I am the one supposedly abducted by the Bandit King than let him know that I'm actually the Bandit Queen."

Irwin blinks.

And I duck my head, unable to look at my kin for this next part. "He helped me defend our ancestors."

I feel Irwin's gaze on me. "You visited the crypt?"

"I said goodbye for both of us. We'll have to have an informal ceremony for Aunt Orpah."

"When we repossess the crypt?"

I shake my head sadly. "I had to . . . seal it. To keep them from . . . defacing it."

Irwin stops walking and turns to me, but I can't tell what his expression is because I don't dare look him in the eyes.

"We can never steal back what they stole from us," he finally whispers.

Unable to speak just now, because my throat is closed off with grief, I just nod.

He places a hand on my shoulder. "Perhaps the *Chazah* Tonic will show a better way."

"I don't forgive you, by the way."

Irwin bristles and almost drops all the lemongrass he's shucking into the beaker.

Knowing the particular nature of the *Chazah* Tonic, I wrench the tonic aside before he can foul it up.

Meredith is sitting on a rock, glaring at us over crossed arms. The *Shamir* on her shoulder seems to feed on her energy rather than on our

Kin Magic, and is likewise glaring. Well, glaring at Irwin, anyway. I've already made it clear I'm far more on her side than his. The only part I'm even on his side with is the importance of making this potion. Not even for its potentially powerful elements, but for the peace it may offer him.

WolfBear, who is steadying the new canvas shelter she's built around the alchemy set, looks up, her ears bent as she looks slightly offended. "I took good care of Lady."

Meredith sighs. "Yes, WolfBear, you did. And I appreciate it." She turns to glare at Irwin. "But I *don't* appreciate being *poisoned*."

I once again have to move the beaker away from Irwin.

"I didn't poison you," he mutters. "It was a benign sleeping powder."

Meredith flicks her hair behind her as she turns her face away in contempt. "I still don't forgive you."

Before this unfortunate conversation can continue, Kennan steps under our canopy, a few raindrops rolling down his face.

I give Irwin a Look to remind him of how important this concoction is to him before handing him back the beaker. Then I approach Kennan.

"Everyone has secured shelter," he says.

"Thank you."

"No." He bows at his waist. "Thank *you*, my lady, for your generosity."

I accept his gratitude with an imperious nod. "Well, I thank you and the others for helping me be so generous."

Kennan salutes and then glances past me. "Is that supposed to happen?"

Turning, I see the liquid in the beaker appears to be on fire.

"Irwin!" I cry, rushing toward him.

But he's already standing right next to the flaming beaker, and I can't stop him from plucking it away from the rudimentary fire it was set on.

Then Irwin brings the internally flaming vial to his nose and inhales.

I watch in horror as all the flames turn to smoke, and all the smoke goes into Irwin's nostrils. Irwin's eyes go so far up in his head, I can see only white. His legs wobble, and then the now-empty vial falls from his hand and shatters on the grass. Then he follows it.

Meredith and I yell, but Kennan is already beside him, catching my cousin before he can hit the ground.

He turns to me, Irwin's unconscious form in his arms. "Where should I place him?"

I mutely point toward the straw bed set up close to the alchemy set. What has my cousin done to himself?

Our tutor specifically said lemongrass could never be used in a poison. Why is he having this adverse effect, then?

Kennan deposits Irwin on the straw bed in a fashion that reminds me of a time long past when Irwin fell asleep while trying to observe an experiment that went too long, and his late father carried him to bed. Before whatever it was that took my uncle from us took him. I was too young to understand at the time, and my parents never tried to explain or even discuss it.

Pushing Kennan aside, I kneel beside my cousin and check his pulse. It's still steady, but the beats are slow. He is deeply asleep.

How deeply? Our tutor warned us that some concoctions, when mixed wrong, could be disastrous, even deadly. And he would know, since he was three hundred years old when my parents hired him.

Suddenly, Irwin starts moving his head back and forth, sweat beading on his shoulder.

I move back an inch, hoping he's just about to wake up and might need room to breathe.

"It can't be so," he mutters.

I move closer again and take his hand. "What is it? What can't be so?"

He keeps rocking his head back and forth, and the movements become more violent. "It can't be so!"

"What can't be so, Irwin?"

Meredith moves to stand behind me. "What do you see?"

"Sunset at dawn," Irwin thrashes his head, turning it from side to side. "*Sunset at dawn*!"

Suddenly, he sits straight up, and his eyes re-open.

I study him, wondering if this is another trick of the potion or an aspect of night sickness. But his eyes, though wide and crazed, are also alert and focused.

"Irwin?" I whisper. "Irwin, are you back?"

He nods. "I'm Irwin. I'm fine."

"What happened?" Meredith is practically on top of me to get closer to Irwin.

Irwin still doesn't meet either of our gazes. "I saw the future."

I frown. "What do you mean?"

Meredith crouches beside me. "What did you see?"

Finally, Irwin tears his eyes from the distance and melds his gaze into mine. "Worlds-shattering war. Deaths both past and planned. The fate of Constantinium in the balance."

I purse my lips, studying him to make sure he's truly awake and back with us.

Meredith kneels beside me, her skirts she must have put on after I asked her to watch Irwin fluttering around her. "Can you be more specific?"

"I can be." He turns to me. "I will be. Elspeth." He closes his eyes and focuses on breathing for a long moment before meeting my gaze again. "I know how we can reclaim what was stolen from us with interest."

I blink. "How?"

"By saving the Empire."

Meredith leans forward. "How?"

"By first saving the Prince."

CHAPTER XIII

Lady Elspeth

Meredith frowns at Irwin's words, some of the awe in her expression wearing away. "How do we know that we have to save the Prince? Or even that you saw anything of value and not a fevered hallucination?"

I purse my lips, knowing how important the *Chazah* Tonic is to our people's history. How else would we have known to store away our sacred texts before Haya fell to Constantinium?

But it is also a difficult tonic, and if he did it wrong, the vision may mean nothing.

Irwin's eyes flash with intensity, and he turns from Meredith to me. He holds out his hand to me, somehow sensing my doubts. "Let me show you."

"Are you sure?" I ask, not sure if he's in the best state for us to harness our Kin Magic to enter his mind together. It is one of the more complicated and exhausting forms of Kin Magic, something only the nobles of our people can afford to learn and practice, along with the even more exhausting ability to swap physical locations.

No, healing kin and sensing their needs are much safer and more commonplace. But with great practice and consent from both parties, the other two can be achieved. Irwin and I have accomplished both before.

Irwin nods, and I place my hand on his. Then I close my eyes and prepare my mind.

"*Hee'neh, hee'neh'nee, heen'nee,*" I say, imagining my mind as a home I have stepped out of and Irwin's as a home I have come to. "I stand at the door and knock."

"*Hee'neh, hee'neh'nee, heen'nee,*" Irwin answers. "I open the door and welcome you with all hospitality."

I close my eyes.

And I see Irwin's home. He opens his door for me, and I step in.

Irwin leads me deeper into his mind, darkness surrounding us, with random flashes of color illuminating the depths on all sides.

"Let me show you what I saw," Irwin says, closing his eyes and reaching into the depths.

Suddenly, the darkness is replaced by a massive, colorful scene that is unfolding around us, yet the scene is clouded somehow. Like we are viewing through a fog.

A blurred figure is sitting on a throne, a crown on his gray head. Even though it is impossible to make out his face, I can only assume that this is the Emperor of the Sun.

As we watch, the Emperor falls from his thrown, his non-existent face hitting the ground, and his crown sliding across the floor.

A second figure steps forward, the long brown robe that sets him apart as a great mortal magic practitioner sliding across the ground, growing larger and larger until it takes up the entire floor.

The Sorcerer bends over and plucks up the fallen crown. He straightens it and places it on his head. Then he lifts one arm in a decisive point.

Suddenly, men come from nowhere, running forward, changing the scene into a swirl of limbs and weapons.

They melt away, revealing the form of another man standing alone in a room brimming with books. His dark hair is not unlike Heinrich's, and a smaller version of the Emperor's crown is perched on his head.

His back is to us, but I can see that he's looking down at something in his hand. A heart, I realize with a jolt.

A heart that has been severed into two parts and is even now bleeding through his fingers and dripping onto the carpet.

Suddenly, the men from earlier rush in and surround the princely figure. Swords and daggers and arrows are drawn and poised to slaughter the young man staring at the broken heart.

Suddenly, the entire scene seems to melt away, and another scene falls from above. The Prince again, this time standing and wielding a broadsword that is clashing against the magic coming from the hands of the dark-robed Sorcerer. Until the Prince seems to dissolve and only the dark-robed man remains, his magic pouring out everywhere with no one to stop him.

In a flash, the scene changes again, this time revealing a gaping hole in the once glorious seat of the Empire, Sitzvononne, that reveals a completely different city that has been wreaked with dust and darkness everywhere within the hole. Only the figure of the Prince is standing just outside the hole.

He glances back, and even though I can't make out his face, I can see the great heaviness on his shoulders and sense the sorrow in his heart.

Then he steps into the hole, and it closes instantly, revealing only Sitzvononne, untouched and whole.

Until suddenly we're seeing the same scene again, only instead of the Prince standing at the entrance of the tear in the tapestry of the scene, it is the Sorcerer. And instead of stepping into the hole, he summons armies out of it. Armies that swarm the capital city, making it resemble more and more the city in the hole, the tear in reality.

Finally, that chaos dissolves, revealing a new scene. This one is the throne the Emperor was sitting on in the first scene. Only now it is empty, the crown sitting next to it. As I watch, the throne seems to alter, becoming the throne that once belonged to my father, and then to me before it was stolen from me .

Bewildered, I step toward it and almost trip over the crown. Bending down, I pluck it up, somewhat surprised that I am touching something tangible in this illusion. But I'm more surprised by how right it feels in my hands.

I bring it up to eye level. In the golden sheen, I see a reflection of the sky. The sun is rising slowly from the horizon, bright and glorious, a new day.

But before the sun can reach its proper position and bring daylight to all, it descends again. Darkness begins to return, but a single star shines where the sun should be and fights against the darkness.

A feeling of overwhelming grief for the lost day overcomes me. The losses of my father and mother, my uncle and aunt, and the life I used to live come flooding back, but there is something else as well. A loss like I've never known before.

I drop the crown, and it clatters to the ground.

Suddenly, my eyes open, and I find myself looking at the dim darkness above, but there is no moon to be seen. Panic overtakes me, and I sit up quickly from where I was lying completely flat on my back.

But then I see that the sun is still in its place, slowly rising. Dawn is still being born.

My body tingles as it reminds me that it still exists and has become quite uncomfortable since I left it. Groaning, I turn to see that Irwin is also sitting up slowly, his eyes clear now like he has regained full control of his mind without either the *Chazah* Tonic influencing it or any trace of me inside it.

"What happened?" Meredith whispers, glancing between us with a worried expression.

WolfBear is standing behind her, looking confused as she scans the area for whatever might have hurt us so she can stop it. Several others around us are watching in concern— the brothers, Kennan, and strangers alike.

I push myself to my feet, my legs wobbling strangely.

WolfBear quickly comes to my side to steady me even as Meredith does the same for Irwin.

And I turn to my audience, my people. "The Emperor is going to die."

A whispered hush comes over the crowd like a blanket.

I lift my chin. "And when he does, the Sorcerer who murders him will try to seize the throne."

Irwin comes to stand beside me on Meredith's arm. "Unless the Prince is rescued from his clutches." His voice is hoarse from inhaling smoke. "There seem to be two paths. One where the Prince is spared from assassination and stands against the Sorcerer who kills the Emperor. And one where the Sorcerer rules without contest."

"The Prince seems to be the only one capable of stopping the Sorcerer from destroying everything," I whisper. "The only one who can rescue our Empire from invaders that appear to be from another world."

I leave it up to Irwin to decide whether to add the final piece that I cannot seem to speak aloud.

The Prince is lost in both scenarios. With one loss, the Empire falls with him. With the other, it is his sacrifice that delivers us all. Sunset at dawn in order to keep the world from falling into darkness.

"So, what do we do?" Abel whispers.

Geoff straightens. "Kill all the Sorcerers?"

Abel turns slowly to his brother and gapes at him for a moment before giving a firm shake of his head.

"Why do anything?" a stranger asks. "What happens to the Empire no longer affects us."

The disrespect of the dream Prince's sacrifice is more than I can bear. I shakily rise to my feet. "But it does. The evil the Sorcerer would unleash— it would find us all."

Kennan holds up a hand to silence his fellows as he studies me. "So, what should we do?"

"We need to rescue the Sacred Prince of the Sun." I utilize the title to put distance between myself and the grief of his loss, but all I can remember is being presented to him in his veils, so full of promise and power and purity. "We need to stand with him against this evil. And we need to make sure the throne goes to someone with a heart for us, the people, and not to a destroyer."

"How will we do any of that?" Meredith asks.

Irwin hurries to his alchemy set and starts taking inventory of his ingredients, as if the answer lies there.

But as I remember the throne and its transformation, I press my hand to my gut as I realize the answer to the third objective, my youthful aspirations turning to dust within me. "I think I know what we will need to do. What *I* have to do."

My head bows under the weight of the knowledge of exactly what I need to do.

Heavy is the head that wears the crown.

"So, we need to travel to the capital city," Kennan says as we cluster into a council as the rain pounds our tarp and splashes mud into our finest "building." "We can go on foot, but we don't exactly know what time the Emperor is appointed to die. It could happen in less than half a fortnight, which is how long it will be to trek there on foot if we take the main road."

I hug my cloak more tightly around me in a vain attempt to hide from the chill there can be no shelter from. "There's an embassy from the Prince staying in my keep. If I can find a way into the party, they can take me directly there with no roadblocks."

Irwin finishes counting his ingredients and looks up. "That's right; you know Heinrich, First Valet to the Sacred Prince of the Sun."

I nod. "He might allow me to ride with them."

Meredith's eyebrows raise into her hairline. "When did any of this happen?"

Since we don't have time to cover the complex answer, I ignore it for now.

Irwin frowns, still mulling over the Heinrich angle. "But isn't he currently at our keep with the man who showed us no mercy? How will you get past that monster when he knows your face?"

Especially since VonTrapp seems to be very keen on hiding what he did to me and mine. And with his massive army, he far outnumbers both my party and what I've seen of Heinrich's. He could kill us all to prevent word from spreading back to the Prince.

But I need to reach the Prince before death does. "I am a master of stealth."

Irwin frowns. "Is Heinrich?"

I remember how loudly he snapped the twigs in the words. "No . . ."

"Perhaps we should consider a disguise."

"I'm already somewhat in disguise." I glance at Meredith.

Irwin shakes his head. "No, something deeper that VonTrapp could never sere through. An illusion."

I narrow my eyes at him. "Only select mortals have any magical capable of creating illusions."

"But our people have long studied their powers and learned how to replicate it with potions." He gestures to his lab equipment. "I have the ingredients I need to create a long-lasting illusion. Save for a strand of hair from the person you'll need to impersonate."

I chew my bottom lip. "Let me see if I can meet with Heinrich and determine if he can smuggle me with him. I have a feeling he would be open to the idea." Unless my behavior last night drove whatever fancies he felt for me out of his mind.

Meredith raises just one eyebrow this time.

"If he can't, though, be sure to get me a strand of his hair." Irwin's face is like stone, and I can tell the vision shook him as deeply as it did me. "We can't afford to lose time."

Still, the thought of betraying Heinrich after helping me defend my ancestors seems wrong and more than I can bear to think of right now. Even if he has irked me exceedingly during our brief acquaintance.

But then I remember the tragedy of the vision and my heart pangs. The Prince deserves the last days on this mortal plane before going wherever that hole takes him to."Fine, prepare the necessary potions for me to take Heinrich's place if I cannot see a way to join his party without being spotted by VonTrapp. And Ii all else fails, we can just steal some horses and find our own bearing."

"And then find our own way into Sitzvononne? The palace?"

I hold up a hand. "Let me meet with Heinrich. From there, we can come up with a plan." My vengeance will not come in death, but in saving a life that he may deliver many more. The Creator shall surely approve.

"We already have a plan." Irwin sets his hard gaze on me. "We rescue the Prince. He rescues the Empire."

"And in between those two events, . . . " I half-choke on the words that need to come next. That *must* come next. The restitution I shall receive from the Empire is a palace to replace my stolen keep, but even that will come at a price. "I wed him. And ensure from the throne that the Night of the Broken Walls never happens again."

CHAPTER XIV

Prince Otello

By the time I reach the rope outside of my tower, my limbs feel as wobbly as they do after with training the broadsword.

Sighing, I wrap the rope around my waist and tie it securely. Then I tug it twice, hoping Heinrich is still awake and able to help me up.

Then, because this has not been my night between fighting in a crypt and then quarreling with my temporary ally, I place my legs on the stones, pulling taught against the rope. Pure determination has me moving my legs like I am walking on a horizontal surface rather than vertical, my wobbling arms reaching up the rope to help pull me upward.

Several yards above the ground, I hear a great turmoil come from the crypt, and see torches start to light up. They are going to be looking for whoever sealed the crypt.

I climb faster. Or at least as fast as I can bear to.

Lights start coming closer, and I wonder if it would be better if I just go still and hope they don't look up.

But no sooner than the thought goes through my mind, the rope starts to move upward itself.

I find new hope and continue my ascent, moving twice as fast as before with the extra help.

Finally, I reach the windowsill and grasp it. Then hands grasp mine and pull me through. Before I collapse on the ground, that was lower than I expected.

"Ow," I groan.

Heinrich stands over me next to a makeshift pulley system he must have put together in my absence. "What happened? What did you learn?"

"VonTrapp is no friend to the family who once owned this castle." Groaning, I sit up and undo my rope.

He helps me pull it free and then stands back. "What are you going to do, my prince?"

"First of all, you are not to call me 'my prince' until we are safe in Sitzvononne."

Heinrich frowns. "But I do not believe Bard Callistus will be following us back."

"There's another issue that has come up. It's probably stupid, but I would feel better to remain in disguise as long as possible."

"What happened?"

I drop onto my mattress and kick off my boots before laying back and throwing my arm over my face. "I think someone saw me use my Heritage."

Heinrich works at undoing his pulley system. "What? *I* haven't even seen you use your Heritage Magic!"

"Yeah, that's just it. Even the secondary heir is kept in the dark of his powers until the time comes that he needs to know how to use it, if it ever does."

"To be fair, your cousin is in the dark about a lot of things besides matters of national security."

"Stop it," I mutter. "He's just a boy."

"A boy without a care in the world, which certainly was never *your* case."

"Well, let's hope that he never *has* to have a care in the world."

Heinrich nods. "Indeed. May your father have a long rule followed by you and your longer reign."

I close my eyes, wondering if I should tell Heinrich about the rest of my encounter with the Lady Meredith.

Lady Meredith. There was never a more perplexing woman. And she is the Bandit King's snares. Honestly, all of this could be a set-up.

What greater treasure could he steal but the secret that Constantinium would pay any price to keep quiet and any other nation would ransom riches to know? How better to bring an Empire to its knees than to know every detail about their greatest defense?

"Heinrich, I cannot stress this enough. You must *be* me for the rest of our trip until we return home." I force my eyes open. "No matter what. Understand?"

He nods solemnly, his gaze analyzing my expression. "On my mother's soul, I shall be you and you shall be me until we pass through the gates of Sitzvononne."

The solemnity of his vow slices through me. I know how sacred a word he has given, not just to him, but also to the Empire. I know the vow will bind Heinrich, but I can't help but wonder if he knows of the secret significance of his words, or if it is a burden I alone bear.

However, my eyelids are heavier than my full armor, and I start to think maybe it would be better to broach the subject in the morning when I can deal with his teasing better.

A sudden banging on the door jars me out of what slumber I had slipped into, though I can't tell if I've been in that state for hours or seconds. Whichever option, it wasn't enough.

Heinrich gestures for me to stay where I am— not that I needed any urging from him to not get out of bed— grabs his sword, and approaches the door.

Before he reaches it, though, the door swings open.

I sit up and reach for my sword before I can register that it is Gerrard the Guard on the other side.

Before I can be relieved, though, I see his expression.

Dropping the sword, I slip out of bed. "What is it?"

"We received word from the royal carrier pigeon." He holds out a letter. "It bears the black seal."

Which means the message within is urgent. Dire.

I stumble toward Gerrard, and if he notices that I'm wearing a tunic instead of a nightshirt, he says nothing. He simply hands me the letter, the black seal shaped like the sun. My family's seal.

Ripping open the letter, I take out the note, expecting to hear something directly from my father. But the words are not from his pen.

My noble prince,

Your father has fallen gravely ill and requests you at his bedside.
— High Sorcerer Adalbert

I drop the letter. "Prepare the horses now and wake everyone. We leave at once."

Gerrard's expression shifts negatively. He never entirely changes his expression from resting anger; it merely shifts up and down. "But, my prince, I cannot guarantee protection when traveling at night. This is the Bandit King's territory, after all."

I hold up a hand. "Do not address me as Prince until we return to Sitzvononne. Which we will leave for at once." Only the most debilitating of diseases would give Adalbert the right to use the Emperor's seal as his own.

Which means my father needs me. And my Empire needs me more.

Because if my father perishes in my absence, that will not be all the authority Adalbert is given.

"I am sorry you have to leave so soon," Baron VonTrapp says.

Heinrich nods in acknowledgement of his words.

But the Baron still doesn't walk away. Or limp away, as the case may be. Not sitting on his throne for once, Vontrapp leans heavily on an ornate cane that is obviously not just for decoration.

I don't have time to rescue him from the conversation and I can trust Heinrich not to give away our suspicions, so I go to see how the stable boys are doing with setting up the horses and if Gerrard the Guard has all the men lined up and ready to go.

Before I can finish my inspection, though, Callistus approaches me and bows.

When he straightens, he gives me a sad smile. "I suppose this is farewell."

I nod. "I suppose so. Would you do me the privilege of keeping your eyes and ears out for the Bandit King? And send me what information you learn?"

Callistus grins. "Of course. But be warned, I may send my observations in verse."

"I suppose I'll have to suffer through it then."

Grinning deeper, Callistus pats me on the shoulder before walking away.

I blink. Has anyone other than Heinrich ever touched me so casually? Is that what non-princes do with each other? Maybe if Princes were allowed more platonic gestures, I would not be so taken with the mysterious Lady Meredith.

Lady Meredith . . . I can almost see the swish of her red skirt going behind a pile of hay stored just outside the stable.

Obviously, the accidental proximity is messing with my mind, making me read too much into things that aren't so.

Except, what else could be that vibrant of red in this area?

Curious, I step forward to investigate and round the rather extensive collection of hay bales, smoothing down the simply cut tunic with imperial coins sewn like buttons over sturdy breeches for travel.

Sure enough, it is Lady Meredith that I find there, her hair once again plaited around her ears, and her dark tunic and leggings replaced by her red dress.

It is hard to say which of those outfits are more becoming on her. And as foolish as it is, I wish I had the opportunity to change into something nicer. But my father is ill, and I shouldn't even be here—

Meredith turns toward me and her face lights up. My heart skips like when I was just a boy, blessing the long lines of young noblewomen being introduced to court.

She approaches me, and I wait for her to make some excuse for last night or else to give some reason for now, but she places her one finger on my lips while the other grips my arm. She tugs at me. My feet are all too willing to comply in following her behind the bales and out of view of my party.

Once she is confident we are beyond others' eyes and ears, she leans toward me, her eyes flashing with earnestness. "I need to go to Sitzvononne."

Grasping her wrist, I pull her finger away from my mouth before I can lose what's left of my reason before a woman I know better than to trust. "Then—" I stop myself from inviting her into my carriage. As much as I would enjoy her company and love that she is safely returned to civilization, out of the clutches of the Bandit King, she still must not learn that I am the Emperor's son. Ever.

"I will arrange transportation for you," I quickly add. "Send back an accompaniment fit for a lady of your stature."

"No, I have to go now." She glances around frantically, and I wonder if someone is watching us even now.

The hairs on the back of my neck rise.

She takes both my hands in hers. "I'm in grave danger. Please smuggle me into the carriage with you. I won't get in the way of your men, I swear."

"I—" My mind frantically goes through all plausible scenarios. "I can't smuggle you. But you may come. I'll alert my men of your presence and the fact that you're under my protection." And that they are not to address me as the Sacred Prince under any circumstances.

She doesn't look convinced by this solution.

"You can even have the carriage alone," I add. "I'll ride ahead." So, I can send word to all the servants that Heinrich will be the figurehead Prince during this time of upheaval.

I nod. Yes, that will work. Grasping her small hand, I move to pull her toward my party with me. Surely Gerrard the Guard has already alerted the men to my wishes of remaining anonymous. When I take a step forward, I see VonTrapp limp by before vanishing out of view behind the hay bales. When I move to take another step forward, I find resistance.

Turning, I find Meredith still standing behind me, her heels dug into the ground and her eyes wide.

I step back toward her. "What is it?"

She uses our joined hands to pull me closer still, and I have to stop myself from stumbling into her.

Which is why I don't notice her next action until her lips are on mine.

I freeze as my mind seems to expand and decrease at the same time while her soft lips skim over mine and her hands reach around my neck. With that grip, she draws me forward.

My feet comply, bringing me closer, the scent of wildflowers encompassing me. My hands wrap around her waist, which appears to be their favorite place to reside. Then my lips dare to mirror hers and return affection. Her kiss is so soft, so sweet, so supple . . .

My forwardness seems to speed up our pace as our movements match each other and the rhythm of my pounding heart. I clutch her more tightly, and she spins us around so that my back is now against a tree. A support I desperately need to keep from collapsing on the forest floor.

Then she pulls her face away from mine.

I stare at her with blurry-eyed wonder as I try to assess what just happened and why it had to end. Then I realize my hands are still on her waist and quickly drop them.

What do I do now? Apologize for my lapse in chivalry? Even if I'm not sorry?

"I'm so sorry," Meredith says, stealing my script as easily as she stole my first kiss.

"What?" My gaze finally focuses enough for me to see the regret on her face. Just in time to get a projectile thrown at my face.

The soft object hits me square on the nose and then explodes in a cloud of dust.

Coughing, I stoop over in an attempt to find some escape from the dust and watch as a scrap of cloth drifts to the ground. The world jolts suddenly, and I feel as though I will soon follow it.

But I force myself to look back up at Meredith, who is watching me with tears in her eyes.

"What did you do?" I gasp. "Was that—" I cough bitterly. "One of your sleeping powders?"

"I'm so sorry," Meredith says again. "I wish there was another way. But this is a matter of national security, and I can't take any more chances than I already have."

"'*National security*?!" I reach for her, and she easily dodges me. The momentum of my movement sends me toppling forward.

This time, Meredith lunges toward me, throwing her arms around me and stopping my descent with all the strength in her lean frame. I sag uselessly into her as she lowers me onto the forest floor. Leaves crunch beneath me and some fly up, joining the dust in the air.

Meredith bends down beside me and puts her hand on my tunic. I want to reach up and push her away from me. But my limbs suddenly seem as heavy as when I take on the properties of stone, only more unwilling to obey my commands.

"I wish I had time to explain, but I don't." She starts unbuttoning my tunic, and I stare at her in shock.

"What are you . . .?" My tongue grows as heavy as my limbs.

"I'll see that no harm comes to you," she adds, yanking the rest of the buttons apart.

I want to tell her to stop this. Demand to know if this is her precious Bandit King's doing. Let her know what I think of the way she's treating me after kissing me just moments ago.

But now the struggle is keeping my eyelids from drooping from their stony weight.

Somehow, my body is not nearly as heavy to her as it is to me, because she pushes me to my side in order to yank my tunic completely away from me.

Then her hands move to my breeches.

Somehow, one hand reaches to grasp her, and I do my best to look up at her in a silent plea before my eyes drift shut for good.

But the rest of my senses are still working for the time being. I feel her other hand come over mine and squeeze it.

Hear her soft, remorseful voice. "I only need your garments, a strand of your hair, and your good name. To save the Empire. But I will not hurt you, nor shall any creature in the forest. Rest easy."

I don't want to listen to her, much less obey without a fight. But I feel my mind already drifting away from the affairs of my body. But I know one thing; I will not comply. I will not rest easy.

Not while my father lies ill and my last chance to make my peace with him is drifting away as quickly as I am under this witch's sleeping spell.

CHAPTER XV

Lady Elspeth

When Heinrich's body goes limp, I know I am now alone at the edge of the forest, in a manner of speaking. With a frantic glance toward the farm, I make sure that we remain that way. The hay bales obscure the view of the gathering party from me— and hopefully me from them.

I pull off both Heinrich's boots before giving a last tug to release the breeches from his ankles. The force almost sends me backward into the tree.

Looking beyond him, I do my best to put aside how horrified I would be if our roles were reversed and focus on the task at hand. This is the beginning of my rescuing the Empire and restoring myself to a position where I will never again have to stoop to such desperate measures.

Glancing back down at the man I'm robbing, I decide that I do not need his braies, too. He certainly needs them more than I.

My gaze goes up his stature, and I feel my face color at the impropriety of it all. Before this moment, I never saw a man in such a state of undress. And most certainly not a man with such a physique. Heinrich must prefer heavier weapons than I to have become so well-muscled.

I feel my skin burn in shame at my thoughts. From what I'm doing. From what I did just before this.

Never in my life have I ever embraced a man in such a manner. Of course, I have kissed him and plenty others on both cheeks in the customary greeting of my people. But this . . . was much different.

And now the man I was kissing—*on the lips* — moments before lies before me, exposed and unconscious, all by my hand.

If the Creator had not already punished me so much for sins I hadn't even committed yet, I would be terrified of His wrath.

I hear a sound and jump before scanning the area, but we are still alone. I can sense that we are, even if I do not feel as though it is true.

As quickly as my now shaking hands can go, I reach behind myself and find the ties to my dress. Normally a lady's maid, or in my case, Meredith, would need to help me in and out of such a contraption. But today I have no time.

Yanking at the ties does nothing, so I have to do yet another thing I regret.

Reaching into my sheath, I take my dagger and then slide it along the ties.

The sound of the beautiful material being sliced apart is what finally causes my tears to escape the prison of my willpower.

Dropping my dagger, I slide out of my dress as quickly as possible, letting it crumple in a lovely red satin puddle at my feet.

I feel exposed changing here, without more trees and foliage to shield me, so I work quickly. Sitting on the grass, I do my best to ignore where the blades bite into the skin my short chemise doesn't cover. Then I tug Heinrich's breeches over my legs.

When I stand up, I see they are a few inches longer than I anticipated. But that will be unnoticeable once I put on his boots.

With another furtive glance around, I see that Heinrich is still asleep and no one else has come upon us yet. But how much longer until his party notices that the First Valet to the Sacred Prince is absent?

In one fluid movement, I tug off my chemise. Trying not to think at all, I take my knife again and slice most of it into a long strip. I wrap the strip around my chest several times, as tightly as I can. Thankfully, as a she-elf, I do not have as large of a bust as most mortal women, but I cannot risk being exposed over such a silly thing.

That done, I tug the tunic over my head and almost fall back at the smell that it surrounds me with. Cedar and soap of the quality only the wealthiest can afford. I did not realize until now that Heinrich had a scent. Something to remind me of what I've done here.

But at least now everyone will smell it on me.

Bending over, I take the rest of my chemise and slice it into smaller rags that I stuff into the boots before shoving my feet into them. It's far from comfortable, but I will learn to mask my footfalls in them the same as when I learned to step on the forest floor without making a sound.

Now that I'm dressed, I turn back to Heinrich.

And feel another pang of guilt at the thought of leaving him here, exposed and alone.

"I'm so sorry," I whisper, as if the more I apologize, the more I mitigate my sin even as I commit it. Then I bend down to my discarded dress, pluck it up, shake it out, and then lay it across him like a blanket.

Finally, I kneel beside him and run a hand down his cheek to check that he's still asleep. When he doesn't move, I move his head to give me a better view of his hair.

Using my dagger again, I slice off a couple of strands of his lovely dark hair. Then I sheathe my weapon and stand.

I fight the urge to apologize again and close my eyes to focus on what I had originally thought would be the hardest part of this mission, the hardest display of Kin Magic of all.

Closing my eyes, I mutter the words Irwin has doubtless been saying on repeat these last few moments while I did what I had to do. What will he think when he sees the fruit of my labor?

No, I need to direct my energies to one of the trickier uses of Kin Magic. I call upon a focusing *Davar.* "*BA'ASHER TELCHI.*"

When I open my eyes, I find myself standing in front of Irwin's lab.

Meredith jumps up from her usual rock. "It actually worked!"

I nod and hand her the tuft of hair I took from Heinrich.

My gaze moves beyond her to where my bow is resting against a tree, my quiver beside it. I'll have to leave those behind for my mission. I feel as exposed as I left Heinrich.

Serves me right.

Sighing, I turn back to Meredith. See my *Shamir* dangling from her ear playfully. "And you'll take care of him?"

She reaches up and pets the *Shamir*. It squeaks in pleasure and nuzzles closer to her. "Of course. And I'll take care of Irwin as well. Even if I haven't forgiven him."

"Thank you. I'll . . . I'll be right back." Taking a deep breath, I close my eyes again and focus. "*Elech*."

This time, I notice a change in the air before I even open my eyes. I'm back beside Heinrich, and he's still asleep. But the sun is getting higher in the sky, and time is passing quickly. How long till he awakens? How long until they look for him— or worse, leave without him/me?

But Irwin said he needed only moments to brew the potion and then we could switch back. I can grab it, and then I can come back. Easy.

In an attempt to take my mind off my nervousness and guilt, I reach to gather all my wayward strands and place them back into my braid. I will need them out of the way in order to perfect the illusion.

Finally, I can't take it any longer, so I just start the chant while I wait. "*BA'ASHER TELCHI. BA'ASHER TELCHI. BA'ASHER TELCHI—*"

Suddenly, I'm back in my camp, and rocking with dizziness for not closing my eyes during the transition.

WolfBear reaches out to steady me.

Finally, the rest of the world steadies, too, and I can make out Meredith watching me wide-eyed and holding out a vial with a purple brew.

This time, her eyes are not filled with awe, but with worry. Because of this potion, or because Irwin told her what I did?

Looking away from another reminder of my guilt, I take the vial and then throw it back.

I'm glad I get it all down at once, because once I register the taste, I know I wouldn't have been able to take another swig. It tastes like something beyond what I've ever consumed before, something obviously not natural.

But the texture is worse. It feels like . . . hair.

I grasp the nearest tree to steady myself until I can focus on not spewing the potion back out.

As I'm still trying to get over the nastiness on the inside, an unnatural warmth comes over my outside. I feel it start at my feet and come up over me, as though an unseen force is pulling a burlap sack up over me and enclosing me in it. As it seems to seal over me, I feel as though I am unable to breathe, even though my lungs and nose are still working perfectly fine. But oxygen seems to be of a lesser quality than it was before.

Meredith, who had been reaching forward in concern, stumbles back. "It— it worked!"

Around me, several of the newer peasants cry out in surprise. Geoff drops the firewood he had been carrying, and Abel trips over it.

I want to hide, wondering why I chose to transform here in the open for all to see. It didn't seem like something that may require privacy until now. But it's too late now, not that I had time for privacy, anyway.

Still, I want to run and hide, curl up somewhere. It is as if my growing years and the uncomfortableness that came with them have come upon me all at once, and a decade of change has been condensed into one moment. A decade of change that never would have happened except unnaturally.

Looking down, I see my hands, only they are not my hands. They are bigger and meatier. Male hands.

Suddenly, I am one of the observers and merely taking in this stranger to the camp who is not me. I do not recognize these feelings or these hands. How could they belong to me?

Yet, I cannot quite see myself from the outside the way the others see me.

A strange curiosity grips me, and I stumble toward a bucket we stole just last night to catch rainwater in. Thanks to the storm, there is plenty of water already inside, and I can make out my reflection clearly.

Only, it is not my reflection. It is Heinrich staring back at me with his thick, dark hair, purple eyes, and firm jaw.

I reach up to touch my jaw and watch my hand go partly through the illusion. I drop my hand, but the sight of what happened still makes me dizzy. As does the feeling of being taller, even though I know I'm not. Irwin told me the potion doesn't change my actual height or shape—which is why it had to be me who took the tonic and not him. It only masks my features with another's.

With Heinrich's.

Who even now lies half-naked in the woods because of me.

I close my eyes as the events of the day overwhelm me. But I don't have time for that. Not now. Not for a long time. One tear, the only tear I allow myself now, escapes as I whisper, "*Elech.*"

Even with my eyes closed, a dizziness overtakes me, probably because of how nauseous I already feel from this potion.

I stumble to the tree I pressed Heinrich against and grasp it for support as I will myself not to be sick. I can't risk spewing out the potion and weakening the illusion.

"For the Sacred Prince of the Sun and the Sanctified Empire of Constantinium," I whisper. "For revenge and for honor."

I finally get enough control of my stomach to glance behind me to where Heinrich is still lying.

Well, for new honor, since my original honor is apparently obsolete.

Taking several calming breaths, I check my sheathes where I have moved them under my tunic, a semblance of familiarity and security to bring with me as I leave behind my own face and go instead to face a powerful enemy.

Hopefully, my tonic will last long enough. Irwin speculates its effects should carry up to a fortnight, but I'm not sure how my metabolism won't dispose of it long before then.

I take one last deep breath and then walk back toward the stables before I can dare think about another thing.

When I step out from behind the hay bales, it's like stepping into another world. The tranquility of the forest has been replaced by the bustle of a royal entourage preparing for a great journey. And since the one man I somewhat knew is sleeping on the forest bed, there are only strangers here.

Also, I have just experienced my first kiss and am now sick to my stomach for multiple reasons, not least of all because I resemble a mortal man.

To my horror, one man— a ginger with a more ragged yet more colorful outfit than the other men, who are adorned in either armor or silks— locks eyes with me.

I look away, hoping he won't approach me until I'm ready to move forward with this deception, which may be a fortnight at the rate I'm going.

But he approaches me nonetheless and puts a hand on my shoulder.

I do my best not to stiffen at the touch from a strange man— after all, friends touch each other all the time, and I'm sure that's who he is to Heinrich.

"Have a good journey, my friend," he says with a slight lilting accent not unlike that of the mercenaries that helped Von Trapp steal my castle from me.

"You're not coming?" I say in my deepest tone, which is easier than I thought it would be with the feeling of the tonic stuck in my throat.

The man gives me a strange look. "I thought we already discussed that? Or was that the other one I spoke to?" He shakes his head to himself. "It makes no difference; I shall miss both you and the Prince."

"And I will miss . . . you." A sudden thought comes to me. "Though I have a favor to ask of you."

The man, who upon closer inspection is as youthful as Heinrich and I are, but with eyes that seem somehow older, gives me a serious expression in contrast to his previous mirth. "Anything, good sir."

"I have deposited some goods I cannot take with me in the woods behind the hay bales. Watch over them for me."

He nods and turns as if to walk toward the bales at that moment.

I feel several beads of sweat dot my temple, and I reach out and grab his elbow. "But don't go there until after you lose sight of the caravan. It is something I prefer the other men not see."

"Ah, I see." He taps his nose. "A secret."

Nodding, I step back. "Exactly. I'm trusting you with this."

"And with correspondence concerning the Bandit King. It is a good thing I'm one of the few *responsible* Bards."

I blink, too tired to gauge whether this is sarcasm or good-natured humor.

The bard winks at me, gives me one last salute, and then saunters off— thankfully not straight toward the hay bales.

"There you are!"

I about jump out of both my skin and the illusion alike. Then I turn to see a man who looks very similar to me. So similar that we— or he and Heinrich, anyway— could be brothers, at least in facial structure and hair style. His blue eyes fall short of Heinrich's rare purple, though.

"Sorry," I mumble. "I'm not feeling all that well."

The man frowns. "Just in time for a long journey."

"But it cannot wait," I quickly add.

"Indeed, not. The Emperor is ill. It's no wonder that you are sick with worry."

The Emperor is ill. The time before the beginning of the end may be shorter than even I anticipated.

Whoever my lookalike is— or whoever is the lookalike to the man I now look like, anyway— leads me toward the one carriage and opens the door for me.

If he's not Heinrich's brother, perhaps he is the first valet to the First Valet?

I walk over to the carriage, and a man wearing armor under a tunic with the insignia of the Emperor's sun opens the door for me. I wait for a long moment for someone to give me a hand up before remembering that I'm disguised as a man now.

Clearing my throat and still not dislodging the feeling of hair in my throat, I duck my head and step inside.

The lookalike steps in also, and as he stoops down, a medallion falls out from beneath his tunic. It is about as large as the palm of my hand and completely silver except for the shimmering gold inlay in the shape of the sun.

The Heritage Medallion of the Crown Prince.

I suddenly find it very hard to breathe past the clog in my throat. Heinrich didn't mention that the Sacred Prince *himself* was part of this entourage. But I suppose I should have expected it; why would the First Valet go on a journey without the man he is supposed to be valeting?

The Prince— Otello— sits beside me rather than across from me. I wait for more riders to step in and validate his need to be beside me, but then the guard closes the door.

Well, I guess this will make it easier to protect him— by being beside him now. Though I wish I were better prepared for the first meeting with my future husband. Even if it will be a short-lived marriage and not based on love at all— only a fool would fall for a man destined to be parted from this realm forever— I still hoped to make a good first . . . well, second impression.

As in, not disguised as a man who looks somewhat like him. His own valet, no less.

Wait, don't valets help attend to sensitive issues? Will I have to help him dress and undress? This man who, when we were first introduced, had to wear veils to protect his purity?

I glance away to keep my cheeks from going red at the thought. My only experience with such a deed was the unfortunate action I took this morning. Which I prefer to never think of again.

Despite my fluster, though, I can't keep myself from glancing sideways at Prince Otello.

Like Heinrich— and me now, I suppose— his dark hair is close to brushing his jaw, which is strong. But maybe not as strong as Heinrich's. And the eyes— I still favor Heinrich's rare purple, which seems better suited for royalty.

Prince Otello is indeed a handsome man, though it seems odd to me that his valet could be counted as more handsome. Aren't there laws against usch things?

The Prince catches my glance and raises one eyebrow at me. "You must really not be feeling well, my . . . friend. To have forgotten that this is always my side of the carriage."

My skin burns again. The carriage ride hasn't even started yet, and I'm already tripping up. "I— uh—"

"Or— this is about the *other* thing, isn't it?" Prince Otello shakes his head.

"Uh— yeah."

"Fine; I suppose if it suits your fancy, I can move."

I'm not even the real First Valet, and I'm unseating the Sacred Prince. This is not going well.

I grasp his arm. "No need. You can stay in your own seat."

"Okay . . ." Prince Otello glances down to where I am still clutching his well-muscled arm.

Quickly dropping my hands, I decide it is much too dangerous for me to be sitting this close to the man I am trying so hard to deceive and eventually both rescue and wed. I stand just as the carriage lurches forward.

I'm not prepared for the sudden momentum, and I topple sideways—onto Prince Otello's lap.

"Pardon!" I cry, jumping up as quickly as possible, hoping he did not notice a decidable difference between my physique and Heinrich's. Then I sit back down in my seat next to the Prince and bury my face in my hands.

"You are really not yourself," Prince Otello says. "Why don't you just rest?"

I mutter my agreement, scared of doing anything else that might betray my identity.

"Especially since, after everything is said and done, you really need to start doing a few more rounds in the training barracks. You're becoming soft."

At this, I don't even dare mutter. I don't dare betray how offended that comment makes me as both woman and a warrior . . . at least one trained as a warrior.

My body will not remain as still as my tongue, though, and my body convulses, I assume in a reaction to the tonic within me.

"Are you well?!"

I try to answer, but my teeth are chattering so hard, and I'm shaking so violently that I cannot even nod.

He touches my forehead and mutters something very unprincely. "You're freezing. Here."

Helplessly, I watch as he stands and takes a piece of luggage down from the overhead compartment and opens it. He pulls out a thick princely tunic not unlike the one he's currently wearing.

He turns with it in his hands, as if to put it on me.

"I c-c-couldn't."

The Prince doesn't listen to me, though, and pulls the tunic over my head.

I fight a flush as he pulls my arms through the sleeves, effectively dressing me. Granted, it's a second layer, but still.

He pulls away and smiles at me with kind eyes. "Better?"

Somewhere deep inside me, I find the strength to nod.

"Good." He pulls me against his side, wrapping his arm around me as if attempting to gift me with his body heat. "What would you do without me?"

I am far too flustered to answer. This is going to be a long, trying journey.

CHAPTER XVI

PRINCE OTELLO

"Father, why did you never remarry?"

The Emperor looked up from sorting through the guild reports to where I sat at my own desk, filing correspondence from our outposts into piles by priority level. But I couldn't focus. The time for the introduction into court of all the noblewomen who had come of age this year was nigh. And as this was the last year before my Unveiling, it was time to turn my mind toward selecting one of those women to be my future Empress.

"Because of my Heritage blood," Father answered, turning back to his paperwork. I was already treading in treacherous waters, coming as close as I did to bringing Mother into the conversation. "You have not experienced it yet, but when it selects who shall propagate the Heritage line, you are helpless against it."

I waited, knowing that already. It was why he wed my mother to begin with. That is not why he hasn't remarried, though.

"The Blood-Bound, as we call it." Father flipped through the report, then set it down and looked me in the eye, his violet gaze meeting mine. "We cannot flee from it. Nor does it allow recovery."

"Sire, wake up. Please, Sir Heinrich, you need to awaken—"

Snorting, I peel one eye open to see who has the audacity to pull me out of such a restful slumber.

Callistus is kneeling over me, his hands on my shoulders as he shakes me.

It occurs to me that I'm feeling too much of his hands. I glance down to see that his fingers are splayed across my bare skin.

I jerk away, slapping at his hands. "What's going on? What are you doing?"

Callistus drops his hands down to his lap and he frowns in concern. "You told me to come out this way after you left, and then I came across *you* lying here in a deep slumber in a less than anticipated state." He gestures to my person.

Almost too scared to look, I glance down and find myself wearing nothing but my braies and the velvet material of Meredith's red dress lying over me.

I push it away from me like it's a venomous snake, or at least like it's as venomous and serpentine as she is. What kind of insult was that supposed to be, on top of everything else she's already done to me?

The sudden movement makes my head spin, and I bring one hand up to soothe it. "Who did you say told you to come find me?"

Callistus furrows his brows together as he takes his satchel off his shoulder. "You. Only, you were still awake and wearing clothes. You told me you had hidden something back here I was not to fetch until your carriage was out of sight."

I feel my stomach sinking. "They already left?" And I'm stranded here without clothing or any way to contact Heinrich, Gerrard, or my father.

My father, who is on his sickbed and needs me with him.

Groaning, I bury my face in my hands. "I need to get to Sitzvononne."

"And I will get you there, my liege. Here."

I part two fingers to peek through and see Callistus offering me some garments from his satchel.

"Oh, thank you." I reach for them just as he pulls back.

"Here I am, offering my lesser garments." Callistus drops his satchel and grabs hold of the tunic he's wearing as if to pull it up.

I hold up my hand. "Your 'lesser' garments will do just fine. There's already been enough nudity in this forest."

"Indeed." Callistus hands me the first option before glancing down at the dress. "And, of course, I wasn't here for the good part."

"None of it was good," I mutter, tugging on the leggings as quickly as I can without tearing them. I did not realize how thin Callistus was. How often does he see a meal when he's not traveling in good company?

"Of course, I know it's not my place to ask . . ." Callistus plucks up the dress and examines it with his back to me, giving me privacy to put on the tunic as well. "But what happened here? It seems like a story worth putting to tune."

"It's a story that I shall never speak of and you had better not popularize."

Callistus sighs deeply. "If you insist, my good sir."

The tunic and leggings are indeed not the finest clothing I've ever worn— never have I worn something so scratchy and rough, and the smell is not what I'm used to. But at least I can feel relief that it is not Callistus' better option and hope that his current apparel is more comfortable.

Though, this is decidedly more comfortable than lying half-naked beneath a dress.

A dress that I never want to see again but still find myself picking up and handing to Callistus to put in his satchel.

"In case we ever find the lady who owned it," I mutter. "She may want it back again."

Callistus furrows his brows. "Very considerate, sire."

"Far from it." I take a staggering step, not liking the feel of rough leaves and too soft grass beneath my feet.

"I bemoan that I have only one pair of shoes, and they would be too small for your feet." Callistus glances down at his cloth shoes that indeed look like I would be lucky to get over half my foot. "But if my liege would prefer them—"

"This is fine. And no need to bereft yourself. Let's just see if we can find someone who can provide shoes and two good horses. And maybe a sword. But definitely the horses." I take a step and a twig scrapes at my skin. "And also some shoes."

If I thought walking on the forest floor was bad, it is nothing compared to the thought of stepping foot inside a stable without protection.

Thankfully, Callistus takes on that role for me, and I watch him as he gestures more wildly the higher his tone rises.

I have half a mind to go in and demand that I am gifted a horse in the Emperor's name, but I don't think it is wise to be going around throwing around my identity with no guard or weapon with which to protect myself. Especially on VonTrapp's land. Or what has become his land, anyway.

"The fool doesn't even know how to properly handle those horses."

Turning, I find a young man, his frame lanky in misfitting clothes and a straw-colored hair falling into his eyes.

"Who are you?" I ask.

"Abel. I used to work in this stable." He gestures to a black stallion separated from the others. "He was my favorite. The finest in all Roden— Middle Imparia even."

"What are you doing here, Abel?"

"Seeing how they are treating my horses." He tears his gaze from the animals and studies me. "You?"

"I'm a traveler down on my luck. My father is ill, but my horse was stolen, and I was hoping to reach him sooner rather than later." I turn forlornly to where Callistus and the stable master have left behind any illusion of decorum in their conversation.

"The former Mistress of this land would have lent out her steed to anyone in need, for only a promise of return. She had a generous heart, our Lady Elspeth."

I glance at him. "Do you know what became of her?"

Abel opens his mouth and then quickly closes it. "I really can't say."

Before I can pester him for more, he glances past me and grins.

I follow his gaze to where the horses that I just saw inside the stable are being led out into the pasture. And a man who appears very similar to Abel is standing at the gate, letting them out into the open land.

We watch in silence as several other people dressed as peasants emerge from the outlying forest and hurry to the gate, where they take the horses' reins and lead them one by one back into the woods.

As I try to process what I'm seeing, Abel steps forward, holding up one finger.

The man at the gate nods and holds back the next person coming for the horse.

Abel then whistles, and the favorite black stallion trots toward him.

I watch as Abel greets the horse by pressing his forehead to his and running his hand through his mane. Then he takes hold of the reins and offers them to me. "His name is Valiant. Ride him well."

My fingers grasp the reins in confusion. "Why are you doing this?"

"Because it's what Lady Elspeth would have wanted," Abel answers. "Because I can see from one moment in your presence that you would be a far kinder master than VonTrapp or his men could ever be. And because we owe your friend one for being such an excellent distraction. Just take care of him, will you?"

I nod, still befuddled.

Abel grins at me and then runs toward where the man at the gate is atop the last stallion from the pasture. He reaches out and grabs ahold of Abel, hoisting him onto the horse with him before they trot into the woods.

And just like that, there is no evidence of whatever it is that just happened, except the reins in my hands and the horse watching me mournfully with big brown eyes.

Suddenly, reality hits me— a bit slowly after the day I've had— and I realize what I've become an accomplice to. Before my conscience can get the better of my judgement, I walk back toward the stable door, doing my best to keep the horse behind me and out of view.

"Callistus!" I whisper-yell.

The Bard turns and gestures at me that he's still working on it.

I nod for him to come out.

He looks confused, but obeys my silent command.

"I'm having trouble getting through to this dense fool," he begins, rounding the corner. Then his gaze falls on the horse and his eyes go wide. "How—"

Using my free hand, I cover his mouth. Then I back all three of us farther away from the door.

When I drop my hand, Callistus whispers, "How?"

"A gift from Emperor-God or the Bandit King, I know not. But now is hardly the time to look a gift horse in the mouth."

Callistus nods. "Agreed."

Then we both climb onto the steed and start her on a steady trot toward the forest. After all, if the others got in and out this way, perhaps we can as well.

"Did you see the Bandit King?" Callistus asks after we've passed through an opening that took us off VonTrapp's land. Words I could tell he's been meaning to utter for a while but didn't dare to while we were still in potentially hostile territory, as though VonTrapp might jump out from behind one of the derelict cabins if he heard us speak.

"I spoke to a former stable boy, and everyone else looked to be peasants, perhaps former serfs. There was no one there who seemed to have any ranking over anyone else."

"Hmm," Callistus says behind me, where he's awkwardly holding onto my shoulders since we have no saddle or anything else but the horse's reins to hold on to. "It is decidedly harder to write a romantic ode about a band of serfs who steal together with no clear leader among them. But perhaps it will make a better tale indeed, for never having been sung before."

"I appreciate you accompanying me to the capital," I say. "Especially since you were so close to your elusive Bandit King."

"I'm sure he will be here when I return. But you are in need now."

Now that we are completely out of view of the VonTrapp estate, I direct the stallion to the main road.

"Is that really the safest option?" Callistus asks. "It may be that bandits or even gysts walk that path."

"It may also be that we can still overtake my party on the way. They may be in graver danger than even my father with a stranger in the midst."

"I still do not understand how a man came to look just like you when there are already two of you in the world."

"I do not think it was a man."

Callistus grips my shoulders more tightly, and I tense. "You think it was not only a woman in the woods with you, but also a woman I spoke to?"

I glance up at the setting sun and keep us riding forward on the stone-paved roads set in place by my ancestors. "Who else could it have been who knew I would not be joining the party anytime soon?"

"Maybe an accomplice? It just seems strange to me to think that I was in the presence of a lady in breeches and had no inkling of an idea."

The thought of Meredith and our last few moments together makes me snort. "Believe me, Callistus, she wasn't a lady by any means."

CHAPTER XVII

Lady Elspeth

The carriage's sudden jarring stop pulls me out of the delusional sleep I had fallen into.

I lift my head to look around . . . and realize with a horrifying jolt that my head had been resting on one of the broad shoulders belonging to Prince Otello.

He's staring down at me stiffly, confusion written all over his face. Then he sees that I'm awake and smirks. "Sleep well?"

"Um . . ." I look away to hide my blush. This is ridiculous. Surely the First Valet isn't so bashful in front of the Prince. I need to think like Heinrich would think.

And not be hoping that Prince Otello never finds out that his future bride appeared to him dressed— and completely disguised— as a man.

"Are you feeling any better?" he asks beside me. "I've never known you to get a full night's sleep the first day of travel."

I look over my shoulder to answer him when the sound of yelling outside cuts me off.

Turning all the way back around to face him, I whisper. "What was that?"

Otello cranes his head to look out the window. "I don't know—"

Suddenly, the carriage lunges forward, throwing us both back. I grip Otello for security before remembering that is most certainly *not* something that a First Valet would do, and releasing him.

To his credit, the Prince shows some concern for me, making sure I'm properly seated before sliding to the window and yelling, "What's going on?"

"We're being pursued!" our driver answers.

I go to the other window and glance out.

In the distance, I can just make out a black horse and two riders. A stallion that reminds me so much of my best breeder, Valiant.

And the horse isn't the only thing that is familiar. Though he is too far away to make out his face, I can't help but note that the front rider has chin-length brown hair so dark it's almost black and is robed in clearly borrowed clothes.

Heinrich. He's caught up with us already.

In a panic, I grab the person most likely to recognize him and pull him away from the window.

"What are you doing?!" Prince Otello cries.

"They could have bows!" I answer.

"I didn't see bows." He goes to the window again to double-check, and I pull him back.

It's at that moment that the carriage hits a rock in the road and jumps. The movement sends us both sprawling to the ground.

I roll to the side, cradling my left arm I landed on. My stomach chooses that moment to remember that I drank hair and says cruel things to me. My head feels like it's going to explode, though whether from terror, physical pain, or guilt, I know not.

The mixture of this is more than I can bear, and my will fails me. Rolling onto my stomach, I'm sick right there under the seats.

"Hey!" Prince Otello cries, diving backward.

"I'm so sorry," I mutter, trying to escape my mess, but my dizziness has me scared I'll fall right into it.

Prince Otello senses my need, grabs my waist as all men seem to do, and pulls me up and away from it.

And cries out.

I have to wait until the vertigo passes from the sudden movement and my vision clears enough to see what caused Prince Otello's horror.

My mess isn't so much the contents of my stomach as it is my own blood.

Confused, I touch my mouth and find a swollen lip and moisture still there that smells as coppery as the taste in my mouth.

I have no reflective surface to see if my illusion remains or if I've thrown up all the tonic within me.

Or maybe it's actually a poison, and I won't outlast its effects.

My head lulls back onto Otello's chest.

He pulls me up and goes to the carriage door to pound it. "Stop the carriage! This is an emergency!"

"We are still being pursued!" the driver answers.

"Then kill them! You're the Emperor's finest, for all the saints' sake. Now I command you to stop this carriage!"

So Heinrich can catch up and expose me. Or worse, be killed. "No . . . don't . . . stop—"

Unfortunately, I don't make a very strong plea for my case because I immediately follow it by coughing blood all over Prince Otello.

If this potion doesn't kill me, mortification might.

Prince Otello thumps the wall of the carriage. "I said *now!*"

It finally skids to a halt, tossing me into him, and this time the darkness that tunnels my vision takes far longer to fade away.

The next thing I know, I'm airborne.

My eyes barely slide open enough to see that Prince Otello is carrying me out of the carriage. Except, he's starting to look less and less like Otello and more and more like Heinrich. Like me.

I squint. Am I hallucinating, or did his eyes just go from blue to purple?

All around us, guards are dismounting and getting into defensive positions. And Otello— I think— sets me down on the grass.

"Do you have any idea what's happening to you?" he asks.

I drank a potion I shouldn't have. "Poison?"

A guard joins the huddle, this one distinguished from the others by a bronze tunic— the symbol of a Captain. "Who could have done this?"

"That's secondary right now," Otello/Heinrich says. "What's important is clearing his system of the tainted blood."

At his words, my body complies, and I roll onto my side enough to spew more blood.

Beyond us, I hear a commotion. Heinrich's horse is so close, I can hear it breathe— and his words are louder. Though, in my state, they are no clearer.

Whatever he's saying, combined with the sight of him, causes the guards to react in confusion, and they glance between him and us.

Then one phrase comes out loud and clear. "She stole my face and now she's erasing his. Can't you see?"

The Captain of the guard glances between Otello and me before suddenly pushing Otello back. "Why do you have the same face?!"

Otello frowns in confusion. "We've always had the same face."

Heinrich pushes into the cluster, shouldered by two guards who realize at the same time as the rest of us— except Otello— that three of us now have the exact same face.

The darkness chooses that exact moment to return. I make my desperate last defense before I lose my grasp of this plane of reality. "I'm Heinrich!"

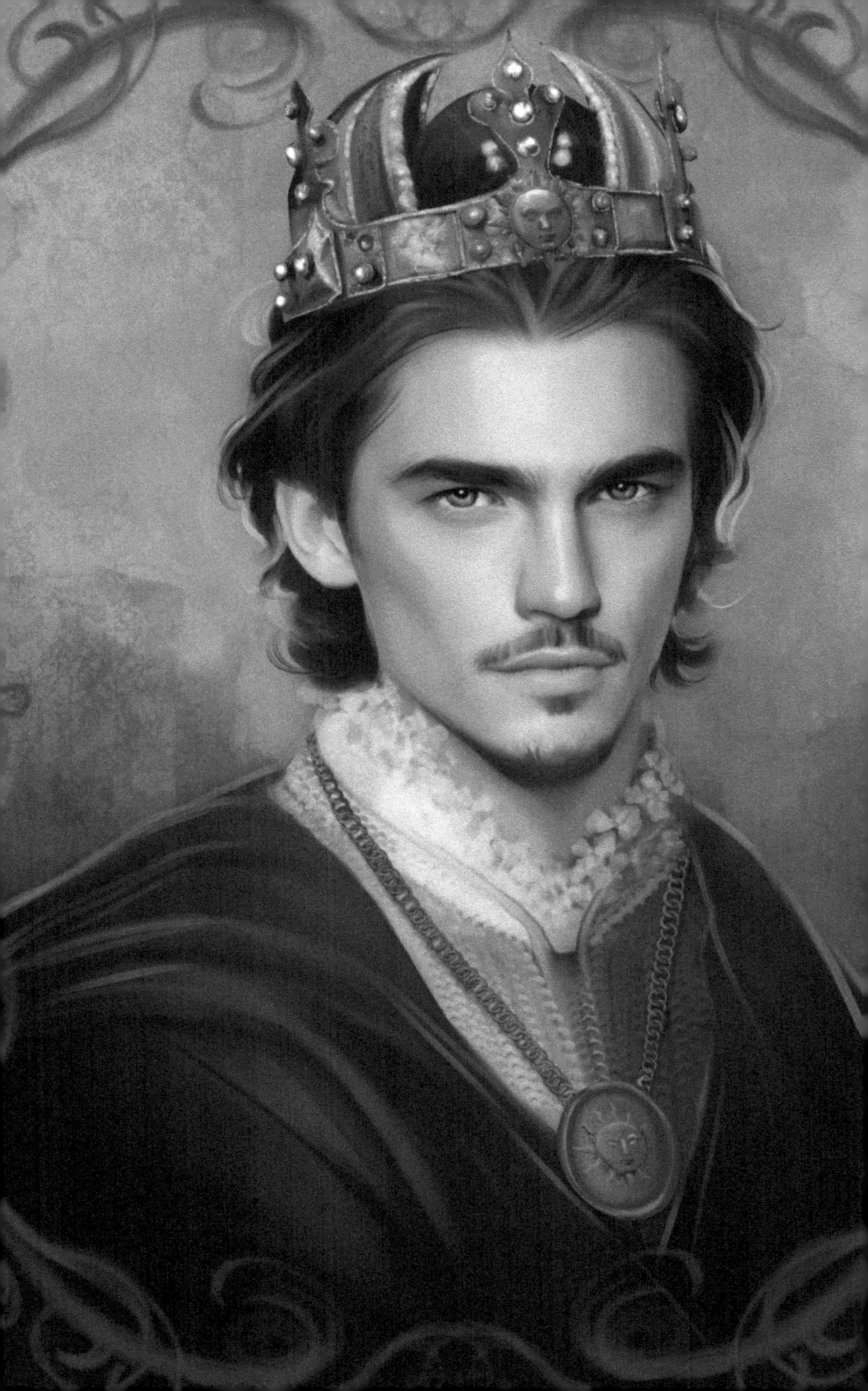

CHAPTER XVIII

Prince Otello

I've had out-of-body experiences before. Fencing lessons that went sour, and my mind had to escape my body for a moment. History tests dropped on me when I wasn't prepared, and Uriel knew it. The eve no one let me kiss my mother goodnight even though she had already finished birthing my brother. The morning after when I was told she did not survive the night.

But in all those cases, I only saw one version of myself from outside, not two.

And I certainly did not see myself lying unconscious on the ground with my other self backing away in shock as he looks between the one on the floor and me. I did not expect to risk confusing my closest friend and my worst enemy.

Or being mixed up with them.

Gerrard the Guard sizes us up in a moment. "What in the Empire is happening?"

"I was attacked before I ever made it to the carriage," I say. "My clothes were stolen, and I was left for dead on the forest floor. I have a witness."

Callistus, flanked by three guards to my two, moves forward. "It is true, Captain. I was told by one of the two men before us to go to that place in the forest after the carriage had departed."

Gerrard scowls. "Which one?"

"I, uh, don't know." Callistus looks between them. "What happened to the one on the ground?"

"Poison." Gerrard grits his teeth at the enemy he could not protect me . . . . or one of me . . . from.

"That is what the wo—" I clear my throat. No need to confuse them more. "*Person* who attacked me used. Some sort of poison to make me sleep."

We all turn to the remaining version of me from the carriage who yet stands.

He holds up his hands in surrender. "It wasn't me. I thought he was acting strange, but I didn't cause it. Look, I have the crest." He holds up a medallion. The sacred sun-crested Heritage Medallion that I entrusted to Heinrich.

Which is who the version of me on the grass cried out he was before passing out.

I turn to the one still awake. "Tell me who you are."

"You know who I am." He holds up the Heritage Medallion again, glancing furtively between Callistus and me, Gerrard, and the version of us on the floor. "Prince . . . Otello."

So, the little wench knew it was me all along when I thought I had hidden my identity so well. And this was her play. Get me out of the picture, and then Heinrich?

I glance at my friend on the floor, who is writhing even in his sleep. "What did you do to him? Was this some sort of ploy to frame him for what you did and then remove him from the picture?"

"I— what? No! Please . . ." He searches my eyes intently, as if trying to find something in them to use.

But he doesn't use my name. Heinrich would have. Well, he'd actually address me by my title just to irk me, but he doesn't do that either. Because he's not Heinrich.

I come to stand before him and grasp hold of my crest. "You are a traitor to your country."

He stares back at me in horror. "I—"

Wrenching the Medallion off his neck, I turn from him to the guards, whose hands are now on their weapons. But they are obviously confused about which of us to protect from the others.

So, I give them clarity. Holding up the Heritage Medallion, I connect with it as a Son of the Sun and focus my power through it potently.

Reaching deep inside of me, I utter the sacred *Davar* that Uriel trained into me. The finest of all party tricks that is used to broadcast my power without giving away all that it is. "As the Emperor-God gave me the sun, so I choose to shine it forth!"

Light shines out of the Heritage Medallion at my command.

Immediately, the guards drop to the ground around me. Then some grab hold of the imposter behind me and secure him. A gag is wrapped around his mouth as he tries to speak again, cutting off his words.

Lowering the Heritage Medallion, I place it securely in my— well, Callistus's— pocket for security until the chain can be repaired. Then I make sure it's not the pocket with the gaping hole in it.

The Heritage Medallion secure, I drop to my knees beside Heinrich. He has ceased writhing, and his chest is rising and falling steadily.

The guard, Archibald, who had remained kneeling by Heinrich's head during all this sets a hand to his forehead. "The fever seems to be broken."

Scooping Heinrich up, I carry him toward the carriage. "Then let us ride straight to Sitzvononne. If we stay on the road and don't stop except when necessary for the horses, we should get there before the end of two days. Uriel will know if there is any poison left and how to remove it." As well as how serious of a sick bed my father is lying on.

"We will get you there with all haste, my liege," Gerrard says before closing the door.

I sit down and then lay Heinrich down in the same row, even if it breaks our once-sacred seating arrangements. But I need to make sure he doesn't get more shaken than necessary.

Pulling his legs onto my lap and placing my hand on his shoulder, I brace us both as the carriage— which has a copper stench about it— starts moving again.

Not able to bear looking at Heinrich in his current state, I turn toward the window, wondering how I can be this nation's future Holy Emperor of the Sanctified Empire of Constantinium when I do not know how my own faith would survive if I lost both of my remaining family to pestilence and poison at once.

Emperor-God, have mercy on us all.

CHAPTER XIX

The Mismatched Duo

Otello:

"I apologize, my prince, but the horses cannot go on at this pace."

I nod at Gerrard the Guard, resigned. I'm prepared to charge all day and night to the palace, but it is not in everyone else's capabilities.

"We are securing you and your valet a room now." Gerrard's gaze drops to where Heinrich is using my lap as a pillow. With his pallor, he would be easily mistaken as dead if not for his frequent body-racking shivers.

Perhaps it will do him good to get out of this carriage that smells like sickness. "See also if you can hire a servant from the inn to clean the carriage in time for our departure."

Gerrard glances toward the filth on the carriage floor but, to his credit, doesn't grimace. "It will be done, your Luminance."

"Thank you, Gerrard the—" I clear my throat. "Gerrard." Then I scoop my arms under Heinrich, preparing to lift.

He mutters something in his sleep and presses closer to me. But I find a grip and rise.

Gerrard takes him from me when I reach the doorway, and I stagger out of the carriage, my legs weak from both the lack of use and from the extra pressure on them for so long.

"This way," Gerrard says, walking toward the inn we first met Callistus in, Heinrich in his arms.

Callistus, who comes right beside me as we walk. "I must say, it has been rather disconcerting to see so many of the same face."

At his words, I glance around, searching for the prisoner, Meredith, or whoever she truly is.

I spot her, still sporting my face as Callistus said, being led to the stables by two guards even as most of the others are tending to the horses.

Meredith spots me from across the way. Violet eyes I'm not used to seeing on anyone other than my father and my reflection meet mine. "I must say, *Heinrich*, when this is all said and done, you really must tell me all about the person who shares your face, your seat, and this night, your bed."

The guards drag him into the stable, but not before I see the half-bemused expression on his face. *My* face, but not my expression. It's quite disconcerting.

Also disconcerting is how she knows that Heinrich and I always share a chamber when traveling as a last line of defense with his wristbands of throwing knives, and that this particular inn only has one cot per room.

Has she been following me that closely? Is my Heritage bloodline already compromised?

Or is she actually Heinrich, and Gerrard is holding the imposter?

I glance over at the man . . . woman? . . . in Gerrard's arms.

The individual moans and reaches out blindly. "My prince . . . my prince!"

Hurrying to catch up with Gerrard, I take Heinrich's hand. "I'm right here. You're in safe arms."

Gerrard harrumphs.

Callistus comes beside me again. "Sleep well . . ." He glances at my Heritage Medallion and bows. "*My prince.*" With that, he goes to greet the barkeep.

How ironic that this charade went so long for Callistus's benefit in case he was a threat, and he was the one who came through when I was abandoned in the woods. It was the fair maiden, the damsel in distress, who was the real danger.

A lesson duly noted.

Gerrard and I climb the stairs to the same room Heinrich and I used before. He deposits my valet on the cot, sweeps the room, and then leaves, making sure the door is shut tight.

And I turn to my half-conscious friend who is wearing my face. My face that looks so wan and pale, sweat beading on his dark brow painted to look like mine even before this foul enchantment took over.

I kneel in front of him and rest my hand on the top of his head. "What am I going to do with you, friend?"

Elspeth:

When my shivering wakes me, I find myself wrapped in unfamiliar arms. Not that any arms would be familiar. "Meredith?" I croak.

"Don't worry, she's not here. The guards have her secure."

I tense, panic over the fate of my friend filling me until my gaze finally clears, giving me a vivid view of Heinrich's face peering down at me.

No, not Heinrich. Otello. *Prince* Otello. My future husband.

And we're already in bed together.

I jolt, a new level of panic filling me.

Otello sits up more and grips me more tightly until I stop flailing. "*Shh*, Heinrich, it is well. Be at peace."

Right. He thinks I'm his valet. His valet who he is tending to.

"I am calm now," I say, and feel Otello's arms loosen around me.

"Finally. You've been flailing all night. I've had to restrain you several times to prevent you from injruing yourself."

Not meeting his gaze, I push away his loosened arms and sit up. I'm still wearing the clothing Prince Otello gave me yesterday. However, the Sacred Prince has stripped down to his braies.

So many thoughts crash like violent waves in my head as he sits up, and the blanket that was giving him some covering falls away.

He and Heinrich look so much the same without outer clothing. Especially while my enchantment still alters his face.

The Sacred Prince looks so much like the man I kissed and left in the woods. My face flushes at the uncanny resemblance.

And now I am that man in his eyes, in the eyes of the man who lay beside me half-dressed all night.

If my mother were still alive, she would surely die of shame. *I'm* on the verge of dying from shame. My cheeks are so hot right now I'm scared I'll burn the rest of the tonic from my system.

Prince Otello sits up straighter and then leans toward me, his face the perfect image of concern that somehow seems so incongruous with his chiseled torso as he leans toward me.

The man has obviously never missed a day of broadsword training.

A large but gentle hand presses against my temple. "I fear your fever is returning."

"I-I'm fine. You shouldn't be tending to me." My mind is a tumble of chaos, like when I mixed too many antagonistic ingredients during Irwin and my alchemy lesson, and I bound off the bed. I'm the valet. I must remember: I'm Heinrich. I need to think like Heinrich, *act* like Heinrich. "Would you like me to draw you a bath, my prince?"

Why did I just say that? I absolutely cannot, under any circumstances, draw him a bath!

Prince Otello looks at me as strangely as I wish I could look at myself. Which would be exactly like this since we share the same face at the moment. "We don't have time, Heinrich. My father—"

"Is dying, yes, of course." What did I just blurt out? Otello is not privy to the prophecy. Has all self-restraint and reason abandoned me this morn?

Otello looks as though I've slapped him as he winces. "Is *sick*, Heinrich. I know no love is lost between you and him, but let us not be too quick to bury him."

Well, there is no love lost between me and the man who stole everything from me. But somehow, seeing the fear, pain, and boyish vulnerability shining in Otello's falsely violet eyes, I cannot find any relish in the thought of my enemy perishing. "Of course. Let us get you dressed and to your father's side post-haste."

"I can dress myself today, Heinrich. You just focus on not keeling over." He moves toward where bright, soft materials are folded at the foot of the bed. "I could not stand the thought of sleeping in Callistus's garments. Thankfully, Gerrard thought to send up a change of clothes."

I have no idea what he's talking about, so I just smile and nod. Which makes me really faint. But I can't stop nodding. Or staring as the Sacred Prince pulls on a pair of breeches.

Why am I still watching? Why am I still smiling? I'm going to faint right off this bed.

"Are you strong enough to ride directly to Sitzvononne?" Prince Otello tugs on a linen undershirt, giving me some relief. Except that it's untied and still gaping at the collar. "I'm anxious for my father, as you know. And I believe Uriel can expunge the last of whatever poison the witch has tainted you with."

Witch? What witch?

Oh, does he mean *me*?

My fingers itch to slap his face, or perhaps make a play to duel for my honor, but I cannot. I'm here to protect him. And he has a right to be mad. Until he sees that it was all for him.

And he's fumbling with tying his shirt closed. It's hard to be upset at him when he is being so boyishly clumsy.

I sigh. "Come here."

To my surprise, Prince Otello obeys, and I find myself helping him with his ties, trying not to brush my illusioned bulky fingers against his skin. But my awkwardness makes me clumsier. I never had this kind of trouble helping Meredith with her ties.

Meredith also never touched a broadsword in her life, so that must be it.

Finally, the shirt is closed, and I drop my hands, looking away as if that can hide my flush again. Is my blush showing through onto Heinrich's face?

The Sacred Prince doesn't seem to notice as he tugs on a tunic and then a cloak. Then he turns back to me. "Do you need any help to dress?"

My eyes nearly pop out of my skull. "No!" I clear my throat. "I mean, it goes against the valet code of honor."

Prince Otello cocks his head to the side. "Since when has there ever been a valet code of honor, much less one you lived by?"

"I, uh, mostly kept it in my mind."

"Since when have you ever kept anything to yourself? Much less had a mind." Prince Otello grins lightheartedly and then tosses my boots at me. Thankfully, he doesn't seem to notice that they have been stuffed as he slides his identical boots on.

When I stand up, though, I only feel stuffing in one of my shoes. The other one is empty.

By the confused expression on Otello's face, he has the filling in his left boot.

As quickly as I can in misfitting boots, I flee from the room, and Otello follows.

At the top of the staircase, Prince Otello turns to me. "Do you need any help?"

"I can manage, thank you." I take one step, land on the stuffing in my boot funny, and proceed to plummet down four wood stairs before I grasp enough of the wall to halt my descent.

I grit my teeth as various parts of my body clamors to bring attention to the pain afflicted upon it, and my pride most of all.

Otello is by my side in an instant. "I didn't doubt your ability to descend, Heinrich. I only questioned your methods of doing so!"

Faking a laugh in a voice that sounds even rougher than what the tonic already makes it, I pull myself to my feet before the Sacred Prince can try to help me up.

The Captain of the Guard, distinguished by his bronze tunic, is waiting on the base of his stairs. He looks as though I shaved ten years off his life in the few moments he must have thought the Crown Prince had taken a tumble.

He looks beyond me to the man whose face I still share. At least his enchantment will likely wear off before mine does, and I can use it as a harbinger of my own façade's looming demise.

Thank goodness the Prince is so determined to get to the capital as quickly as possible.

"The horses have been tended to, the carriage has been cleaned, and the prisoner has been prepared for departure likewise. We are ready to leave at your word."

Otello nods. "Then we shall go now. I can eat on the way."

The man I sent to find Heinrich in the woods steps forward, his eyes bright in a handsome face that is a contrast to his thin, dirty garments. He holds out several carefully wrapped parcels. "I made sure the innkeeper made enough for you two." He glances between us. "I apologize, but I am not sure which to address as the Prince."

Otello takes the parcels. "Makes no difference; thank you, Callistus. Will you be parting with us, then?"

"Not yet. The Bandit King can wait. I feel as though I should see you safely to the outskirts of Sitzvononne. At least as far as the next Rose and Crown Inn before charting my return."

Prince Otello nods. "You shall be welcome even within the palace walls if you so choose."

Callistus waves away the Prince's words, his voice strangely lyrical. "I could not think to impose myself on such a grand affair in my current state. Mayhap I will take you up on your offer, though, once I have made a name for myself as worthy of singing before royalty."

With that, he practically skips toward the door.

Otello turns to me. "He's an odd one, that Bard."

I nod. "Indeed."

We follow Callistus out to the bustle of guards preparing their mounts around the royal carriage. It all falls away from view, though, when my gaze falls on the real Heinrich.

He is being assisted onto a horse on account of the bindings keeping his hands from being of any use. Strands of straw stick out of his hair, giving me a good impression of where he slept last night.

Meanwhile, I slept in a fine bed for the first time in so long.

Guilt causes me to drop my gaze.

But not before he notes the two of us still falsely bearing his face. "Ay, now, did you both sleep well?" He sounds altogether far too merry for a man who knows I've robbed him of his life.

"Quiet, witch," Prince Otello growls, gesturing for me to climb into the carriage first.

"As you wish, *Heinrich*." Heinrich's gaze is pointedly on the Prince himself. Has he mixed up which one of us is the one who robbed him and which one is royalty in the confusion of our shared faces?

Then his gaze turns to me, and the same sardonic expression remains in place. "He can be such a *dummkopf*, can he not?"

I blink at Heinrich in confusion before I'm pushed into the carriage by Otello.

The moment he settles in, the Prince buries his face in his hands and groans.

For a long moment, I study him, not sure what to say to comfort him as the carriage lurches forward, taking us on our way.

And Otello remains hidden behind his hands.

"My prince?"

"She's right, you know." The Sacred Prince finally drops his hands so that he can lean his head wearily against the cushioned seat. "I am such a *dummkopf.*"

It takes me far too long to realize that the "she" Otello is referring to is Heinrich. By then, it's too late to assure him.

"I am supposed to wed and give my Empire an heir," Otello continues. "It is my sovereign duty to pass on my Heritage bloodline. But apparently that is just another one of the responsibilities I am far from ready to shoulder should my father . . . should he pass on."

I chew my lip nervously. "What do you mean? Why do you say you failed?"

The Prince is too distraught to elaborate, so he just shakes his head. "And on the matter of my insufficiencies, I could not even find the lost Lady Elspeth."

My heart almost stops. He was . . . looking for me?

Perhaps arranging our marriage will not be so difficult after all. Once we do not look exactly alike, that is.

"My prince," I begin, not exactly sure how I mean to continue.

Suddenly, the carriage jolts beneath us, and then we seem to reach new levels of speed.

Otello goes to the window and pulls aside the curtains of the carriage that is too fine for me to have been sick in. "What is going on?"

"We're being pursued, sire," answers the lyrical voice of Bard Callistus.

Terror grips me. But it's Otello who asks, "By whom?"

"I believe, though scarcely so, that our pursuers are gysts."

CHAPTER XX

Lady Elspeth

"Gysts?" I whisper. "That can't be possible. Gysts don't exist."

"Now is not the time to be a skeptic, Heinrich. We live in the same household as a blood-sucking, life-force drinking demon, after all." Otello sticks his head out the window, I suppose to get a better bearing.

I think about doing the same for a moment, if only to see a gyst with my own eyes. But then my stomach goes queasy at making such a daring move, though not from fear. My tonic is making its wrath known once again.

Of all the times to get sick . . .

Suddenly, the carriage hits something with such a jolt it sends me flying out of my seat. For a moment, all I can think about is keeping the contents of my stomach and whatever remains of the tonic down.

Then the outside world jars into my focus as the carriage jolts again, sending me sprawling onto what was once the side.

And sending Otello crashing into me.

"I'm dying! I'm dying!" I scream blindly. There is so much pressure on top of me, along with the fear that I won't be able to breathe that keeps me from testing my lungs. And I need to breathe so I won't be sick.

The window across from the one we're lying in opens and the curtains are yanked to the side as a hand reaches through.

For a moment, the pain is gone as I watch the strange intruder reach down until it touches the top of the Prince's head.

Otello looks up and sees the same completely human yet also unfamiliar limb.

Just as it clenches around a tuft of his hair and yanks him upward.

I gasp as the pressure of his body lifts and releases me. Then I watch in terror as Otello gets lifted enough that his head comes partially out the window. Though his shoulders won't let the ascension continue.

"There's another one in here!" cries a voice with an accent not unlike the one shared by the mercenaries that helped VonTrapp take over my castle.

Then Otello is released.

I throw myself to the side of the carriage just as he crashes down behind me.

"*Son of a werwölfe,*" Otello gasps behind me, and I try to decide if I'm surprised to hear the Sacred Prince curse or still just surprised at the turn of events.

Our carriage shakes again, and I try to brace myself as it rises.

We both slide forward and then stumble to the actual floor of the carriage as it turns upright.

The carriage door swings open, and a greasy-haired man wearing undyed sheep skin over his pale, gaunt frame peers in at us. The grimace falls off his face when he sees two identical faces. "There's another *two.*"

Then he reaches in and grabs us both by our hair, and I have a horrifying thought that he'll tug my carefully plaited hair out from under its illusion. Instead, he just yanks us out with strength that doesn't align with his frame.

I hit the grass on my hands and knees. And then I can't hold it in any longer. Blood and bile tear out of me, my body's desperate attempt to purge itself of the unnatural tonic.

Otello sits up and wraps his arm around my waist to keep me from falling face-first into my mess as all strength deserts me.

"Is this all of you, then?"

Trembling, I lift my head enough to find Heinrich also on his knees on the grass, still bound. I lift my face still higher to make out the man who threw Otello and me down, snarling down at us. Behind him, a man similarly dressed has a dagger to Callistus' throat.

Beyond them, I spot the Captain watching the scene likewise. He's still alive. He can deliver us from these gysts or bandits or whatever they are . . .

The Captain is standing in a strange position, leaned back slightly even though he appears to be trying to stand at attention. And— is that a fist protruding from his chest?

Just behind him is another greasy man, his arm vanishing into the back of the good Captain.

Gysts. This is what makes them so terrifying compared to estries and werwölves. At least those are bound to the same blood magic the rest of us are.

These seem bound to nothing on this earth.

Turning, I see more of the same horrifying scene. Soldiers contorted in various shapes, with gysts standing around them, reaching *into* them. We outnumber the gysts, but the gysts have two arms and that's all they need to incapacitate the Emperor's finest.

"Well, now." The gyst who dragged us out steps toward us, and for a terrifying moment, I think he's going to put his hand into me and grasp my heart. Instead, he just stares between Otello and me and then Heinrich as though trying to solve a problem. "This here is a bit of a predicament. Which of yous is the so-called Sacred Prince?"

At this point, I'm shaking so hard from a mixture of sickness and terror that I couldn't betray my betrothed even if I wanted to. Neither Heinrich nor Otello speak up either.

So, he turns to Callistus. "Well, which is it?"

"How should I know—?" Callistus's voice becomes extremely high-pitched as the dagger presses tighter against his throat.

"Come now, boy," rasps the man holding the dagger. "Only one of them needs to die today."

A fevered chill runs through me, and I almost collapse.

Heinrich twitches, and for a moment, I think he's going to accuse me. And what can I do then? Betray him again? I certainly can't oust the real Prince.

Is this the prophecy unfolding now? Nothing is like what I expected.

But it's Callistus who speaks. "They are all the sons of prominent men. Each one could afford you a grand ransom."

The man with his hand in the Captain's chest snarls. "Why don't we's all of us just kill all of them?"

The Captain moves as if to clobber the man, but then his eyes roll up in his skull and he stills.

As for Callistus, his eyes look ready to *jump* out of his skull. "No, no, you most certainly do not want to do that. I'm sure whoever paid you to do this dark deed would castigate you if you slay the wrong man. What if one of these before you was his son or some such?" Callistus looks at him pointedly.

The man doesn't look too convinced. However, the man interrogating us does. "Just tell us which one is the Prince, and we can be done with this whole affair."

I drop my gaze and stare down at my sickness. Is this how I rescue the Prince? By turning myself in to die in his stead so he can redeem the Empire from certain death?

Never get to see my vindication or my vengeance.

Lifting my gaze, I take one last look at Otello and see the determination in his expression as he weighs the pros and cons of what he can do.

But even without knowledge of the prophecy, he knows what will happen to the kingdom if the purest line of the Heritage Blood dwindles to nothing. Our enemies will see it as weakness and attack with their own Heritage bloodlines.

Blood.

My gaze drops to where I have spilled enough of my own onto the grass. Blood isn't only Otello's source of magic. It's mine.

I look up again, this time at Heinrich, who is studying Otello intently. But when he senses my stare, he turns to me with the face I accidentally made infectious.

With my blood. My blood, which I can control with my Kin Magic.

The crude words of the men holding us captive and the desperate protests from Callistus fall away as I focus on my blood. I have no *Davar* for this use of my magic, and I'm not sure the Creator would even respond if I did after all I've done.

But my blood responds.

I watch it snake through the grass like a red serpent until it reaches the sandaled feet of the gyst who dragged us from the carriage.

Lifting my gaze again, I watch as he continues to move his mouth. But that mouth starts to look less and less like his face. And more and more like Heinrich's as the tonic infects him likewise.

Around him, the gysts cry out as they watch the change come over their fellow, even causing a full head of brown, clean hair to overtake his nasty scalp.

Several men release their holds on the guards, who then collapse. "What witchcraft is this?!"

Otello tenses and then glances at Heinrich, who shrugs at him and then turns to me.

I stare blankly ahead to keep my powers secret even as my blood snakes through the grass, reaching for more victims.

More guards are released as more Heinrichs are created. Some guards manage to stand, grasping their weapons and rushing at their former captors, and chaos dissolves around us.

The gyst who yanked me out turns to me and somehow, he seems to *know* I'm at fault, because he stalks toward me, taking an ax off his back and holding it out as if to behead me.

I don't have the strength to flee. Maybe if I throw myself backward, my head can remain on my neck . . .

Otello's grip on me strengthens, and I wonder if he can pull me away in time. Or if he'll foolishly sacrifice himself when he is the one we all must keep alive.

Out of the corner of my eye, Heinrich moves. Pulls something out of his boot. Stands. Throws.

A small blade barely as long as a thumb embeds itself into the jugular of the gyst who was approaching me.

The gyst looks down, quite befuddled. Then he vanishes before my eyes, the blade falling to the grass.

Heinrich smirks. "No one calls her witch but us."

I wait for the gyst to reappear and correct him, but he never does.

Around us, the guards are still fighting, all free now except for the Captain, who appears to have the most stubborn of all the gysts.

Sweat beads on the Captain's brows as he grabs hold of the hand protruding from his chest. And breaks one of the fingers.

The gyst cries out and yanks his arm from out of the Captain's chest in a way that makes him fall to his knees, crying out, but free.

And the gyst steps through him before becoming material as he stands where his vanished companion once stood. "I say it's time to kill the whole lot of yous and see where the pieces fall afterward." Grasping his ax from where it was sheathed at his waist, he charges at us with a savage battle cry.

Otello releases me and jumps up, throwing his gold Heritage Medallion out so that the ax hits it instead of him. "As the Emperor-God gave me the sun, I choose to shine it forth!"

Immediately, blinding light shines out from it, piercing into the gyst.

Who disintegrates even as night before the rising sun.

"Go back to Purgatory!" Otello yells, turning. His Heritage Medallion continues to shine out, driving the gysts away.

And then there are only three of us with Heinrich's face left.

The Sacred Prince drops his Heritage Medallion, panting.

Around him, the guards come to themselves except for the Captain, who remains on the ground. Heinrich tries to collect his blade, but one guard grabs his wrist. Callistus drops to one knee before Otello as though preparing to be knighted. "My prince."

And no one goes to Otello's side to steady him after such a powerful outpouring of magic. No one sees what he needs, only what he represents.

"My prince . . ." I mutter, pushing myself to my feet to go to him. But I stood too quickly, because the world tips around wildly.

Then darkness rushes to shut out the painful spinning.

I think I fall, but before I hit the ground, strong arms wrap around me. Then I know nothing at all.

CHAPTER XXI

PRINCE OTELLO

Worry knots my stomach as Heinrich remains unconscious beside me and Gerrard lies across from me as the rather worse-for-wear carriage rushes us toward Sitzvononne, rising higher and higher the closer we come.

Even though I grew up here, there is something about the city carved from the mountain that never ceases to amaze me. The white stone of Kreuzschlafen, the palace my family has called home for four generations, gleams in the sunlight.

But even that majesty built on the pinnacle of the mountain pales compared to the steep waterfall pouring down from the neighboring mountain and pouring into the holy pool that pilgrims come from across Constantinium and even beyond the Empire. They also visit alongside the First Cathedral of the Emperor-God encased in gold that reflects the dancing water that cascades down the western side of the mountain Sitzvononne sits upon.

We call the waterfall Heaven's Grace. Even its roar as we cross the bridge over its resulting river doesn't wake Heinrich.

In fact, Heinrich doesn't awaken until the carriage is pulling into the palace courtyard.

He opens one eye and then the other, before looking up at me groggily. "Which one are you?"

"Otello," I answer, wondering what kind of trial he went through in the carriage alone with the witch.

Probably almost on par with the trial I suffered with her.

"Oh, marry," he whispers before smiling. "And I'm Heinrich."

I pat his leg. "I know."

He looks at my hand for a long moment and I pull away. "How are you faring?"

Moaning, he closes his eyes again. "The world is still spinning, but my stomach is calm."

"Good. I want you to rest. Hopefully, the remaining poison will wear off soon."

He grunts at that.

Then the carriage door closes, and the doors swing open.

I turn to Henri, Gerrard's second-in-command, and the flock of servants who have come to greet us. "See that Heinrich and Gerrard are taken to their rooms and made comfortable. Send for the Court Physician for them both." And perhaps Uriel can give further guidance on how we can expel whatever enchantment has altered Heinrich's features to match my own once the more pressing matters are seen to.

"And the other . . ." Henri frowns. "You?"

"Take her to a holding room. She is the least of my problems right now." And hopefully, when I do have the time to interrogate her, she will have reverted to her true form. If her being a beautiful woman even *is* her true form.

A horror sinks in my stomach, but I push that aside. Imagining someone I kissed having my face right now is sickening enough without the added complication of whatever else she might be hiding.

"Her?" Henri asks, eyes wide with surprise and he glances toward Meredith.

She bats her eyes at him and blows a kiss. Which is unnerving to see on my face.

Henri cautiously gestures for guards to take Meredith's elbows and leade her away. Which she does with gusto, putting more sway in her hips than any man or woman ever used before. That of course look like my hips.

The men are going to have a hard time looking at me the same way.

"My prince."

I turn to find Uriel coming to meet me the moment I step outside of the carriage.

"How is he?" I ask.

Uriel's solemn expression says it all. "He hasn't left his bed in two days."

I don't need to hear any more before charging toward the entrance of the corridors that will take me to my father.

The guards open the door for me without question— the news of the little multiplication of my face hasn't spread throughout the palace yet, obviously.

Due to the angle of the room, I have to walk already inside the darkened room, all outside light muffled by the darkest drapes produced for the gravest of illnesses, in order to see his bed.

The bed, which is about twice as large as the carriage, makes my usually regal-looking father look dwarf-like in comparison.

I approach him quietly, and every step closer fills me with trepidation. There are more wrinkles on his face, less hair on his head, and there is something off about the color of his skin, but I cannot quite tell what tint it has taken in this darkness.

"The Emperor is resting now."

Startling, I turn to find Adalbert standing in the corner.

"What are you doing here?" I demand.

"My magic is sustaining him."

I sink onto the velvet chair by my father's bedside at those words. "Is it that serious?"

"Indeed."

The spice of the incense burning all around the room makes the room as choked as I feel. But somehow, I still smell the stench of something beyond it. Death, or at least the omen of it.

My hand reaches to my father's. Because of the length of the bed, I have to sit on it in order to find his hand.

His hand is cold and dry. I squeeze it anyway. "Return to me, Father."

He gives no response. After all, the Holy Emperor of the Sun is not one to follow orders.

I stay like that for another moment before seeing that there is nothing more I can do here. Repositioning his hand under the sheets to warm it somewhat, I go to the doorway.

There, I pause and glance back for one last look at my father, terrified that it is the last time I'll see him alive.

Then Uriel gestures for me to come to him.

Frowning, I follow him, having a few things of my own to tell him. Before I can, though, Uriel glances at the guards at the door and then pulls me farther down the corridor.

"I was going to ask for you to also stand guard over my father," I say. "Unlike Adalbert, I trust you. And your magic bloodline is far purer than his."

"If that is what you request, my prince, it will be done. But I have a request of my own for you, if you'll allow me."

I blink at the earnestness in his voice. "Yes, Uriel?"

"Should the terrible tragedy of the Emperor's passing come upon us sooner rather than later, I ask that you be prepared."

"Prepared for what?"

"Either I or someone I trust shall go to you, no matter the hour. Go with them, and they will take you somewhere safe until I am sure your throne is secure."

I frown. "Why would my throne not be secure? My people have no quarrel with me."

"I do not mean your people." Sorrow passes over Uriel's face. "I feel a dark magic in this place. But I have no evidence to present. So, until I do, or until I am sure it has passed, your safety is of first importance. After the Night of the Broken Walls, Constantinium lost the illusion of security. To lose you likewise would be a devastating blow."

Nodding slowly, I glance back toward my father's bedchamber. "Pray we never reach that point. I know I shall." Even as I begin to pray, so many things rush to mind. Not only would I have to give up what little liberty I enjoy now, but also, I will no longer be able to investigate the Bandit King and the fate of the Lady Elspeth. Others will have to do that in my stead as I see if my training was sufficient to prepare me for all the responsibilities before the Holy Emperor of the Sun.

Not to mention I'll have to wed quickly and produce an heir, or else the crown would be passed to my cousin at my demise. How can I even think of getting married when my first kiss ended so disastrously?

The air suddenly seems far too thin.

Uriel bows his head. "I will surely pray to the Creator, my liege." With that, he goes back to the bedchamber to obey my command.

And I make my way to the palace chapel to obey my own command.

The chapel is housed in the left wing of the palace, an extension added after my grandfather's vision that led him to convert himself and all his people to be Followers of the Way. Or rather, try to. Some people in the more distant provinces cling to our forefathers' pagan practices even while carrying out the new customs of the Way. And the elves proudly claim to have served the Emperor-God of the Way by His earliest name before my grandfather ever met Him.

When I reach the large wooden doors that serve as protection to any who seek sanctuary at the chapel, I slip out of my boots, as this is holy ground.

A guard slides one door open for me, and I step inside, ignoring how cold the stones of the holy ground are.

It is sunset outside, which I can see by the way the light is shining through the stained-glass windows illustrating the life of the Sunrise from on High, the Son of the Emperor-God and yet Emperor-God Himself.

I walk between the wooden pews that are strangely unoccupied for the time of day, toward the broken altar at the end of the room that signifies the way the Sunrise from on High was the ultimate sacrifice, redeeming mortal and elf alike. We humans were to turn from our false sacrifice to the pagan gods, and the elf-folk could finally cease their constant sacrifices to the Emperor-God as He sacrificed Himself on their behalf.

Bowing at the stair that leads up to the broken altar, I look more closely at the windows, that filled me with curiosity as a child and encouragement as a man.

The scene furthest left depicts the Sunset from on High stepping down from his rightful throne in the third Heaven and filling a stable with His light as a newborn babe. Next to that window is the image of the Sunset from on High, now the Final Sacrifice. He is nailed to the cruel execution device of my forefathers' forefathers, the Empire that came before Constantinium and bore us into existence as it crumpled.

I turn my head to the window directly to the right of the broken altar. It depicts the Final Sacrifice standing beside His now empty tomb, taking the title of Unbroken Conqueror. The final window depicts the Unbroken Conqueror once again in the third and highest Heaven, sitting on a greater throne as the Emperor-God until He returns to conquer one last time at the sunset of time.

Bowing my head, I beseech the Emperor-God to spare my father and allow me to resist my ascension for a little longer.

CHAPTER XXII

Lady Elspeth

I have never felt so comfortable in my entire life.

Peeling open my eyes, I find myself looking up at a canopy. A larger canopy than my old bed even. And this feather mattress is even softer.

Confusion muddles my comfort, and I turn to find Heinrich napping on a cot beside my bed.

Startling, I jump back, pulling the silk sheets up over my chest until everything comes rushing back.

The man resting beside me is Prince Otello, whose face was altered after coming into contact with my blood. And he believes me to be Heinrich.

I hasten to the washbasin set up on the other side of the bed to check my reflection.

That same masculine face stares up at me. It is the same visage shared by the man no doubt locked in a prison tower.

Perhaps Irwin's potion was more potent than we realized for it to have lasted this long, despite my becoming sick— not to mention its ability to spread as it did.

"Heinrich?"

I turn, remembering just in time to deepen my voice, since the sense of hair in my throat is diminished. "Yes?"

"Sorry for collapsing in here like that." Prince Otello rubs his face. "I was praying all night in the chapel."

"For your father?"

He nods. Worry, sorrow, and fear churn in his eyes.

My heart breaks for him, and I want to comfort him, but I cannot lie to him when I know his father is not long for this world. And I cannot yet tell him how much I understand the loss of a father.

Even if my father's legacy was ultimately betrayed by the Emperor he faithfully served, who is unfortunately the other father in question.

"He's still resting, so I thought I'd check on you."

Even though it feels quite inappropriate in the current company, I lay back down on the bed. "And when you saw I was still resting?"

"I thought I'd rest, too. Father's room is noxious with incense, and Adalbert won't leave his side. So I thought I'd make sure you needed for nothing this night."

I make an understanding grunt, hoping that it is the appropriate response here.

Glancing under the covers, I find that I'm still wearing the tunic Otello put on me in the carriage and the breeches I stole from the real Heinrich. Since I don't have to worry about my wrappings being exposed, I slide out of bed to wash my face in the basin waiting for me.

"Do you think I should consider being wed?"

I accidentally drink some of the face water and choke on it.

"Constantinium has been without an Empress for a decade. But when the time comes for me to take the throne, which will hopefully be a great while from now, it may give my people more confidence in my regime to have an Empress again."

I stop washing my face before I drown myself. "I think you should most certainly wed. The people see women as the stabilizing unit in a marriage, a family. They would see an Empress as a stabilizing power over the Empire. Especially in the face of your youth."

And it would give them someone to follow when they lose their prince so young.

Prince Otello mulls over my words several moments before speaking. "How should I go about getting wed?"

Marry me. "You should marry a noblewoman."

I hear Prince Otello begin to pace behind me. "I should marry inside the land? Not pursue a marriage alliance? Our relationship with Ehyptio is strained."

Taking a deep breath, I turn to face Otello. "I didn't say not to pursue a marriage alliance. But there is unrest within our own borders, between mortals and elf-folk."

He nods, still pacing. "And I will go back to seeking to rectify that once my father is well again."

"No restitution will be enough. The elf-folk are a proud people, and they do not easily forget. They will never again feel safe in these lands. Unless you marry one of their own."

Otello stops mid-pace and turns to face me. "You think I should marry a she-elf?"

"A *noble* she-elf."

He stares at me. "From where?"

"They are out there. We need only find one."

Otello sighs and puts his face in his hands. "I couldn't even find Lady Elspeth."

Just wait until the Lady Elspeth he's sought after rescues him from certain death. There is already practically a crown on my head.

Smiling to myself, I glance down . . . and find myself looking at two different hands. One is a large, masculine hand that matches Prince Otello's right now. And the other is daintier with long, slender fingers. My hand.

The potion is wearing off.

Otello drops his arm just as I drop my transforming hand into the fold of my borrowed tunic.

"I could host a ball like my father did," Otello says, smirking now. "But somehow I feel like the elves would think that was a trap."

He's seriously considering me? Of course, he is; he thinks I'm his First Valet. Probably his closest confidant.

My foot starts to tingle.

Glancing down, I see that whoever brought me to bed must have removed my boots, and one of my feet is obviously shrinking.

I place it behind my other foot quickly and pretend that I'm scratching the back of my ankle.

Thankfully, Otello doesn't seem to notice my feet, but he does frown at my expression. "Is something the matter?"

"Oh? Nothing. I'm just thinking about how much I would like to . . . bathe." Yes. And use that as a moment of privacy so I can disappear into the shadows of the palace until it comes time to extract the Prince.

"Right, of course. That carriage was rank. And so were Callistus's clothes. Don't tell him I said that, though. He's staying in an inn outside the city."

I smile and nod, no idea what he's talking about as I hope my facial illusion doesn't fall off while he's looking at me.

Otello turns from me to sniff himself, and I glance back down at the washbasin.

"Yep, still smell both the carriage and Callistus on me."

I watch my reflection in horror as my nose reappears on the wrong face, a grave mismatch.

"I will have to have the servants draw me a bath as well. Even if it means I'll have to figure out how to dress myself since my First Valet had to get himself poisoned."

My attempt at silently slipping back under the sheets is disrupted by those words, and I face-plant instead.

"Are you all right?" Otello asks.

"I'm fine," I say, swooping the sheets over my head. "I just felt very cold all of the sudden."

When my eyes acclimate to the darkness under the sheets, I see a long tendril of my hair lying on my pillow beside me. It has escaped from both its plaited braid and the illusion enchantment.

"Should I send for the Physician?"

"No, that's fine. I'm sure he's busy with you father, anyway."

"You are like my brother, Heinrich. Don't be so dismissive about your wellbeing."

"I— thank you. You're like a brother to me as well." My voice comes out a bit higher than I mean, and I clear my throat.

"Here, let me get you some water."

I wince. Why can't he just leave?

A moment later, I sense him next to my mattress.

Just to make him go away, I reach out the hand that wasn't transformed a moment ago.

"Heinrich, your hand! It's so . . . dainty."

Abandoning the water, I pull my hand back under the sheets. Apparently, the illusion has faded in both my hands.

And I've just made myself look guilty.

Suddenly, the sheets are yanked off of me, and Otello is staring down at me.

His eyes widen, and the tankard of water falls from his hands, spilling onto the mattress and drenching me.

I close my eyes, knowing that I have failed not only my Empire, but my elvish heritage.

I've been caught.

I don't fight as Otello drags me out of the bedchamber, even though it is such a sorrowful thing to be parted from that lovely bed.

"Guards!" he yells, causing men to materialize from nowhere.

"Release Heinrich from the tower at once!" he bellows. "And escort this prisoner there in his stead."

At his words, even tighter grips come down on both of my arms now, releasing me from Otello's hold. Then I'm dragged down the hallway almost faster than I can keep up.

We pass a large doorway with several more guards posted outside it, speaking to a man in brown robes of a Sorcerer. Thankfully, these do not join the posse.

The man in brown glances up, though, and his gaze meets mine. A surge of hate flashes across his visage.

And I know. This is the Sorcerer from the vision. The man who wants to put Otello to death and betray the Empire to destruction.

But a woman being dragged to the dungeon is in no place to expose a high-ranking official of evil based only on a potion-induced dream, so I hold my tongue.

As I try not to lose my balance and become literally dragged across the castle, I also try to focus on my surroundings. How many chambers we pass, how many corridors up and down.

The time shall come soon when I will need to know how to make it to the Prince's chambers. Before the Sorcerer in the dark robes can.

Finally, we reach a rounded wall that indicates the base of a tower. The wooden door is open, and Otello is already there, speaking to a man who also has the face we all shared until very recently.

"I am so sorry, Heinrich," Otello blurts, taking a gag out of his mouth. "I chose the wrong you."

Heinrich glances at me, and I expect to see rage twisting his face for everything I've done to him, but he just shrugs. "I can see why. She's quite beautiful. I would choose her, too."

And that's the last I see of the scene before I'm pushed into the tower and the door is closed behind me, leaving me in complete darkness with only the Creator.

If ever He was with me in the first place.

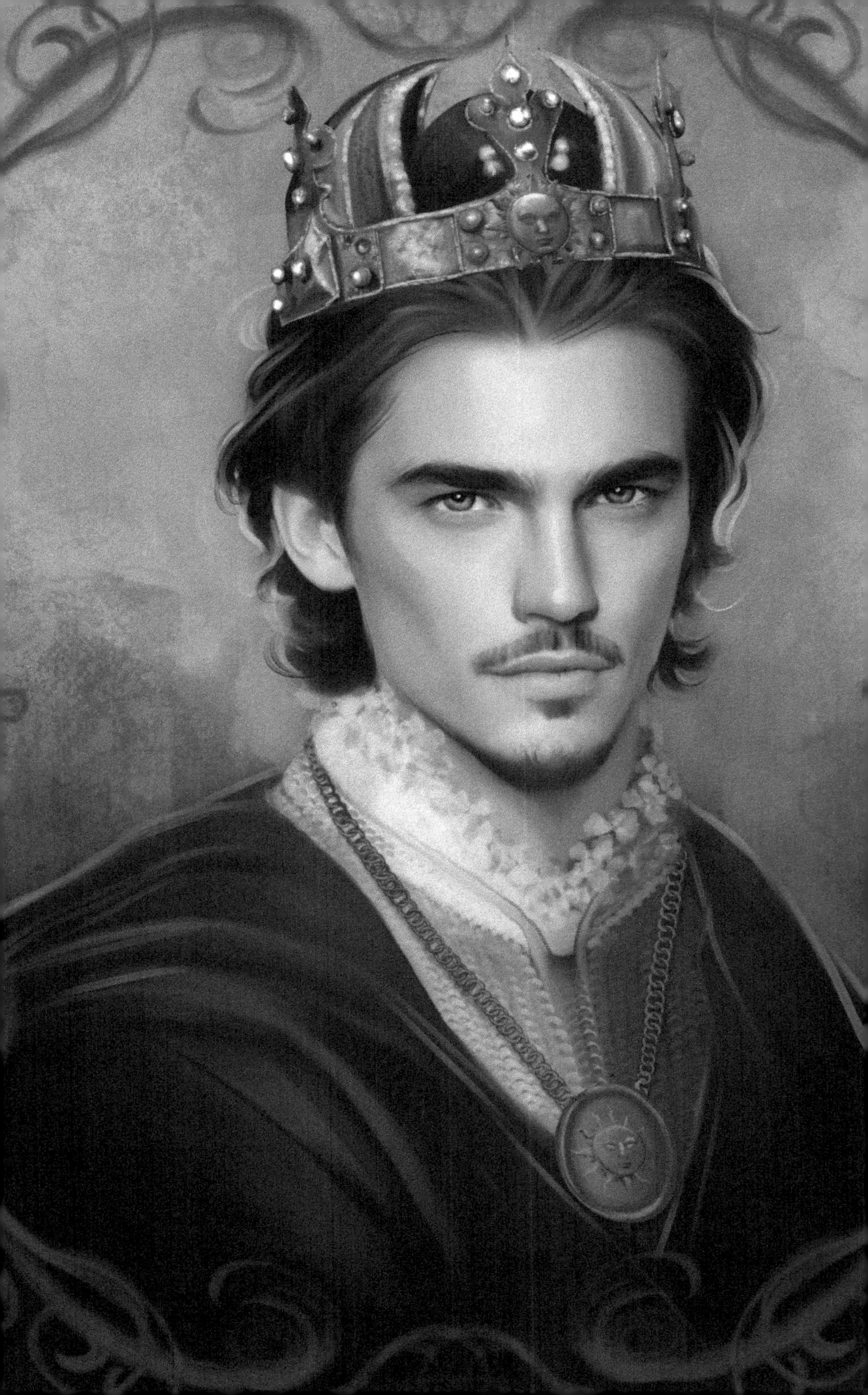

CHAPTER XXIII

PRINCE OTELLO

I roll my eyes at Heinrich's words. How could I have mistaken him for anyone else?

Then I see a smudge of dirt on his face and remember how dearly Heinrich hates dirt. This little experience must have been torture to him.

Beyond him, I see several servants watching. I gesture to them. "Take him to his room and see that he is properly tended to, fed, and cleaned."

Heinrich grins. "So, all this time, all I had to do to get the royal treatment was get usurped by a lady?"

Shoving him, I grin. "Get out of here."

One of the servants, Godwin, steps toward me with the sackcloth that had been intended for Heinrich to put on, as is the tradition for new prisoners. But he appears to have somehow wheedled himself out of that fate.

We'll see if the witch can do the same.

"Give it here," I say, taking the garment and excusing Godwin.

Then I turn toward the tower that had been holding my closest friend, and now contains the woman who did that to him. Who made *me* do that to him.

Not to mention the creature who kissed me and left me half-naked in the woods.

I grab hold of the arm of another passing servant, also named Godwin. "In my room, you will find a torn red dress. Bring it hither."

Even though my command is odd, he just nods before rushing off, his head bowed.

And I stride toward the tower that has, within the vespers, housed both my dearest friend and my worst enemy. My fists clench at my side and I charge toward the tower.

Henri is at the door, taking this prisoner seriously after everything that has transpired. “Do you want me to go in with you?”

A question he wouldn’t even leave up to me to answer if this were a male prisoner; perhaps he’s not taking it seriously after all. But this better suits my purpose. “No. I need to face this alone.”

Godwin returns with both speed and grace to place the dress in my hands.

Henri glances down at the delivery and raises an eyebrow. But he says nothing as he opens the door.

I move toward the darkness, and another servant hands me a lamp.

“If you need me, just raise your voice and I will be at your side, my prince,” Henri says before closing the door behind me.

It takes my eyes a moment to adjust to just the light from the lantern. When they do, I see a small wooden table, a single chair, a straw cot, and a chamber pot.

Panic grips me when I don’t see Meredith right away. Even if she’s just a slip of a thing, she did overpower me.

But panic is quickly replaced by embarrassment when I find her huddled in the corner, hugging her tunic-clad legs to her chest and staring up at me with wide eyes that gleam an unearthly blue shade in this lighting.

“I can explain,” she whispers. “I had a good reason to do this.”

“Oh, really?” I sit down on the single chair, because this is going to be something. “There are good reasons for seduction and robbery these days? And what about making an innocent man pay for your crimes?”

“I thought it was the only way. I saw a vision—“

I stand up so hard the chair falls over. “You did this all because you had a *dream*?”

She licks her lips, drawing my gaze there. For a long moment, I stare at them, remembering what they felt like against mine. Wondering if they would still taste so sweet . . .

“I know dreams mean little to your kind,” she says, snapping me out of her spell, “but for my people—“

What does she mean "her kind"? That she's a woman and I'm a man? I do respect dreams. When they come to me from someone I trust, namely Uriel, who as the Keeper of Knowledge, knows what he's speaking of at all times.

"You can regale your fellow prisoners with your dreams," I say. "I'm sure they'll love to hear all about them. Especially since they are almost all men and apparently can't dream on their own."

Meredith launches to her feet, and my hand goes unconsciously to my saber.

"You can't throw me into the dungeon with them! I'm a lady— a noblewoman of rank! There are laws for how we are treated in these situations."

I grunt and gesture at her slender form wearing my clothing. "You don't look much like a woman." That is actually a lie. She looks very feminine, and not even despite the clothes. Rather, as I see the shapeliness of her breeches-clad legs, I'm not sure how I didn't notice before. "And you gave up your rank as a noblewoman when you threw in your lot with the Bandit King and did what you did. You will be treated with the same respect I would give him or any of his other lackeys."

Meredith has tears falling from her beautiful eyes now, and she's trembling. I have never in my life made a woman cry before, and I can see now that it isn't something I want to repeat. Actually, all I want to do is gather her in my arms and tell her it's all right; I'm never going to let a man hurt her.

No, I need to keep it together. A Prince does not show favoritism. He metes out justice with an even hand.

"And don't think you'll be wearing stolen clothes, either."

Meredith looks down at herself and then back up at me, expressionless.

First, I toss her the sackcloth that had been offered Heinrich.

She plucks it up and stretches it out. The garment was clearly created merely to cover a prisoner and not keep them warm.

But it would do nothing to cover her. At least, not in any way that wouldn't draw the male eye to her still more.

Meredith seems to realize this as I do, because she drops it and rushes toward the table.

"How *dare* you."

I blink, startled that the words that are coming out of her mouth aren't 'I beg of you.' "Pardon?"

"You are cruel! You have the authority over so many people and claim your Emperor-God gave it to you. But did the Creator give your father the right to rob from His first people? Does the Creator let you choose to honor the rights for some and not for others based on how you feel that day?"

Reeling back as if she'd slapped me, I almost reach out to the wall for support. "I, uh—"

My gaze falls on her torn dress still in my hands, my memory of why I am treating her so returning to me.

"Fine, don't wear the rags. Wear one of your own gowns, as is the noblewoman's right." I drop it in front of her and watch the way her eyes widen at the sight of it. "And ask yourself, does the Emperor-God approve of what you did to His Sacred Prince in the woods?"

She lowers her gaze in shame.

"Now dress yourself in whichever option you choose, but know that you will not spend another moment wearing *my* garments."

Meredith jerks her gaze back up to meet mine. "Surely you do not mean for me to change in front of you."

"Like I asked you not to strip me in the woods?" I cross my arms and straighten my back, reminding myself exactly what she did. Exactly why I need to mete out justice right now and not mercy. "At least I am allowing you to tend to yourself. But if you would like me to summon a guard to attend to you . . ."

She utters something in old Elvish, likely taught to her by her lost friend, the Lady Elspeth.

"How could you?"

Feeling as though Elspeth is speaking to me from beyond the grave or wherever she has been taken to, I drop my gaze from Meredith to where she is snatching up both garments that I've offered her, shame filling me and mixing horribly with the embarrassment I already feel from the forest.

Deciding to avert my gaze, I take one last glance up at Meredith to ensure that she won't attack me the moment my back is turned. Her own back is already to me, and she tugs off my tunic as I watch. The action reveals her smooth, pale skin covered by only cloth bindings that were doubtless used as part of her disguise along with my trousers that she's still wearing.

Forgetting all possibility of danger, I turn my back to her and stare at the dark stone wall. Blinking rapidly, I try to remove the image of her so vulnerable from my mind's eye.

Something hits me from behind, and I whirl around just in time to get my own trousers flung onto my face.

When I peel them off, I find my tunic on the ground from where it's fallen after hitting me. Then I look up to Elspeth and find her wearing the crimson dress she wore when she lured me into the forest. Her eyes are flashing as she grits her teeth at me.

"Marry, why so gloomy?" I ask, mock bowing at my waist and snatching up my stolen tunic. "I'm sure with your great skill of removing your clothing and others', you will be able to barter for your freedom soon enough."

Meredith balls her fists and takes a step forward. I realize she must be wearing the sackcloth also underneath her dress, since I don't see any sign of it. "Do you torment all within your power so cruelly, *Sir* Heinrich?"

"No, only the seductresses, *Lady* Meredith."

"Oh, seductress, am I?" Meredith steps closer and then closer still.

It takes me a moment to remember that I can call her off, or at least step back, but then she's upon me. Her wildflower scent surrounds me, paralyzing me in place. Her warmth invades my space. And then she's leaning ever closer to me, her chest brushing against mine.

"If I'm the seductress . . ." Her hands brush across my shoulders, her fingers playing with my neck.

My neck! She's an enemy, and I've let her come too close. I need to get away.

But I only want to lean closer. To taste her sweet lips once again. She's like a spider, injecting me with her poison. Only what am I, that I want more of it?

It's like Meredith can read my mind as she looks up into my eyes. "Then what are you?"

A simpleton addicted to folly. My head is already dipping toward hers.

Her lips find mine, filling my senses once again with her. Meredith's lips are soft, a caress on my mouth. Mine are far less gentle in return as I drink her in, tasting wildflowers and ale from the inn. More than that though, she feels like temptation and danger and everything I didn't know I wanted, somewhere deep in my soul.

To be in here, unchaperoned, kissing a prisoner whom I loathe is not just foolish; it's forbidden. As my hands clutch her tiny waist, I feel far less sacred than I should.

And I'm not sure that I mind. But I need to.

Even as she tries to deepen the kiss and I follow blindly after, my hands rise to find her shoulders. I draw one more desperate taste of her before pushing her away before I can drown.

Meredith blinks at me in confusion before a coy smile once again returns to those too-tempting lips. "Well? What does that make you?"

"A man who knows what seductresses are good for." With that, I step through and slam the door behind me before I can lose the rest of my self-control. The little witch can rot in there for all I care.

CHAPTER XXIV

The Mismatched Duo

Elspeth:

Judging by the level of rage in every step Heinrich takes away from me, rotting in this dark room would be the least of all evils should my fate remain in his hands.

But my fate is far too grand to fit in his tiny hands.

And when I get my *own* hands on *him* . . .

My hands fist over the royal Heritage Medallion I slipped off Heinrich's neck. What was a valet doing with this, anyway? Is he doubling for Otello until they determine whether I worked alone?

Shaking my head, I do my best to brush away my anger, grief, and fear so I can focus. Focus on balancing myself, and in that balance, I find my focus.

"*Modaath*," I whisper.

"*Modaath*," I hear Irwin echo in my soul when it would be impossible to hear with my ears.

"They have me in a tower," I say. "There are no windows and only one door. He threatened to move me to the dungeon soon."

"We made it to the city. We're coming to rescue you. I won't let that them take you into that pit."

I lean back against the cold wall, doing my best to banish all doubt so he won't sense it. "I know. I believe in you."

Otello:

I can't believe this is happening. No, actually, I can. It's been long enough since my father got sick that I have become accustomed to it. Even if it is harder to become acclimated to the chaos that has since fallen upon my life.

But now, with my valet recovering from wrongful imprisonment, a she-devil in my tower, and the secret of my Heritage Magic threatened, the thing I least expect is the premonition of evil that washes over me.

That, and the sudden hand on my shoulder.

I turn, surprised by the gesture. No servant would ever be so bold.

Adalbert is standing behind me, his face solemn. "Your father is hosting a banquet. He requests that you be there."

"A banquet?" His words are more shocking than his touch, and I stumble backwards before glancing at his room. "Is he well enough? Or—?"

"Your father will dine this night and would have you dine with him." With that, he turns away, his brown cloak sweeping at the ground he walks across.

Elspeth:

My skirt sweeps across the filthy floor as I pace back and forth. Back and forth.

I believe in Irwin and the rest of them. I really do. Well, I believe in Irwin, WolfBear, and Meredith. I'm not so sure about the brothers, though.

Not when I'm locked in the most secure building in the Empire.

Then again, I used to think that of my own keep, and that proved me so very wrong.

The cool of the tower has frozen my feet and chills through my dress. As uncomfortable as the scratchy sackcloth that I wear beneath is, at least it offers additional warmth— as well as covering for my back where my dress leaves me exposed now.

I may deserve this for what I did to Heinrich, but he has more than taken his vengeance out on me. So now I owe him some in return.

But first I need to fight for my freedom.

"So, it is true."

I almost jump out of my skin at the strange voice that interrupts my solitude.

Whirling around, I face an elf wearing green robes standing in the doorway of my cell.

"Cousin?" I say in the customary greeting of our people, even among those where no kinship can be traced for the last twelve generations.

"It's been so many years." His expression softens as he studies me beneath his green hood and patches of silver hair. "I wasn't sure I would be able to recognize you when the time came, but you have only grown in grace and beauty."

I glance down at my tattered red dress before looking back at him. "Do you know me, kinsman? Have you come to rescue me?"

"Not yet, little sister. Night is drawing near, and I will need you near in order to spirit away the sun."

"Are your referring to . . . the Prince?"

He gives me the barest of nods, and I'm not even sure that I see it. "I will see you freed from here, but the Empire has dire need of you yet."

With that, he turns and leaves the room so subtly that I almost doubt he was ever here.

I hurry to the door and attempt to open it, but no, it's still bolted shut from the other side.

Sighing, I go back to pacing because first, I need to wait for Irwin to rescue me.

Otello:

Heinrich isn't here to help me prepare, so I do it alone. I pull on my ceremonial robe, feeling as though I'm missing something. My mind is still dazed from the kiss I took from Meredith in vengeance for the one she stole from me in the Great Wald.

And I'm not sure that I mind. But I must push such things from my mind and focus on my duties as the Sacred Prince. Whether I like it or not, it is important to my people that I represent myself as a leader, no matter what I'm struggling with.

I go to stand in front of my floor mirror. But the man staring back at me dressed as an Emperor is no leader. He's only a lonely little boy.

How am I supposed to rule— alone?

Elspeth:

I'm no longer alone.

Well, in this room, I'm alone. But just outside— I sense a friendly soul.

I sense my kinfolk. My true cousin whose bloodline and loyalty are both known to me.

I go to the door. "Irwin?"

I'm coming. Stole a fine silver dagger you need to see.

Irwin, focus.

Not to worry; all the guards seem to be elsewhere. Oh, wait, never mind.

Be careful!

Don't worry. I'm stealthy.

I bite my lip.

Oh, but Meredith isn't.

Grasping the door like I can open it to assist him, I end up just clutching it like a support.

Don't worry; WolfBear is really strong. She just knocked him clean out.

I exhale.

Oh, no, he had friends!

I about fall over.

But WolfBear is still strong. She just knocked them out at the same time.

Clutching the door handle, I steady myself.

Oh, but those friends had a lot more friends!

A desperate prayer escapes my lips.

And . . . WolfBear is even stronger than I thought. They're climbing all over her and she's just throwing them down—

The door shakes as if something is thrown against it, and I step back.

Then the door finally swings open, revealing my wide-eyed cousin.

"Irwin!" I rush forward to hug him.

He pulls away. "No time. We have to go before we find the limit to WolfBear's strength." He turns to where WolfBear is standing in the middle of about twelve fallen guards.

"Right. Let's go." I point toward a side staircase. "Let's take the servant's route."

Irwin happily falls in behind me, the way it has always been as we begin the rest of the escape.

Otello:

I shouldn't be thinking about escape. A masterful spread with every type of meat the palace farms have to offer is steaming before me, but I have no appetite.

The stench of death and decay works to overpower the meal despite all the perfumes and powders that are obviously trying to combat it. And as much as I would like to deny it, the repugnant mixture is coming from my father.

I glance at the sitting Holy Emperor of the Sun, but he seems to stare right through me with a dead expression in his eyes.

"Father?" I whisper, my voice sounding more like the scared little boy stealing seconds with his father by hiding behind his throne to be near him, and not the one man who will soon sit on that throne himself.

"Son . . ." Father drawls, still not quite looking at me.

I turn away so to hide my pain from Adalbert, who remains standing just behind my father.

My gaze falls on the doorway to the servant's hallway that they have been weaving in and out to keep the food on the table fresh.

Just in time to see none other than the prisoner I left in the tower slide by. Meredith freezes when she sees me, her eyes widening. Then she turns, revealing rough, brown sackcloth where the red of her dress parts.

One hand reaches back and grabs hold of another, tugging a male elf after her, his back to me, but his stature telling the truth of his bloodline.

And in that moment, I realize that I'm not as angry about her having escaped this far so much as I'm furious for her having escaped into the arms of this man. This woman who kissed *me*.

I stand up so suddenly, my chair falls over. Before I can make chase, though, my father chokes.

Turning to him, I find him gagging and gurgling as though he might never breathe again. I rush to his side and take his arm. "I'm here, Father. Steady, steady—"

His hand is already as cold as a corpse as I raise it, trying to dislodge what he must be choking on. But then he dribbles a dark liquid from his mouth.

I drop his hand and grab his shoulders instead to steady him. Then I turn to the nearest guards. "He's been poisoned!" I turn to Adalbert. "Do something!"

But Adalbert seems strangely stricken, too, frozen in his place, his eyes rolling upward and his hands beginning to shake.

"*Father*," I whisper, turning back to my father and clutching him to myself. If only the enemy was outside, so I could stop them and not inside where I cannot touch, cannot defeat.

The image of a blue-eyed angel with deceitful innocence traipsing past the servant's kitchen flashes through my mind's eye.

And then my father goes still in my arms.

"Father? Father!" I press my ear to his heart but hear nothing. "No . . . no!" I clutch him more tightly, as if I can somehow keep his soul inside his body.

But then it pulses out. Or something does, an invisible force that throws me backward against the stone wall.

Too afraid to feel the pain, I stare as my father's body crumples.

I stand on shaking legs, knowing the rites I must say, but not sure if I have to strength to utter the sacred words. "So sets the Son of the Sun . . ."

And so rises the Son of the Son of the Sun. I need to finish the last rite, but not from here, like an impersonal witness. I move to return to my father, but a hand grabs me by the back of my royal robe and tugs me back, into the back servant's passage.

"Let me go!" I cry, tears tightening my throat.

"I *am* letting you go," Uriel says, suddenly stripping me of my robe.

I stare down at the puddle of purple and furs on the floor. "Wh-what?" My brain is so inundated with the way the world is falling apart around me, I cannot think of any reason for his actions or logic left in the world.

"I have someone in place who will get you out of here. But you need to wait for her in my chambers."

"Get me out of here?" Suddenly, a simple green cloak is pulled over my shoulders and its hood tugged over my head.

"He'll have all the doors heavily guarded, so you'll have to escape through the window. But wait for her. She is wise in the ways of my people; she can get you out of the city."

"*Who?!*" I demand. "What is happening?"

As if to give me more reason to question, the surrounding air tints green.

Uriel pushes me toward the stairs. "Go. Go!"

My mind is under too much pressure to think, so my body obeys his words blindly. I hurry up the stairs and down the upper hallway toward the chamber above the library that belongs to Uriel, just as it belonged to the Keeper of Knowledge before him. If there ever was a Keeper of Knowledge before him. Suddenly, I'm not so sure.

I pass two servants crouched down, apparently in pain. Backing up, I turn to them, scared that perhaps they were exposed to some of the poison. "Have you eaten recently?"

They look up in unison, and I'm stunned to see that they both have cat-green eyes. I can't speak for the woman, but I'm certain Godwin didn't have green eyes just earlier this morn.

Startled, I step back.

"Kill the Prince," they say in unison.

I take another step back. "Don't speak like that. It's treason."

They don't seem to care, though, as they lunge for me.

Instinct takes over and I turn so that the woman rams into my shoulder. Then I reach behind me for Godwin, grab onto him, and throw him into the wall. He crumples and falls, but the woman just reaches her hands around my neck.

I throw my head back, colliding with her face. I feel her crumple to the ground behind me.

But I don't turn to see my handiwork as I take off running toward the library.

My feet don't take me directly there though. My heart leads me elsewhere, one wing down where I know my remaining family is staying.

CHAPTER XXV

The Mismatched Duo

Elspeth:

Along with my only remaining family, I flee for my life and for freedom through the servants' wings, toward where intuitive thinking tells me the stable entrance should eventually present itself.

I pause when I see a few silver coins laid carelessly on a table next to a leather pouch, no doubt containing more, and a vase of violets. I snatch up the coins and the pouch, leaving the lovely flowers because I'm generous like that.

"Over here!" Irwin calls at an open doorway.

Picking up my pace, I follow him and the others. I'm assaulted by both the stench of horse and an arm grabbing my elbow.

Shrieking, I pull back, ready to flail at whoever and whatever prohibits my escape.

Until my gaze falls once again on the elf wearing green robes and an earnest but not unkind expression.

I open my mouth to ask who he is *before* I lash out at him, in respect for his elvish descent. But he speaks first. "The time has come. You must rescue the Prince."

"I— uh— what?" Irwin blinks in surprise. "How do you know about that?"

"Prince?" Meredith whispers behind me, and I turn to find a strange swirling in her green eyes.

The man steps back and gestures to several steeds saddled and ready to ride. "I have prepared these for your company. They must leave immediately." He gestures to Meredith, who is wavering slightly.

Irwin steadies her, and she lets him, which causes me great levels of concern.

WolfBear grunts. "WolfBear go where Mistress goes."

"And she will go to you as well," assures the green-clad elf. "After she adds the Prince to your party. But you must take your friends who bear mortal blood outside the borders of the city first, or else they will become your enemies as well."

I glance back at Abel and find him wobbling as his eyes flash green when they should be blue. "What is happening?"

"I have no time to explain, but a powerful burst of dark magic has been released and is enveloping the city even now. But it has no power over kin blood." He glances at WolfBear. "Or mixed blood, so it would seem. But the Prince's time is running out."

And if that is true, so is the world's.

I turn to WolfBear. "Get Abel and Meredith outside the city, to Rose Crown Inn. Irwin and I will join you shortly."

WolfBear gives me no quarrel as she yanks our two mortal companions to her and leads them to the horses.

Irwin stares after Meredith in concern, but I turn back to the kinsman. "Where is the Prince?"

If the elf harbors any surprise at my implicit belief in his story, he doesn't show it. Or perhaps he simply has no time to show it. Likely I don't either, if the Prince I came to rescue is in danger even now.

The elf holds out a piece of black fabric toward me. "Take the Cowl of Shadows. You must wear it until you are safely out of the city with the Prince."

I take it from him and shake it out. The shimmering black fabric tumbles down, a cape almost as tall as I am, capped by a hood, with a brooch inscribed with the symbol of a moon in silver to keep it together.

Taking it from the kinsman, I wrap it around me with a flourish and clasp the brooch together.

The elf reaches forward, grasps the hood where it is bundled at my shoulders, and pulls it over my head, enclosing me in its shadow.

And making my body vanish.

Irwin cries out as I try to find my hands, my feet, my torso, anything. Then I push the hood back and see them all at once.

"An invisibility cloak?" Irwin breathes, his horror fading to awe.

I try pulling the cloak back on and off again to the same result as before. "Do you have another for the Prince?"

"All you keep under the cloak with you while the hood is up will also be invisible. But it is imperative that the Prince himself does not see your face until outside the city wall."

Dropping the hood again, I look up. "And when we are outside?"

"Find somewhere safe to hide, or if there is none, continue forward to where you can keep him safe. I will catch up to give more direction. When he asks who you are, merely tell him that Uriel, Keeper of Knowledge, sent you."

Crashes echo from inside the palace, and the elf takes my shoulders and pushes me toward the stable entrance leading to the courtyard. "You must go. You will find the Prince in the library, which you will find by its wall of glass. Tell him Uriel, Keeper of Knowledge sent you. Your kin shall have your horses prepared for you. Now go!"

Stumbling out into the direct sunlight, I pull my hood back over my head. Then I glance around, searching for the wall of glass.

Otello:

Glancing around to make sure there are no potential hostiles, I go to open the door.

And find Heinrich out of bed and doubled over, his hands over his head as if trying to stave off blows. But no one else is in the room. "Heinrich!"

He jerks up suddenly, his eyes an eerie shade of green he wasn't born with, just like the servants.

I back away a step. "What is happening?"

Heinrich's eyes turn blue again for a moment. "I don't know. But you need to get out. Get away. Run!" The green shimmers in his eyes and he stoops over again.

"I'm not leaving without you." I move forward again and grab his arm.

Only to be backhanded almost into the wall.

"Heinrich—"

He charges at me, pushing me all the way to the wall, slamming my head against it hard.

The room spins momentarily, and I feel a sickness roiling in my gut.

When my vision clears, I see Heinrich's fist coming for my face.

I duck and hear him cry out as it hits the wall. Then I slide down and crawl out from between Heinrich and the wall, moving toward the door.

Hands grasp my ankles and yank me back.

Grabbing at the rug, I try to stop my backward movement and end up tugging up the woven piece and overturning a table.

Then I'm flipped around so that I'm on my back, staring up at Heinrich with his unnatural green eyes and his fist pulled back.

"Kill the Prince," he whispers.

"Heinrich," I whisper. "*Brother.*"

The title he never seized and the truth I never uttered wavers between us, an entity all its own.

The green in Heinrich's eyes flicker, and for a moment, I see him gazing back at me, our kinship even more evident in this moment.

And I know that he knew, after all.

"*Run*," Heinrich whispers. "I can't hold it off forever."

"Hold *what* off?"

"I don't know. But it's returning." Face twisting in horror, Heinrich rears, his hands grasping his head again.

Half-stumbling, half-crawling, I move away from him, using the door to help myself up to my feet.

When I turn back to him, the green eyes are back, and he's snatching a letter knife from off the floor near the overturned table.

I shut the door behind me and flee toward the library, unwilling to fight my half-brother. Reluctant to let my blood be on his hands.

Whether or not he follows me, I can't tell, because I barely even process the ground beneath my feet until I turn into the library. Then I push two tables in front of the door before turning to take in the rest of the room.

It's mercifully devoid of further individuals with unnaturally green eyes. My only company is the books filling the shelves that line the walls of the room, which is three levels high, with sliding ladders throughout.

Except for one wall, which is entirely made of glass.

In a panic, I go to examine the gardens on the other side of the windows. I half-expect more friends with unnaturally green eyes to be slobbering on the glass, trying to hurt me for no known reason.

But only flowers occupy the gardens.

Which makes it all the more alarming when the glass suddenly breaks.

I jump back and watch as the rest of the windowpane gives out before a rock that appears to be floating on the other side.

Backing toward the display housing an ancestral, ornate blade on one of the shelves, I try unsuccessfully to take it in hand. It's welded in place because apparently, no one was ever attacked in a library before.

The stone falls onto the garden outdoors, and the overwhelming sense that I am no longer alone in this room comes upon me. "Who goes there?"

"I am kin of Uriel, Keeper of Knowledge," calls a disembodied female voice. "He has sent me to take you from the city."

"What is going on?" I ask, making out a shadow of human form on the ground, but not seeing the form itself. My hand reaches for the knife sheathed on my waist.

A great force rams into the outer library doors, causing them to rattle.

"My prince, we have no time." The shadow moves until it is cast just to my left.

Then a hand I cannot see grasps mine, and the unnaturalness of it all frays at my last nerves.

"Keep your knife ready," the invisible woman breathes. "You may have need of it."

Then, her hand tightening its grip on mine, she tugs me toward the opening she made in the window. I have no strength or reason enough to even consider fighting her as I duck between the jagged edges of glass.

The library door bursts open, revealing a dozen of servants, all with eyes of green. Heinrich stands at the head of them.

"Duck low, my prince," orders my invisible savior.

I crouch slightly, not sure what it will do when the bushes barely reach my knees.

Her hand releases mine, and then two hands are on my shoulders, pushing me lower.

"He's there!" I hear Heinrich call, but while the voice is his, there is nothing of him in the words.

Something sweeps over me, and I am shrouded in darkness.

"What are you doing?" I demand in a hiss.

"Where did he go?" calls Macon, the royal steward.

"We are invisible," the woman says just beside me, and I feel her warmth and, her breath. "But we must move. I need you to wrap your arms around me, so we operate as a unit."

Not sure what else to do, I reach toward the voice and immediately brush velvet.

"Oy!" Hands grab mine and move them downward before wrapping my arms around what feels like her waist. "Careful, there."

"Many pardons. I am unused to hiding behind a lady's skirts."

She snorts in a decidedly unladylike manner, most likely to make me feel better, and then her hands grasp my hunched shoulders. "We must move side-wise together."

"Lead the way."

CHAPTER XXVI

Prince Otello

I feel the shrouded woman move beneath me and take steps to keep up with her, which is more of a struggle than I anticipated while bent in this strange position.

"I'm going to make a sharp turn toward the right," she says.

I move with her, feeling somewhat as though we are dancing. If ever I danced with someone who stood twice as tall as I, that is.

A horse whinnies suddenly, and I become aware of the smell of the stable somewhere outside this cloak and its encompassing scent of wildflowers.

"I must uncover you now," she says. "Mount the horse beside us immediately. Do not look back, but follow the he-elf out of the city. I will be right behind you."

With that, her hands drop from my shoulders and push my hands from her. Then I'm overwhelmed by fresh air and sunlight as the cloak is suddenly yanked from me.

Gulping in stable-stained fresh air, I turn to see my own pure white stallion beside me, already saddled.

I hear the shouts of many servants, more than had come into the library, and hoist myself onto Mythos. I turn to find that the guards have joined their number, and the maid who rescued me is still invisible to my eyes.

But just ahead of me is an elf male astride a brown mare. He glances back at me, and I have a nagging feeling that he lurks in one of my memories. But I feel as though I've never seen him clearly before . . .

He's Meredith's companion that she was so protective of when we met outside the crypt.

His eyes widen in surprise to mirror mine, but then the sound of arrows being drawn back stirs us both into action.

The elf nods at me, and then his horse charges forward.

With a nudge of my knees, Mythos charges after.

Ahead of us, the gates begin to close.

I lower my form to reduce resistance and increase our speed.

The elf ahead makes it through, and then so do I. Only then do I peer back in time to see a riderless horse barely escape the courtyard just as the gate closes.

No, not riderless. The brown stallion has someone pulling at his reins.

My heart lightens to know that my invisible savior is still in my company. Until I see the great volley of arrows coming down from the gate towers toward us.

I watch as the arrows rain down on rooftops and cobblestone roads. One slices through the air and stabs through the male elf's left arm. He cries out in pain, and his horse rears in surprise.

"Irwin!" the invisible rider cries, and her horse comes alongside Irwin's. An unseen hand appears to grasp the horse's reins and guide it back to the ground.

Another volley of arrows is being pulled back.

"Hurry!" I yell back. "We're almost out of range!"

Irwin nods, grasping his arm and looking pale, but he urges his horse forward alongside the invisible rider.

And I turn back to guide my own horse. I have to watch the cobblestones as we descend to make sure he doesn't slip on the cobbles or trample a hapless peasant.

Though there are definitely a lot of peasants on the road. And a lot more are swarming.

I look up from the cobblestone road to see a sea of green gazes.

"Kill the Prince," they drone in unison, pressing so closely that I have to pull my horse up to keep from trampling them.

One peasant grabs a hold of one of my legs, then another, and another. Then I'm yanked off my horse and into a swarm of hands and bodies, dragging me down, down, down.

The moment I hit the cobblestones, they swarm over me, blocking out my view of the sun of my calling, stifling even the air. I try to wrap my arms around my neck to hide my face, but I feel them all piling on top of me, crushing me—

"Otello!"

It's startling to hear a woman use my given name with no title attached. But I don't have time to decide whether I like it or not as life becomes more and more pressure and darkness and void . . .

A sliver of light pierces through as someone is tossed backward. Then another and another. It seems like there is always someone there to replace a peasant who is so easily dragged away, yet the gap of light is growing. Whatever enchantment has them in its grips is dulling their ability to react. They are mindless.

Suddenly, through the gap of light, I feel another pressure come down on me. A lithe, female body presses over me, limbs on both sides of my torso, and my breathing is further inhibited by the feeling of an unseen cloak falling over me.

Around us, peasants cry out in confusion and start to disperse. The gap of light gets wider and wider.

"Kill the Prince? Kill the Prince!"

Then all the pressure is gone except for the woman on top of me. Her arms reach under me. "Can you stand?"

"I think so." I push myself to my hands and knees as she adjusts herself around me, still trying to keep the cloak in place.

We stand together, and I stagger slightly as my body seeks to reassure itself that nothing was too damaged during the stifling.

Irwin stands in the pavilion of the First Cathedral that overhangs Heaven's Grace. "Elspeth?!"

I jerk my head around, as though I might somehow make out this so-called Elspeth's face while she holds her invisibility cloak over me. Blindly, we stagger toward her companion.

"Elspeth?" Irwin says again, not seeing that we've joined him on the balcony. He looks down at his blood-soaked sleeve from where the arrow punctured him. Then he collapses.

"Irwin!" Elspeth cries, and then she and the cloak are gone.

I gasp in the clear, cold air that I never thought I'd breathe again as I stand before the three-story cathedral plated in gold to match and reflect the sunlight.

The large cathedral doors burst open, and a flood of monks pile out, their robes red and their scalps bald.

And their eyes are emerald green.

I turn back and find that the swarm of peasants has reached the entrance to the temple courtyard, trapping us here with the monks.

"There's no way out," I whisper.

"Over here!" the woman— Elspeth— calls, her voice almost drowned out by the falls. I assume she's near Irwin working some kind of healer's magic, as his blood appears to have stopped flowing, and color is returning to his face.

I move to join them, but then hands grasp my tunic from behind. So many hands wanting to drag me backward.

Turning, I smack away the hands grasping my other arm. I use both hands to push back the monk taking the lead, knocking him to the ground.

He immediately starts crawling toward me and reaches for my ankles.

I kick him, and he falls backward.

"Otello!" Elspeth says, and her voice is far closer to me now.

As are the other monks, stepping over their fallen companion to get to me. "Kill the Prince. Kill the Prince."

Striking out with one arm, I smack several in the face. And they grab at my arm.

These monks are pacifists. What dark magic has driven them to forget their vows and rise against their ruler?

And forced me to strike back even though they dedicate their lives to serve the Emperor-God? Like me, they are under the protection of the sun.

But the sun seems to withhold its protections over me. A betrayal when we were both appointed to serve the Emperor-God as His rulers by day.

As if to mock me, the sun, despite on its way to abandon me to night, glints off the Cathedral into my eyes. Now that I'm temporarily blinded, another monk grasps my ankle and almost sends me flailing onto the cobblestones.

"Oh!" Elspeth yells, and I hear another form hit the cobblestone beside me.

I reach for where I heard her fall, and my fingers find something else instead. My Heritage Medallion on a broken chain and lying on the cobblestones between us.

My Heritage Medallion.

Ignoring the hands grasping at me and the roar of the peasants closing in, I hold up the medal toward the temple. "As the Emperor-God gave me the sun, I choose to shine it forth!"

Light beams out, striking the First Cathedral, and reflecting backward in a light that would be blinding if my Heritage Magic did not give me the very essence of light at this moment.

The monks fall away from me in shock, and the crowds stop their charge.

I scan the area. "Elspeth?"

"Right behind you. Go to Irwin!"

Obeying the one thing that somehow makes sense in all this chaos, I go to where Irwin has regained consciousness and is slowly standing. An unseen force suddenly seems help him stand faster.

Of course. Because if this truly is my Elspeth, she is an elf. And elves are far swifter than mortals.

"We're going to have to jump," calls Elspeth's disembodied voice from beside Irwin.

Some of Irwin's previous pallor returns.

I back away a step until I hear footfalls echo behind me on the cobblestone.

Turning, I see Heinrich striding toward me, his hand out to protect some of his vision from the light as he steps over convulsing peasants and monks, his gaze set on me.

His gaze that is still very green.

"My prince, we have to jump!" Elspeth cries behind me, and Irwin is climbing over the wall already at her words, perched and ready to fly.

Before me, Heinrich takes one of his throwing knives from the inside of his sleeves to his fingers, preparing to flick it at me.

Then he blinks rapidly, his eyes swirling blue through the green. His expression fades from hardened to heartbroken. "Otello, don't let me kill you!"

The green washes over the blue in his eyes, a storm swallowing all that defies it.

Behind me, Irwin jumps.

Before me, Heinrich pulls back his wrist.

Another hand clutches my wrist. An invisible one, tugging me toward Angel's Grace. The setting sun glints off the waters.

Yet I can't tear my gaze away from Heinrich. It's not him I truly see, though, but a vision in my mind's eye. Heinrich's hand finding his blade. That blade finding my neck.. My Heritage blood flow impotent from my veins. Elspeth's desperate words of *"How could you*?"

There comes a time even in the life of an Emperor to follow orders. So, I do.

"Saints save us all," I mutter.

Turning, I throw myself over the balcony, and into the waiting arms of the falls.

CHAPTER XXVII

LADY ELSPETH

I regret every decision I ever made that led me to his point, plummeting down Heaven's Grace. The strength of the current alone keeps me from being snatched by the air and dropped in a straight drop with nothing to ease my fall.

Worse yet, I am not alone in my descent; I cannot fear for my life alone. Somewhere out of my view, the last of my kin has stupidly propelled himself off the cliff because I was going to. Just like my mother's sister always chided him against doing.

And the Sacred Prince himself jumped merely because I *told* him to. I, a disgraced noblewoman and self-proclaimed queen of criminals, commanded the man who would be Emperor to share my fate.

And so, he has. Even though I am the woman who has altered his face by magic that somehow has not faded yet.

Oh, Creator have mercy on us all.

Choking on the water flowing under my body and sometimes over, I am struck by a desperate thought as my mind tries to take me anywhere but here with my body.

How did everyone, from servants to peasants to monks, know Otello was the Prince that they sought to kill, when he wore Heinrich's face? Surely the spell that numbed their mind into becoming subservient to another's will did not also lend them deeper perception?

A horrifying thought grips me as the water takes me almost straight downward, so I am falling upright down the last lengths of the fall.

Did I grab the wrong person standing by the wall of glass? Or . . . or . . .

Was it somehow the Sacred Prince *himself* that I drugged and disrobed in the woods?

I tumble into the water pooling at the bottom of the falls, sinking so deep from the force that I fear I will never again rise.

But I must. I must rise so that I can see to it that Irwin does as well. And the Prince.

So that the Sacred Prince may someday fall in return for the rise of our Empire from death or whatever dark fate the prophecy foretold.

Kicking, I search for the surface, but I realize I do not even know which direction to rise, my head whirling from my fall and my eyes stinging with water.

Panic grips me more tightly than I knew it could, seeping into my very soul until I think it will drown me before the water can.

Until I realize what a thorough job my damp dress is doing in dragging me downward.

So, I propel myself opposite that kicking as much as I can with the wet material wrapping around my legs.

But now that I am looking in the right direction, I see the sunlight trailing down. I must reach it; I must not die where the sun cannot see me.

I burst upward, breaking the surface and choking out water, but hardly daring to trust the air again when so many previous breaths failed me.

My lungs override my distrust, and I take one gasping swallow of air as I see movement out of the side of my eye. Irwin?

Before I can tell for sure, the force of the downward currents, strong with proximity to the falls, grab hold of my leaden skirts again. They drag me back down, away from the air, the sun, and all that I love.

Even as my vision clouds, I see the figure swimming toward me.

Renewed hope fills me, and I try to swim up toward the incoming figure, but my skirt continues to drag me down. In desperation, I tear at my sleeves, trying to yank them off my shoulders. If this gown wants to drown, let it. But I must return to the light, to my kin.

The figure, who must be the Prince only because he's too tall to be Irwin, reaches for me. I see a flash of a dagger in his hand.

He must be the man from the woods. Why else would he slice that knife down the front of my bodice?

I should have let the water consume me . . .

The Sacred Prince bites his knife between his teeth, grabs hold of my sleeves, and tugs downward until the dress. Now that it's cut in both the front and the back, the gown slides down to my waist.

I realize what he's doing before the skirts tug me back down, under the surface. Reaching down, I grasp the material clustered around my hips and wrench it down over them.

The water greedily grasps and drags the tatters down my legs the rest of the way, freeing me. I watch it flow down, red like the blood that was almost shed above, before we fled into Heaven's Grace.

Suddenly, arms wrap around my sackcloth-clad torso and propel me upward.

I break the surface, and gasp for air. I don't care if I go back down again in the future, if only I can enjoy this taste of life one more time.

The brawny arms just under my chest do not seem to share my reckless abandon. Those arms lean me backward, while still keeping my head out of the water as I'm guided away from the waterfall.

"Elspeth!" Irwin calls from somewhere I can't place because of the deafening roar of the falls.

But then he's beside me, taking my arm and helping to carry me to the shore.

My feet finally touch the ground, and I do my best to support my weight as we stumble onto the grassy shore. Where all three of us collapse, partially upon each other.

"We made it," I gasp, my throat hoarse from choking and my nostrils stinging from the water that flowed through them. "We're absolutely mad, but we made it."

"Land," Irwin gasps, crawling out of our pile to better caress the grass. "Sweet, sweet land."

I smile to see him still alive and whole after our perilous encounter. Beside me lies the Prince, who is still heavily breathing against the shore-line.

When my neck grows too weary to keep my head upright, I let my chin drop. Thank all three Heavens that the sacred Heritage Medallion is still clenched in my fist. I tie a knot in the chain and tuck it quickly beneath my soggy sackcloth for the time being. Concerning the sackcloth, the material is dark enough to not have become translucent, but there is still far too little of it over my long legs.

Of course, this is what I must be wearing before my prince, my betrothed-to-be. Not even Irwin should have to see this much of my limbs.

With a desperate glance, I search for some kind of covering, as though clothing grows in between blades of grass. The Creator is merciful, though, and I find the black folds of the Cowl of Shadows still around me. It strikes me suddenly that even though I wore it while swimming, I felt no extra burden from it then. Unlike my traitorous dress. May it rot in the depths of Heaven's Grace forever. Even now, the Cowl of Shadows is eerily dry to the touch.

The Creator is merciful indeed.

Wrapping the cloak tightly around me for warmth as well as modesty, I can't help but wonder why the green-robed kinsman did not tell me to clad the Prince with it since the crowds only cared about him. What would my face have to do with anything?

I turn back to the Sacred Prince. "I am decent now, your Luminance."

His dark hair is plastered to his strong jaw. While who I hope very dearly is the Prince is still lying on his stomach, he has pushed himself up slightly and is resting on his elbows. And he's pointedly looking away from me.

My face burns at the thought that I have embarrassed the Prince by my state of dress. Even if he was the one who cut my dress off me.

At that thought, I am sure my face is as red as my dress was. Thankfully, Irwin has wandered farther into the sparse forest around us, getting our bearings.

"Lady Elspeth, I have been searching everywhere for you." The Prince's voice is also hoarse from our impromptu swim, but still steady.

My eyes widen. "Y-you have?"

"Indeed, I want to apologize. And now I must thank you." He finally turns to me, and I feel his gaze going up the folds of my cloak before coming to rest on my face.

His eyes widen, and I see recognition flash through his gaze.

And the truth of who he is slices through my heart. Even as lies tear apart at the seams before us. "Y-you *are* the Prince, aren't you?"

"The Emperor, actually." He pushes himself up to his knees, and I can feel the fury radiating from him. "Because you killed my father."

"What? No!"

But he doesn't seem to hear me as he lunges at me, knocking me back hard on the ground. I wince as my head makes impact, and then his body looms over me, his arms clutching my shoulders and his knees resting on either side of my hips.

"Get off of me!" I cry, lifting my knee and making contact. Then I grab him by his soaked jerkin and try to roll him off me. I succeed in rolling him over, but his clutch on me brings me with him, so that I'm now on top of him.

"I didn't kill your father," I gasp. "Though he is responsible for the death of my aunt and the loss of my home, my title— everything!"

Otello studies me through narrowed eyes, not looking convinced. "You left me drugged and disrobed in the forest!"

"Because I was trying to save the Prince!" I yank his hands from me and jerk away. "Should have saved myself the trouble."

I try to crawl away, but then strong hands circle my hips, dragging me back down.

Glancing down, I find Otello clinging to me, wrapped around my legs that are way too bare, with the sackcloth only covering me halfway down my thighs.

"Hullo!" Irwin cries suddenly, and I look up to see him rushing back over. "Unhand her this instant!"

Otello looks down and seems to realize that he's touching my skin, because he jerks back. I kick at him before pushing myself up and rushing toward Irwin.

Before I reach him, though, Otello overtakes me, and he presses me into a tree trunk.

I spin around as he grasps my wrists and holds them up above me.

The Prince's purple eyes flash dangerously, warning of mysterious Heritage Magic and all the unknown ways it could destroy me. "Your name isn't Meredith." His voice is little more than a growl.

Lifting my chin, I meet his gaze, wishing the flames of anger I feel within me could lick out and burn him. Smite him before he can smite me. "And yours isn't Heinrich."

For a moment, we stand that way, glaring each other down.

In hindsight, mayhap I made a botch of all this running off to claim my own revenge and restitution without the Creator's help. But I did what seemed right at the time in the only way I knew would lead to my seeing some return for my grief in my lifetime. My people have been waiting for *Haya* for generations, after all. And we don't have generations to save the Empire.

Suddenly, Irwin is grasping both our shoulders. "Stop this nonsense this instant and— and look!"

Growling, Otello turns to my cousin. "*What*?"

Irwin points up, where a dark form throws itself from the Cathedral's outlook and into the Heaven's Grace. Whatever it is, it's more determined than the cluster of people pressed against the edge and peering on to find the Sacred Prince. Though even now some are moving away from the ledge, perhaps realizing that they can catch up to us eventually if they go down to the city gates.

"*Dark Ritual*," Otello curses before releasing me. "What matter of magic is this?"

"The darkest kind," I whisper, grasping Otello's wrist without realizing it. I suppose because I don't want it to be in vain that I swam down a waterfall to save the Prince.

My other hand grasps Irwin's hand, and together the three of us rush into the forest.

"I think I saw some tracks ahead," Irwin says. "I recognized WolfBear's heavy footfalls."

Otello turns to him. "WolfBear?"

Irwin grunts. "Yeah. I'd advise you keep your paws off my dear Elspeth in the future, or else her bodyguard will tear your arms clean off."

Otello glances at Irwin, but I tug them both forward. "We'll worry about catching up with our party soon enough. For now, we need to hide." I scan the area, looking for a denser place to hide between trees and bushes.

"Perhaps your new cloak, Elspeth?"

I turn to Irwin and shake my head. "Of course. Behind those trees."

We rush between a cove of several trees grown closely together. Then I hold out the folds of my cloak.

Irwin hugs my waist in the most appropriate embrace he can manage.

Otello kneels close to me and braces his hands on either side of my feet, as though unwilling to touch me again.

I drop my cloak down over us, hoping that we vanish as completely as we did before.

For a moment, we are all still, balancing out our breathing that, for me, at least, is coming out much too heavy after the plummet, near-drowning experience, and then wrestling match with the Sacred Prince.

Or is he the Emperor now? Did he say his father had passed on?

I almost choke on air as it all hits me at once. The prophecy is unfolding before our eyes. Only different. Heinrich is actually Otello. He hates me— for good reason.

And I still have to marry him.

The entire mass of ensorcelled villages has left my view. Because the spell has worn off, or because they are even now seeking an alternate route down the mountain?

I am a long way from being the Baroness of a backwoods but beautiful patch of land far away from where anything ever happens.

Then a figure robed in a black cloak not unlike my own emerges from the pool, his hood pulled back to reveal a face so pale I half expect him to collapse from consumption.

Instead, he glides through the pool, emerging without any moisture dripping from his cloak that shimmers as mine does. When he pulls the hood back up over his head, though, he doesn't vanish. But something potent seems to wave over him all the same.

And even though I've never seen him before, I know exactly who he is. There is a power about him that has nothing to do with the magic he currently wears.

"The Emperor's Shadow," I mouth.

Below me, I hear confirmation as Otello mutters what sounds like a curse.

The Shadow seems to have heard us, and he turns to face us, his face completely darkened by his hood so not to betray his expression.

To my great horror, he steps toward us.

If I could, I would bring my hands up to touch my forehead and each shoulder to bring blessing upon us, but I stand frozen and hope to remain invisible a little longer to the only legal estrie. An undead assassin. The deceased killer.

My heart stutters at the approach of a monster that is not born from the womb, but in sacrilege. They conduct a dark ritual in which they consume either a mortal's or an elf's blood. Then they carve out their own heart.

My hand grips Irwin's shoulder to assure myself that he's there even as Otello's hand clutches my calf, I assume to keep me steady. The unexpected touch has the opposite effect, though, and almost sends me keeling backward.

Sheer willpower and Otello's tightening grip keep me from doing so. Nothing can keep me from trembling, though, as the estrie continues to move forward, walking straight toward us.

Surely, he can't see us. *I* can't even see us . . .

He comes to stand right in front of me, so close that if it weren't for his hood, I would probably feel his breath on my face. I don't dare blink.

Suddenly, his hand darts out, grasps my neck, and pushes me back hard into the tree, hitting my head against the bark. Pain shoots through my scalp and darkness threatens to close in.

My body has no choice but to follow after my head, bringing my cloak with it and exposing both Otello and Irwin.

Thankfully, the Shadow doesn't seem to have noticed them yet as he continues to apply terrible pressure to my throat, banishing all air from my lungs. Then, his other hand snaps at my face, tugging my hood off.

Light exposes my gasping face. The Shadow's fingers do lax somewhat when he realizes he's strangling a stranger.

And behind him, Irwin creeps forward with the stealth our ancestors passed down to us and our parents honed in us. A dagger gleams in his hands.

To avoid giving him away, I let my eyes roll upward.

Then the Emperor's Shadow speaks, his voice sounding as dead as autumn leaves crinkling under foot. "Where is the Sacred Prince?"

The Prince, apparently not seeing Irwin's approach, makes himself known by jumping up from the leaves and throwing his body into the estrie.

I gasp as the hand is wrenched from my neck, claws tearing through my skin. Choking on air, I bend over, one hand against my bleeding throat and the other clutching the tree for support.

Irwin comes to my side, his hunt forgotten as his wide eyes search mine. "Are you all right?"

Since I'm not sure I can speak right now, I point toward where Otello is even now wrestling with the shade. From my vantage, it's hard to tell who is winning.

Irwin doesn't look very keen to leave me, but I glare at him until he does. Then my cousin stabs his newly stolen silver dagger into the Shade's back before it can bring its claws down the face of the man I'm supposed to marry.

I realize just how much damage could be done to not only my hope of taking over the Empire, but also my groom's one good attribute— his good looks.

Pushing myself to my feet, I waver, darkness closing in on my vision. I stand very still for a moment, trying to push the darkness back, one hand clinging to the tree while my other hand reaches for my throat. My neck feels odd somehow, like it's starting to swell.

I bring my hand that had been pressing into my neck up to my eye-level. Blood and black liquid both drip from my fingers.

The sight banishes the last of the strength from my legs and light from my eyes, and I crumble in a heap, gone before I can feel the full effect of my fall, swallowed up in the curse of an estrie's touch.

Surely . . . surely this is not how the Bandit Queen perishes.

CHAPTER XXVIII

PRINCE OTELLO

I always did my best to avoid my father's Shadow while I was in court.

But it is rather difficult to ignore him when he's lying on top of me, trying to infect me with the poison flowing through his veins.

"Unhand me!" I demand, grasping the wrist of his gloved hands. The gloves have the tips cut off so black, curled nails can be available as a weapon. "I am your emperor, and you must obey me!"

"You are merely a boy." The rasping voice doesn't sound like it comes from the creature on top of me, but from somewhere in the sky above him.

The estrie shifts its body so that it no longer needs its other hand to support it, and those claws move for my face.

I try to move off my other hand that I've fallen on top of when the Shadow took control of the struggle and moved on top of me.

Suddenly, the sky roars, and it takes me a moment to realize that the sound is coming from the faceless estrie as he rears backward, the strike missing my face.

Seizing the opportunity, I knee the Shadow and use my hold on his wrist to move him to the side so I can roll off my hand and back onto him.

But he uses the inertia to roll back onto me, and I lack the strength I need to continue moving.

I look up to see the royal assassin pull back his hand, his long nails tipped with poison.

Before the blow can land, though, his hand jerks back as if in some sort of reaction, one that has him rearing back.

With the last of my strength, I push him off me. This time I jump to my feet instead of trying to hold him down. I waver a bit on my feet, the blood rushing to my head as I look down on the creature reaching back to where a dagger is embedded deep in his back.

Irwin, the ally to the woman who has either rescued me or abducted me, is standing behind the estrie. His face is pale and somewhat green as he looks down at the damage only he could have caused since I do not see the woman here.

Glancing beyond him, I spot Meredith— no, *Elspeth*— still against the tree. The no-longer disguised she-elf has her hands pressed her neck. As I watch, she pulls her hand back. A red and black mixture drips from her hand and her neck wound.

The monster poisoned her.

And I probably helped cause it with my impetuous actions.

Glancing down at the Shadow struggling to reach for the blade that must be crafted from silver to cause such a reaction in him. Bending down, I grasp it before he can reach it and wrench it out. Then I turn it hard, driving it down further.

Through the tears in the Shadow's cloak, I can see the blackened veins flowing under his skin. The color dilutes as silver spreads through the veins, now covering an area about the size of my hand but growing.

I step back as the estrie stops struggling, a paralysis coming over him in reaction to the silver contaminating his blood.

Then I turn and hurry to Elspeth's side. For the magnitude of her personality and prowess before, she seems so small and vulnerable now. Now when she lies unconscious on the forest floor, wearing only sack-cloth and a cloak.

Just as she left me in the woods, unconscious, with only my braies and a discarded dress.

"She's been poisoned!" Irwin cries, dropping to his knees beside her.

For a moment, there is a temptation like a presence standing just behind me, whispering to leave them both and flee. It would be fitting justice for her, after all.

But my father is dead, and Heinrich isn't . . . Heinrich. A crushing loneliness weighs on my soul. And these two unlikely allies are all that stand between it and me with the barest hint of a promise of a purpose they can lead me to.

"It doesn't matter where you take her, Adalbert! I will find her!"

I blink at the sudden words. *My* words, if my memory serves me well, which I cannot trust at this moment. Can't trust anything right now, except my need to get away from here and illuminate the truths that have been hidden for far too long. Starting with why I dreamed of Elspeth before I ever met her, going by Meredith's name or otherwise.

To my right, the Shadow twitches. And to my left, the waterfall still roars, a landmark that other potential assassins can use to easily find us.

Justice or not, I can't leave them to die.

Without another thought, I stoop down, pushing Irwin away from where his hands are brushing Elspeth's neck.

"Let me heal her!" he cries. "You have to let me heal her before the poison takes hold!"

"You will," I blurt, barely knowing what I'm saying as the part of my mind that knows how to thrive with danger takes hold. I reach one hand beneath Elspeth's head, the other one catching her under her bared knees. Then I hoist her dead weight as I rise to my feet. She's lighter than I expected, like her bones are composed of a lighter material than most.

Because the woman is a she-elf?

I have no time to ponder this out, though. My feet drive me deeper into the forest, her cloak not quite touching the ground it seeks to trail across.

"Where are you going!" Irwin calls, keeping pace with me, his eyes wild with worry.

"Somewhere safer than here."

"If the poison takes hold, there will be nowhere safe for her."

I don't slow my pace, but I do scan the area I had been blindly running through.

My gaze falls on a jutting rock formation partially hidden under moss. I redirect my steps there.

By the time I reach the overhang, my body remembers all that it went through this day, and my legs buckles beneath me. I almost drop Elspeth, but sheer will keeps me from throwing her across the grass.

I lay her down as gently as I can and then steady myself by grasping the overhang so that I don't crash down on top of her.

Then Irwin is sliding across the grass, coming to a stop beside her on his knees, his stature kneeling just short enough to be erect while under the overhang. He gingerly brushes his finger against her raw neck, still bleeding red and black.

Elspeth's frail frame convulses in reaction.

"Can you help her?" I whisper.

Irwin nods and places his hand firmly on the side of her neck now. Then he opens his eyes, and all blood seems to leave his face.

I glance back at Elspeth, and see that he's pulled his hand away somewhat, but it's still hovering. And the black is extending out of the cuts onto his hands, collecting into a black mass.

The lines of ink thin out and then dissipate into nothing, and all that remains is the mass on his palm.

Irwin pulls his hand back and then tosses the black mass behind him before falling back hard on his rump after kneeling beside Elspeth. The blood slowly returns to his face.

"H-how did you do that?" I cradle Elspeth's head as color slowly returns to her face as well.

"Kin Magic." Irwin leans back on the balls of his feet.

"You are kin, then?"

"All elf-folk are kin, but yes, in your terms, we are family. Cousins." Irwin glances back down at Elspeth.

And I find a strange welling of relief in myself at the realization that the two are related and not bound by something else.

Because apparently, I'm a fool and don't learn a lesson the first time around.

"Where's the Shadow?" Elspeth cranes her head as if to peer beyond me. She falters slightly, and her cousin hurries to steady her.

"We left him behind." I glance behind me likewise. "He is immobilized for now. But we need to move before dusk."

It is impossible to completely kill an estrie by day when their spirit clings to their body. The injuries he sustained our grievous, but he has one last night for his spirit to leave his body to hunt. Should he consume blood this night, his body shall recover.

That nocturnal spirit-form is when the estrie is most powerful. It can move invisibly except to the keenest eyes, and it can suck the life-force from any sleeping victim it comes upon. Or waking, if it so chooses. Its spirit-fang venom may not be as lethal as its physical talon poison, but it can paralyze with a single bite.

One shudders to think of what it might do, even to someone who remains vigilant to an opponent they cannot hope to see. Especially since it is already sunset and we are too near.

"Trail." Elspeth turns to her kin. "See if you can find the trail that will lead us to the Rose Crown Inn."

He searches her face. "Are you sure?"

"Yes, hurry! The sooner we regroup, the better." Elspeth pushes herself backward in the grass until her back is flush to the stone overhang. She relaxes.

"You have a party waiting for as at Rose Crown Inn?" I ask.

Elspeth nods. "They will be our escort back to where my army is stationed."

"Your . . . army?"

She cocks her head to one side as she looks at me. "Well, who did you think was going to help us defeat the Sorcerer taking over your Empire even now? Who's going to help you reclaim your throne?"

So many things whirl around in my head. Elspeth thinks a Sorcerer is behind this? Adalbert? Or is she trying to frame him for her crime? And . . . an army?

I suppose my own army seems to have turned against me. Will the spell ever break? Of course, it will. Heinrich cannot be turned against me forever. He simply cannot.

"Take me to your army," I demand, raising myself up to my royal stature as much as I can under this overhang. Which isn't much. "I will reward you. Whatever you desire."

"Oh, you will." A wicked smile twists across her lips that had only a moment ago been filling me with encouragement. The memory of her assurance fades away to dread now, and I suspect I've just signed away my firstborn child somehow. "You will reward me most handsomely, Holy Emperor of the Sanctified Empire of Constantinium."

EPILOGUE

The False Prince

"I anoint you as the Holy Emperor of the Sanctified Empire of Constantinium."

Strange words scratch at my inner ear unpleasantly, and I peel one eye open to see the cause of my discomfort.

Brown robes are stooped over me. It takes my vision a moment longer to focus on the face of High Sorcerer Adalbert, his face expressionless.

"S-sire?" I whisper, my voice as hoarse as my mind is cloudy. What kind of ale did I get into?

I try to rise to properly salute the High Sorcerer's station even though I share Otello's mistrust of the man himself.

Adalbert gestures for me to lie back down. "Peace, Heinrich."

"Wh-what is happening?" The room we're in is small and dark, and shaped in a perfect circle. I don't recognize it, nor do I recall coming here.

The last I remember is . . . is . . . *"Otello, don't let me kill you!"*

I jerk upward as the memory stabs my soul. I'm prevented from sitting all the way up, though, by the chains around my wrist that are binding me to the stone slab I am lying on.

There's no time to think about that, though. "Otello, is he well? Is he . . . alive?"

"You are Otello."

I blink. "Sorry?" Memories of the strange enchantment come to mind. "Oh, no, I'm Heinrich. My face was just temporarily altered by exposure to some sort of tonic."

"I will keep the tonic from lapsing," Adalbert assures me, as though that is something I'd find comforting. He stoops over an alchemy kit that has somehow been crammed into this tiny room alongside the stone slab.

"You misunderstand; I want it to wear off. And I want to see Otello." I scan the dark room, but we are alone.

Two torches alone illuminate the room, showing what appears to be a door bolted shut from our side on one part of the room, and etchings of some kind of ritual on another part of the wall. It must herald back to the country's pagan origin, for there is nothing Christian about the figures dancing around the stone altar bearing a human sacrifice.

"*You* misunderstand, boy." Adalbert turns back to me now that whatever mixture he was working on is flowing through the beakers. "It does not matter what you wish for. Only what *I* desire."

"I serve the Prince, not you." I tug at my chains. "Where is he?"

"*You* are he." Adalbert comes to loom over me. "The Emperor's body did not last as long as I required, and someone has spirited his son away. Thus, I have need of another puppet to serve me from the throne."

I strain at my chains. "The Holy Emperor has passed?"

"Oh, he passed long ago." Adalbert reaches into his robes and removes a curved dagger made of ebony, or else dipped in black poison.

He places it on the alchemy table and reaches for a silver chalice. "It was not meant to be like this, child. However, you proved far more resistant than I anticipated while under the powerful spell woven from the release of my necromantic control. And I have no time for such willfulness."

I stare at the dagger dumbly as Adalbert's words echo in my head. The Emperor is dead. *Has* been dead. Necromancy.

Adalbert picks up the dagger again, and I tense, wondering how to fight when I am pinned down as I am.

However, he brings the blade to his own wrist. I watch in macabre fascination as he slices open his own skin and drips blood into the silver chalice.

"What you speak of," I whisper, needing to know more. Needing to know if there is some way I can transmit this information to Gerrard or someone before Adalbert carries out whatever scheme he has for me. "It's treason."

"Constantinium has blasphemously served the so-called Emperor-God for far too long. We never should have forsaken the gods of old. They knew what real power was." Adalbert thrusts the chalice filled with his blood to my lips. "Drink."

I recoil. "Never!"

The silver slams into my teeth, nearly cracking them, and the cup is tipped upward.

I choke as warm, coppery liquid is poured into my mouth and drips from my lips to my bared chest.

The moment the cup is passed away from me, I turn and spew out as much as I can. Focus on the thought of expelling the rest . . .

Before I can drain my system of the poison, Adalbert grabs me by my hair and forces me back down onto the stone slab.

"Stop your retching, boy," Adalbert hisses. "This is a glorious event. The time has come for the shadows to no longer hide from the sun. The gods of old shall rise again. And you shall no longer be outshined by your half-brother. You shall *be* him."

"Never!" I cry. "I will never be Emperor, nor shall I be your slave!"

"I already informed you, young one, that your will means nothing now. You will be an obedient child." He uses the dagger to slice at my torso. Just enough to part skin, but not enough to cause blood to gush out.

The pain blinds me for a moment, but then I come to a single, clarifying realization.

The stone slab I am chained to is the altar from the mural.

"Necromancy leaves no room for the corpse to possess a will," Adalbert says, lifting his knife high.

"Creator have mercy!" I cry, but there is no mercy to be found as Adalbert plunges the blade into my heart.

For a horrid moment, I feel pain and shock, and the slicing of skin and spirit.

And then I feel nothing at all.

TO BE CONTINUED...

Treason & Thievery
His throne was stolen from him.
The Bandit Queen will help reclaim it—
With the condition that he wed her.

Elspeth has performed her greatest heist yet: stealing the Sacred Prince from the capital just as a release of dark magic turned its citizens against him. That was the easy part. Now she has to safely deliver the reluctant refugee across the province to her camp where he believes the Bandit King will bargain with his army to help Otello reclaim his stolen throne. Except, she is the Bandit King, and that bargain is a marriage arrangement.

Otello's life was turned upside-down in a single moment. Now he's forced to ally himself with the woman who betrayed him with a kiss if he wants to survive, let alone have a chance at seizing back the seat of his empire from the necromancer who wants his blood. As does everything else, it seems, from vampires to gysts. All that is, except the one the magic in his veins has imprinted on, the right hand of the Bandit King, who he knows better than to trust with anything, let alone his heart.

He is prophesied to save the Empire. She is destined to destroy him.

Releasing now on Kindle Vella

ABOUT THE AUTHOR

Jes Drew is the author of the Cursed Fae of Orphydice Manor series, the Sunset at Dawn trilogy, the Ninja and Hunter trilogy, the Howling Twenty trilogy, the Kristian Clark saga/The Man on the Run series, the Castaways trilogy, The Dystopian Takeover trilogy, Summers of Yesteryear series, The Clockwork Faerie Tale Novellas, the Legends of the Master Spy series, The New ESE Files series, *Tales from Parallel Worlds, Genie and Serena, Accidentally on the Run, This Side of Heaven,* and *The Death of a Hero.*

She has three degrees, including a Master of Arts in Behavioral Counseling. Also, she has about five million houseplants (and counting— the plants and not the degrees . . . unless she relapses). She is still debating if having a fae husband is worth the hassle. Contact her at author.jes.dre w@gmail.com.

ABOUT THE SERIES

Sunset at Dawn is a three season romantic fantasy adventure following Elspeth and Otello. After each season releases individually, first on Kindle Vella and then on KDP, it will be compiled into one volume and will be the pilot of the chronicles of the *Cousins of Constantinium*. The series will be connected by setting and characters, but each book will feature a standalone romance following a different couple as they also fall in love, fight evil, and face the sacrifices they must make for the sake of the Empire.

Acknowledgments

This book has been a passion project which has practically written itself. With some help from me, of course, and I had help from many others.

For one thing, there's all my readers on Kindle Vella who read the story even without all the extra art.

For another thing, I always have to thank my editor, Katy Maureman. And there is a long and talented artists I have to thank for the artwork for this story: Maddy Moore, Hannah Rogers, Mageonduty, and saintjupit3rgr4phic.

Next, I have to thank my Royal Spies for being my street team. You help so much!

Then there's my family, every crazy one of you. But especially Nicki Chapelway, who gave me the push I needed to branch back into fantasy and I have certainly not regretted it. Those covid afternoons playing Elder Scrolls really paid off for both of us.

Finally, all gratitude to God for gifting me this story to be steward over. Much appreciated.

AFTERWORD

If you enjoyed this book, or even if you did not, please consider putting up a review wherever you review books. Reviews help authors and other readers alike. Thank you for your consideration.

And if you answered "yes" to enjoying this book, check out these other books by Jes Drew coming soon or now available in ebook, print, and audiobooks:

Also by Jes Drew

Thankfully

Sunset at Dawn, Season Two: *Treason & Thievery* (Currently releasing as a serial)

Cursed Fae of Orphydice Manor Book 0.5: *Entreaty of Shadows*
Cursed Fae of Orphydice Manor Book One: *Embrace of Shadows*
Cursed Fae of Orphydice Manor Book 1.5: *Blood of Destruction*
Cursed Fae of Orphydice Manor Book Two: *Bond of Destruction*

The Samurai's Student, Season One: *Year of the Tiger* (Currently releasing as a serial)

The Ninja and Hunter Trilogy, Book One: *The Time I Saved the Day*
The Ninja and Hunter Trilogy, Book Two: *The Time I Saved a Damsel in Distress*
The Ninja and Hunter Trilogy, Book Three: *The Time I Saved the World*

The Castaways Trilogy, Book One: *Castaways*
The Castaways Trilogy, Book Two: *Fugitives*
The Castaways Trilogy, Book Three: *Targets*

The Dystopian Takeover Trilogy, Book One: *Mind of Darkness*
The Dystopian Takeover Trilogy, Book Two: *Fists of Injustice*
The Dystopian Takeover Trilogy, Book Three: *Heart of Steel*

The Summers of Yesteryear Series, Book One: *At Summer's End*
The Summers of Yesteryear Series, Book Two: *Echoes of Summer*
The Summers of Yesteryear Series, Book Three: *Summer Again*

The Death of a Hero (And other Peacemaker short stories) (All profit goes to Exodus Road)

The Howling Twenties Trilogy, Book One: *Wolf Claw*
The Howling Twenties Trilogy, Book Two: *Wolf Curse*
The Howling Twenties Trilogy, Book Three: *Wolf Cure*

Tales of Parallel Worlds (An anthology of short stories and poems from The Howling Twenties Trilogy and beyond) (All profit goes to Polaris)
Genie and Serena, PI (All profit goes to Polaris)

The Clockwork Faerie Tale Novellas, Book One: *Red as Blood* (A Snow White and the Seven Dwarves/Snow White and Rose Red retelling)
The Clockwork Faerie Tale Novellas, Book Two: *Sleep Like Poison* (A Sleeping Beauty retelling)
The Clockwork Faerie Tale Novellas, Book Three: *Wisps at Night* (An Aladdin and the Magic Lamp retelling)
The Clockwork Faerie Tale Novellas, Book Four: *Ship to Nowhere* (A Sindbad and the Seven Seas retelling)

Kristian Clark and the Agency Trap, Book One: *The Bachelor Missions*
Kristian Clark and the Agency Trap, Book Two: *In the Rogue*
Kristian Clark and the Agency Trap, Book 2.5: *Ruptured Reality* (And other short stories) (All profit goes to Human Coalition)
Marina Ivanov, PI (A Kristian Clark short story) (All profit goes to Human Coalition)
Codename: Christmas Carol (A Kristian Clark short story)

Kristian Clark and the American Agenda, Book One: *Agents Adam and Eve*
Kristian Clark and the American Agenda, Book Two: *Operation Paradise Lost*

Kristian Clark and the American Agenda, Book 2.5: *Eden In-Between* (And other short stories) (All profit goes to Human Coalition)
Eitan Cohren, MIA (A Kristian Clark short story) (All profit goes to Human Coalition)

The Man on the Run Season One, Episode One: *Kristian Clark and the Holy Heist* (A Kristian Clark re-release)

Legends of the Master Spy, Book One: *My Wife, the President*
Legends of the Master Spy, Book Two: *The First First Gentleman*

The New ESE Files, Book One: *The Ghost of You*
The New ESE Files, Book Two: *New Teacher in Town*

The Accidental Superheroes series, book one: *Accidentally on the Run*

This Side of Heaven (A Poetry Collection)(All profit goes to Birthright)

COMING SOON

LORD WILLING

Sunset at Dawn, Book Two: *Treason & Thievery*

Cursed Fae of Orphydice Manor, Book 2.5: *King of Unraveling*
Cursed Fae of Orphydice Manor, Book Three: *Kiss of Unraveling*

The Man on the Run, Season One, Episode Two: *Kristian Clark and the Kidnapped Code* (A Kristian Clark re-release)

Legends of the Master Spy, Book Three: *We the Elite*

The New ESE Files, Book Three: *The Assassin Next Door*

The Clockwork Faerie Novellas, Book Five: *Rose with Thorns* (A Beauty and the Beast retelling)

The Faith Trilogy, Book One: *Invisible Faith*

Jesse's Angels, Book One: *College Royale*

BY NICKI CHAPELWAY

My Time in Amar:
Book One: *A Week of Werewolves, Faeries, and Fancy Dresses*
Book Two: *A Time of Tribulation, Pirates, and Lost Princesses*
Book Three: *A Season of Subterfuge, Courtiers, and War Councils*

Return to Amar:
Book One: *A Certain Sort of Madness*
Book Two: *A Matter of Curiosity*

Winter Cursed:
Winter Cursed
A Winter Grim and Lonely
A Winter Dark and Deadly

Of Dreams and Nightmares:
Book One: *Of Gold and Iron*
Book Two: *Of Stars and Shadows*

Rage like the gods:
Book 0.5: *Between gods and Demigods*
Book One: *Rage like the gods*
A Legend of Ruskhazar: *A Tale of gods and Glory*

A Tale of Loki and Sigyn
Book One: *Harbinger of the End*

An Apprentice of Death:
Book One: *An Apprentice of Death*

Ingram Content Group UK Ltd.
Milton Keynes UK
UKHW020022190423
420401UK00020B/270/J

9 781088 086308